TERROR LAKE

BY

EDWARD J. MCFADDEN III

TERROR LAKE

WWW.SEVEREDPRESS.COM

ISBN: 978-1-923165-08-3

“There was an iciness, a sinking, a sickening of the heart—an unredeemed dreariness of thought which no goading of the imagination could torture into aught of the sublime.” – Edgar Allen Poe

PROLOGUE:

Terimore Lake, Alaska, ***12:19 AM AKST, March 10th, 1999***

The lake ice glowed with an ethereal light.

James Wyatt eased his Pathfinder to a stop behind his brother's battered red pickup, the crunch of cracking ice rising above the howling wind. Big Red was covered in a blanket of snow, and the truck looked like it hadn't moved in a couple of days, its oversized tires frozen to the snowpack.

Cotton candy clouds fleeted across a star-dabbled sky, the reflected light of a gibbous moon painting the world in harsh black and white. Mountains clogged the horizon in every direction, and out on the frozen lake a single fishing tent glowed orange like a forlorn Easter egg.

He sighed, killed the SUV's lights, and shut down the engine. Darkness pressed on him, and James felt the ghost of cold working its way into the cab. He zipped his jacket, pulled up his hood, slipped on his gloves, and got out of the truck.

A wolf howled, its angry call carrying on the wind, snow twirling across the snowpack, silvery shadows reaching out from the surrounding forest. The primal call was answered by two others.

James popped the Pathfinder's rear hatch and retrieved a flashlight and a rifle. The SUV's interior light drove away the suffocating blackness, and suddenly he felt exposed. He locked the truck and the SUV went dark. Clouds of vapor flowed from his mouth and nose like dragon's breath, and James felt the heat draining from his extremities as his eyes adjusted.

He rolled his shoulders and cracked his neck, pushing away his anger and frustration. James had spent too much of his life chasing down his brother and he had little patience left for Kenny. His brother had lost his job at the fish processing plant, and he hadn't taken well to being unemployed. James understood. Kenny had never been a pillar of society, but he had a kid now and his brother needed to think about his family.

So when Beth called and told him she hadn't seen or heard from Kenny in two days, James knew what he needed to do. His nephew Terry was only thirteen years old, and a teenage boy needed his father.

The trail that led down to the lake was a well-trodden path of foot-stomped snow, but James took his time anyway. Slick patches of ice pocked the snow like sores, and rocks, twigs, roots, and pricker vines protruded from the snowpack, all of them eager to aid in his fall.

To the south at the head of the lake, the lights of Mount Aire sparkled in the blackness, a cloud of mist hanging over the town like a halo. Lights from the houses that surrounded the lake sparkled in the evergreen forest, tall shadows falling on the shimmering wind-blown ice.

A clucking-clicking sound echoed on the wind, the tinkle of snow sifting over ice like millions of cockroaches scuttling over glass.

The trail fell steeply to the lake's edge, and James cursed his brother as he slipped and slid down the last section, grabbing at vegetation, his rifle hanging by its shoulder strap and smacking his legs.

Several other fishing tents and shanties dotted the frozen lake, but they were dark, and there were no footprints in the fresh snow that covered portions of the ice. In spots, the wind had scoured the lake, and patches of pale light glowed from beneath the ice as if a spaceship was climbing from the depths.

Terimore Lake, which the locals called Terror Lake, was roughly two miles wide and six miles long. Its official maximum depth was 946 feet at its center, but legends said some sections were much deeper. The lake was one of many that dotted the Kenai Peninsula and received drainage from Tustumena Glacier.

James paused at the lake's edge, the wind gusting, bits of ice nipping at his face. The evergreens creaked and moaned, and the heat of concern warmed him as James stared out at the orange tent. It shone in the darkness, the light from within pressing through the thin weatherproof fabric. He smiled, pushing away the growing aggravation and anger building in him like a storm. He should be home relaxing with his family, drinking coffee and bourbon as he watched the idiot-box. But no, his depressed brother had gone on another bender, and it was up to him to bail him out. Again.

He hugged himself, driving away the cold, memories of good times with his brother warming his chest yet cooling his anger. Kenny had won the Terimore 200 sled dog race at the age of twenty-three, but sadly that's where his brother had peaked. In time his local fame had faded, and when he failed three times to qualify for the Iditarod, butchering fish was the only employment he could find.

Jobs weren't exactly plentiful on the peninsula, and the commute to Anchorage was expensive and time-consuming. With a population of 1316 as of the last census, Mount Aire was the lone outpost along the lake. Cooper Landing was forty miles to the east, the vast beautiful nothingness of Kenai National Wildlife Refuge to the south.

Pale moonlight angled over the frozen wasteland, shadows writhed, and tree branches creaked and moaned as James made his way across the ice, the glacier encroaching to the northern edge of the lake a huge white frozen tongue licking the blackness.

A loud pop, then a series of thuds, deep hollow booms, and cracking ice rose above the wind.

James stopped walking, skin crawling with invisible ants, head pounding in rhythm with his galloping heart. He knew the ice was thick and there was no way he could fall through, but still his nerves danced on a wire. Thoughts of being trapped beneath the ice, unable to find his way out, had been a recurring dream his entire life.

Loud cooing and cawing cut through the arguing wind. James looked back and a field of yellow eyes filled the darkness beneath the tree canopy. A barking and braying mixed with snarls and chuffs carried over the ice, and a wolf inched from the cover of the evergreens.

James saw only the beast's dark shadow, but there weren't many species of beasts that ran in packs on the peninsula. He pulled his flashlight and turned it on, harsh LED light knifing into the trees and silencing the wolves.

The alpha stopped advancing, his head angled toward the sky as he sniffed the air. Two pack mates slipped from the forest, falling in behind their leader.

James lifted the rifle, put the stock to his shoulder, and used the flashlight like a scope, holding it as he supported the rifle's forestock.

More beasts slunk into the cloud of light, yellow eyes shining, teeth bared as they growled.

It was illegal to shoot a wolf unless it posed a threat to human life, but James didn't see a game warden, and he cared little for the longevity of gray wolves. They stole chickens, eggs, and livestock, raided farms, and occasionally attacked humans.

He ranged the gun over the forest, counting sets of eyes, deciding if he should make an example of the alpha. He was a hundred yards out on the lake, and there was no cover. If the pack decided he was vulnerable they might attack, and wolves were always hungry.

Before he could decide a cackle-like bark, followed by a thin, mournful cry that sounded like a whale in pain pierced the night.

The alpha wolf looked back, saw his mates deserting him, turned tail, and loped back into the woods. Like the power had been cutoff, all the eyes disappeared as the beasts scattered, James's flashlight beam revealing only snow-laden evergreens and the dark shadows of night.

He panned the light three-hundred-and-sixty degrees, and nothing moved on the flat expanse of windswept ice and snow.

Kenny's tent was fifty yards off, and James heard canvas fluttering in the wind. He shined the flashlight toward the orange glow and called out Kenny's name.

Nothing but the bitching wind and snow sifting over ice.

A thick cloud floated across the moon and a ghostly grayness crept over the lake, like the moon was dropping below the horizon at a fantastic rate. Shadows danced, and something dark moved beneath the ice.

James almost dropped the flashlight as he stepped back.

Before him, the ice was opaque and partially covered in sculpted snowdrifts, but James saw a black-and-white shape circling beneath the ice. It was big. Much larger than any fish that should be in the lake. His brother's voice rattled in his head, preaching about the legend, how it was a year of the beast.

Cold sweat dripped down his back as he called out for Kenny again, and once more received no response. Warning lights sprouted all over his mental dashboard, his stomach sinking as imaginary mice marched up his spine, all senses telling him to turn around and go home. Get in the truck and don't look back.

But Kenny was his brother. The orange tent beckoned, but no shadows moved therein.

For the first time, James truly feared for his brother. Had Kenny gotten so drunk that he'd passed out and frozen to death? Had he wandered out onto the lake to urinate only to get lost and freeze in his intoxicated state? What would he tell Beth and the kids? He knew he was making assumptions. He didn't know for sure if his brother was drinking, but though he'd be ashamed to do so, he'd bet everything he had that Kenny was lit like a Christmas tree because that was his permanent state these days.

With images of his brother's blue face driving him on, James continued across the lake. The knot in his chest tightened with each step, the wind and cold working together to find every kink in his wool and polyester armor.

A beaten trail appeared in the snow before him, boot prints heading toward his brother's tent. The paths leading to other icehouses were filled with snow, and only shallow depressions could be seen trailing away into darkness.

Something shiny caught his eye and James trained the flashlight on it. A blue object stuck from a drift of snow, and he headed toward it but paused when he came across a pair of tracks. The prints had been made by a beast walking on all fours.

The prints were like nothing James had ever seen, thin slashes in the snow that looked like an alligator or giant snake had slithered over the ice, though he knew that wasn't possible.

James panned the flashlight around and a squeal escaped his lips.

A blue glove stuck from the snowpack, splotches of black all around it. His breath caught in his throat as he got closer and saw that there was still a hand in the glove.

Bone, sinew, muscle, and fat stuck from the glove like bloody hair, dark stains trailing across the ice to the tent. Canvas snapped in the wind, and James flinched as his vision went blurry. Bile crept up his throat and it took all the control James had to keep from throwing up his dinner. Heat spread through him, then a deep cold, his body cycling through panic, fear, and apprehension.

The tent was torn open, its door flapping in the wind, long rips in the fabric sides spilling light like open wounds. The ice was splattered with blood, and his brother's fishing pole lay broken as if he'd refused to give up on a fish that had turned the tables on him.

James stuck the tip of the rifle into the tent and eased his head inside.

The coppery stink of blood and the rank smell of human waste assailed him, and this time James did toss his cookies. Vomit sprayed the inside of the tent, splattering what remained of his brother's sleeping bag and gear. The gas lantern connected to the propane tank, which had a heater attached to it, hissed and snapped, puke pelting the heater's core. Blood stains marred the canvas, the cooler was torn up, and empty beer cans and several empty whiskey bottles littered the tent's floor. The ice hole had frozen over, his brother's fishing line frozen in place, the line trailing out through the open tent flap to where the pole lay forlorn on the ice. There was a black rifle and James hefted it and sniffed the barrel. Whatever had happened, it was over fast because his brother's gun hadn't been fired recently.

A deep growl of fury carried on the breeze, and James turned, frantically panning the flashlight through the open tent door.

Patches of white writhed in the darkness, shadows encroaching on the tent.

"Who's there?" he said, but his words were lost in the angry wind.

Dread burrowed through James, a deep soul-crushing sense of loss. His brother was dead. James could feel it.

The ice creaked and popped as something large moved across the frozen lake.

Suddenly James didn't want to draw attention to himself. He turned off the propane, the hissing ceased, and the flame sputtered out, the orange glow of the heater fading to black. James killed his flashlight and silvery darkness pressed into the tent.

With the wind chanting and the torn neoprene snapping, he slipped from the tent and searched its perimeter. He found a blood slick trailing north toward the glacier. It glistened black in the moonlight, and when he saw the arm James dropped to his knees, tears building in his eyes.

Bloody gristle hung from both ends of the severed appendage and the sleeve of his brother's deep green army jacket was unmistakable. James splayed the flashlight around, trying to find the blue glove with the hand still inside it, but he saw only contoured snow drifts, the dark tent, and the eldritch glare of the ice.

The crunch of footsteps, cracking and snapping ice.

James pressed to his feet and lurched into motion, rifle up. His limbs felt like they were filled with concrete. A sharp ringing filled his head, and it grew in strength as he staggered across the lake, knowing what he was going to find but hoping beyond hope that he was wrong.

He saw his brother as a young boy in his mind's eye, his mischievous grin. James had always respected that grin, knew it was the precursor of things to come, both good and bad. Kenny wasn't a bad person, but he'd done some questionable things when he was younger—poaching, theft, and vandalism came to mind. But did he deserve to die on the frozen tundra at fifty?

Pain cramped James's back, his knees threatening to come unhinged, when he found his brother.

What was left of Kenny lay tangled in a snowdrift, streaks of blue ice spidering out from the pile like lightning bolts. Black pools of blood surrounded the body, and the reek of death and decay carried on the breeze.

In addition to the right arm, both his brother's legs were gone, and the white ball joints of his hip cavity glistened in the moonlight. Bloody wounds marred the torso, the green jacket torn to shreds. Kenny's neck was twisted severely, and from James's viewpoint, it looked like it had turned one hundred and eighty degrees.

A gash cut across Kenny's face, dark blood congealing in his three-day salt and pepper stubble. One eye was missing, but the other stared blankly at the star-filled sky, his mouth curved into one last smirk.

What had his brother thought in that final moment? Did he regret his life? Did he think about his family? Or was he too drunk to understand that the end was near, and there was no time to make amends? It made James think about his own life, and that sent a tremor of angst and sorrow through him. He had time to figure things out, but his brother didn't.

A sharp growl, followed by an angry roar snapped James from his reverie. Ice cracked and popped as something huge ran across the icepack.

James aimed the gun at nothing as he spun like a top, his breaths coming in ragged bursts, his heart racing.

Chuffing, growling, and clicking as the ice cracked and screamed.

With nothing left to do James flicked on his flashlight, and the last things he saw were slick streaks of black and white, and a wicked smile of pointy teeth below two shining eyes as they surged from the blackness.

1

Terimore Lake, Alaska, ***10:43 AM AKST, February 6th, 2017***

The snowmobile's engine gurgled and sang as Wildlife Trooper Terry Wyatt goosed the machine's throttle. Bright morning sunlight angled through the mountain peaks and reflected off the thin sheet of verglas that covered the accumulated snow, and as the trail plunged toward the lake, tiny starbursts of multicolored light danced in the icy mist that twisted in the air like smoke. Snowdrifts towered over the path, and evergreens laden with snow climbed from the snowpack. The crisp winter air chilled his cheeks and made his nose run, the faint scent of gasoline carrying on the breeze. The Polaris Pro was eco-friendly, but burning petrol was burning petrol.

Wyatt eased off the throttle and the machine slowed. Pebbles and dirt spit from beneath the snowmobile's thick rubber tread, the snowmobile vibrating, and a rifle in its scabbard, which was mounted to the left of the handlebars, tapped the Polaris's gas tank with each bump in the trail. He brought the rig to a stop, the sound of cracking ice rising above the squeak and snap of the trees.

He killed the engine, and an unreal silence eased his thumping heart. Birds tittered, and a varmint eyed him from just inside the tree break as he lifted his goggles and took off his helmet. The forest fell away before him, the sun's glare painting the lake a shimmering silvery-white.

The trees whispered of days long gone, and as Wyatt looked around, he realized he was at the spot where his father and uncle's vehicles were found the night they were…

Murdered? Over the years he'd been forced to accept the fact that he would never know—not with one hundred percent certainty—what had happened to his father and Uncle James. Most believed the massacre had been the work of a rabid polar bear, though no bear prints were found anywhere near where his uncle and father's remains were discovered.

Some believed his father and uncle had been taken by an Akhlut, a beast that legends said appeared every six years in search of prey to feed its young. Wyatt didn't know what to believe anymore. It was a long time ago, and he would never forget, but as time went on, and his father's image faded from memory, the legend of the cycle of the beast became more unrealistic.

When it was suggested that the annual Terimore 200 sled dog race be canceled because 2017 was a year of the beast, there hadn't been a single vote in favor of skipping a year. Even those who believed the legends wouldn't sacrifice one of the peninsula's biggest events, and the mountains, lakes, and forests of the Kenai Peninsula didn't attract wallflowers.

Plus, people died on the peninsula all the time. Adventurers, hunters, fishermen, mushers, trappers, and tourists that rode bikes, paddled, cross-country skied, and hiked almost every inch of the peninsula's majestic fjords, mountains, and tranquil lakes.

Joining the troopers after his service in the Navy had always been the plan, but he'd be lying to himself if he said joining the Rabbit Rangers had nothing to do with the death of his father and uncle.

He reached into a pocket on the front of his orange tactical vest and drew out his father's utility knife. It had been found in the snow by his fishing tent the night he was killed, and he always kept it near. Wyatt and his father hadn't been close, and he wasn't surprised when his father died. As a thirteen-year-old boy, he'd believed his father would drink himself to death and he had simply run out of time.

What did that say about how he felt about his only son? A man who hadn't cared enough about him to give him his name? He turned the knife over in his hand before putting it away, the cold metal giving him a shock.

Now Uncle James, well, he was just in the wrong place at the wrong time. Wyatt had fond memories of him, though his children and Aunt Beth kept their distance from him and his mum. Their father had been killed because his dad couldn't get his shit together. It was sad, unfair, and heartbreaking, but true.

He shifted his position as he pulled his binoculars and the snowmobile's pleather seat squeaked. Wyatt had a good view of the racecourse and the tongue of ice that spilled onto the frozen lake in the north like a dirty wave perpetually frozen in time. The trail of the annual two-hundred-mile sled dog race cut across Terror Lake, a dirty track marked with thin orange poles running off the glacier and across the lake.

Three cooing black-capped chickadees perched in a nearby tree fell silent, the gentle wind singing as snow sifted over ice, tree branches popping. Beneath it all Wyatt heard the distant growl of thunder, a faint static that carried on the breeze.

He pressed the binoculars to his eyes.

Static burst from his radio, then fell silent.

The rumble was getting closer and thin ribbons of frozen mist cycled over the glacier, a frosty rainbow forming over the tongue of ice.

Wyatt focused the binoculars as the cloud grew, the sound of barking breaking the stillness.

A sled pulled by a team of huskies emerged from the mist and bounded down the face of the glacier, the musher's red jacket sticking out like a drop of blood on a pristine white carpet. Barks, yips, and howls of exertion and excitement, the rumble of the sled, and the yelling of the musher leaked into the forest.

He couldn't tell which racer it was, but as the musher got closer, he heard the man yelling commands at his team.

"*Sose! Sose!*" came the calls, the thunder of the dogs' paws churning the snowpack growing, a rooster tail of snow trailing behind the sled.

It was the musher from Finland, Sven Sortisein, and he was driving his team forward in his native tongue. The Fin's face shield caught the light like Darth Vader's helmet, dazzling multicolored shards shooting toward the heavens.

Five dogs pulled the sled, two on each side and a lead malamute out front. The buckles along the gangline sparkled in the sun, the dogs struggling against their bonds as they surged forward through the snow. Sven held the drag break handle with one hand, his other gripping the sled's driving bow. The sled's runners shrieked as the sleigh ran over ice, and the Fin yelled, "*Gee! Gee! Gee!*"

The dogs arced right, away from a section of overflow where the ice was so thick that the lake water had nowhere to go and had pushed up and over the ice. The area was marked like ground under repair on a golf course because overflow sites usually have a thin layer of ice covering the water.

The team of dogs was loud now, their barks and cries driving out all other sounds. Twenty bootie-covered feet pounded the ground, and as the sled tore past, Wyatt thought of his father. He'd won the Terimore 200, but he'd never been able to make it to the super bowl of sled dog racing, the Iditarod. His father's failure had driven Wyatt to be different, to have a purpose beyond himself, and the wildlife of Alaska had filled that void.

"*Haw! Haw! Haw!*" Sven screamed, and the team shifted its course, turning left, and the sled plunged into the forest, leaving a swirling cloud of frozen mist behind.

The fog settled, and the chickadees chirped as the steady thrumming of the dogs faded.

Wyatt ate a power bar as he waited for the next competitor, the minutes slipping away. The race captain had told him two racers would be coming his way within the hour, but as time faded, and the second racer didn't appear, an uneasy feeling crept through Wyatt like a penetrating cold.

He brushed it off. Things happened out on the racecourse all the time. Dogs needed to be tended, there were always sled breakdowns, broken ganglines, and a myriad of other unforeseen obstacles which made sled dog racing such a challenge. Wyatt pulled his water bottle, took a long pull, then sucked in some crisp Alaskan air, his angst fading.

The squawk of his radio broke the peaceful trance.

"Wyatt, do you copy?" said lead race coordinator Jada Harvnor. She was one of the race's few committee members who wasn't a musher, so on race days she was the one left carrying the bag containing all the responsibilities.

He pulled his radio and responded, "I copy, Jada. What's up?"

"Racer Seventeen, Jesse Ombridge, didn't make it to Checkpoint Eight."

Wyatt called up a map of the racecourse in his mind's eye. Checkpoint Eight was just north of his position.

"Get up there and check it out. Please," she said. "And keep in touch. I need to know what's going on."

"10-4."

He buttoned up, put on his helmet, and started the snowmobile, the cackle of the engine driving away the chickadees. The birds squawked and bitched as they dropped from their perches and took flight, their black heads like hats atop their white bodies.

Wyatt twisted the machine's throttle and the rig leaped from the snowpack, throwing pebbles, sticks, and dirt.

Checkpoint Eight was at the center of an open field and consisted of a heated yellow tent where racers could restock water and emergency supplies. Mushers were expected to carry basic gear, though like any race vehicle, carrying as little weight as possible was a key to success. The post was manned by a volunteer, and as Wyatt came over a rise and plunged toward the field, he saw Kim Farret's yellow ski jacket standing out against the whiteness. She was pacing back and forth, clouds of frozen mist surrounding her head.

Wyatt and Kim had gone out a few times, and he liked her, but the spark between them seemed to have run its course, though he thought of her often. He brought the snowmobile to a stop and killed the engine, his ears ringing, cold biting his face as he lifted his goggles.

"Hi, Wyatt. I figured they'd send you."

"It is my territory."

"So it is."

The wind whistled and snow cycled over verglas.

When Wyatt could wait no more, he said, "How long overdue is Jesse?"

She hiked her shoulders.

Jesse Ombridge was a race organizer and had been a committee member for twenty years. He'd competed in the Iditarod four times, but a third-place finish was the best he had to show for his efforts.

The icy fingers of worry and fear massaged Wyatt's back. Jesse was an experienced musher, not prone to mistakes. Perhaps one of his sled runners had broken? Or maybe one of his team had fallen ill… But no, Jesse could easily deal with both those problems—any race problem, really. He'd seen it all, and he had a radio and could call for help if he had no other option.

"Alright," Wyatt said. If Jesse was in trouble time might be short. "I'll be in touch as soon as I know something."

She nodded.

"Update central, please. Let them know I was here and that I'm venturing further up the route," he said.

She nodded again.

Wyatt cranked the snowmobile back up, remounted his goggles, and gunned the throttle. The machine darted forward, engine wailing as the thick black rubber tread spit dirty snow.

The race route cut into the forest to the east, and the snowmobile bounced along the trail, Wyatt working the handlebars as the rumble of the engine echoed through the forest.

He'd gone a mile, and Wyatt hadn't seen any sign of Jesse, when a deer blocked the trail. The four-pointer stared defiantly at the approaching snow machine, its eyes glowing in the gloom beneath the tree canopy which was laden with snow and ice. A sunbeam angled through the ceiling of brown and white and fell on the beast. It stomped the ground and lowered its head, its narrow mouth pecking at something on the trail, vapor jetting from its nostrils.

Wyatt slowed the snowmobile, brought it to a stop, and shut it down. He dismounted, took off his helmet, and placed it on the seat. Nervous pain cramping his legs, Wyatt stalked the deer. When he was fifteen feet away a tree branch snapped and the buck sprang into the forest, disappearing into the shadowy grayness.

He drew his Glock 19 and chambered a round, but the gun wasn't needed. A chipmunk charged from the trees. He rolled his shoulders, holstered his weapon, and dropped to a knee.

Whatever morsel the beast had been enjoying was gone, but a splotch of blood marred the dirty snow-covered trail.

He looked around, the feeling that he was being watched eating at him, and paranoia elbowed its way to the forefront of his mental priority line. But just because you're paranoid doesn't mean someone… or something, wasn't out to get him. He thought of the Akhlut.

The wind chanted, and beneath it, Wyatt thought he heard a voice calling for help, but when he listened hard there was nothing but the cajoling breeze.

Back on the snowmobile, sweat dripping down his back despite the cold, Wyatt powered forward as fast as the machine would go. Tension tap danced on his spine, tears forming in his eyes from the cold chilling his face.

Braying and barking could be heard on the trail ahead, dogs whining and chirping as if distressed. He coaxed every bit of speed he could from the snow machine, his mind spinning a series of scenarios that could explain Jesse's full stop during a qualifying race.

The crying huskies got louder, and ahead the gleam of metal pierced the snow clouds.

Wyatt's heart sank when he saw the smashed sled, three dogs still tethered to the gangline, a blood slick trailing into a hole in cracked ice.

The trail passed over a crude log bridge that crossed one of the many creeks that fed Terror Lake. The sled was broken in two, half still on the path, the other half sticking from the cracked ice of the creek. But none of that was what drew Wyatt's eye.

To the south of the path, thirty feet from the log bridge, there was a ragged hole in the ice where something huge had broken through the ice sheet covering the creek.

He brought the machine to a stop and killed the motor, the gentle breeze, cooing birds, and sifting snow doing nothing to ease the tension growing in his stomach like a tumor. There was no sign of Jesse… well, not no sign. The snow and ice all around the sled were splattered crimson, the trail of blood leading into the ice hole leaving little doubt as to what had occurred.

Jesse had run up on a polar bear. They were rare in these parts, but it wasn't uncommon for the beasts to venture south in winter. But no… There were claw-like gashes in the snow all around the broken sled, but he didn't see any paw prints.

He gasped, bile burning his throat.

A severed leg stuck from a snowdrift along the trail.

Pain lanced Wyatt's chest, all the moisture draining from his mouth as he opened a channel to race command. "Jada! Do you copy?"

"I'm here, Wyatt. Go ahead."

"Get out here," he said. "Get everybody out here."

"Wyatt, what is it? What—"

Wyatt blocked her out, an itch he couldn't scratch tickling his nerves. The beast was getting an early start this cycle.

He closed his eyes and licked his cracked lips.

It was all happening again.

2

Ferocious barking broke the stillness, and Wyatt pulled his gaze from the severed leg as his radio fell silent.

A large huskie charged through the mist, mouth open in a vicious snarl, teeth bared, but when the beast saw Wyatt it slowed and much of its fury drained. Wind dusted the huskie with a shower of snow, and the sled dog whined and fidgeted as it skidded to a stop and sat before Wyatt. The dog's long fur was white streaked with gray and black, its snout stained with dried blood, and a long bloody gash ran across the beast's right flank.

Wyatt knew the animal. "Tia, come here, sweetie," he cooed, but the dog was spooked, and the beast remained sitting, shifting uncomfortably as she stared up at Wyatt with glassy gray eyes.

"Where is Jesse?"

The huskie swayed as the beast looked over her shoulder toward her three teammates who were still connected to the destroyed sled. The dogs lay on their bellies watching Wyatt and Tia, whimpering and crying.

The distant sound of rotor foils pounding the air echoed through whispering trees, and the wind chortled as a low growl carried down the trail.

With a hand on the handle of the Glock, Wyatt threaded through the crime scene, being careful not to step in any of the blood that decorated the snow like a Jackson Pollock painting.

Tia wasn't so careful, and she stepped in blood and left red pawprints on the dirty white snow. The dog was jumping from her skin as she followed Wyatt, her training and instinct telling the beast the human would make everything right.

He disconnected the gangline from the destroyed sled and the dogs strained against their rigging, yipping and struggling. Using the gangline and a snub line, Wyatt tied the three dogs to a tree and attached Tia's neck line.

With the dogs secured, and the *womp womp* of the helicopter growing closer, he pulled his phone and began documenting the scene as best he could.

The tracks of the destroyed sled showed that when Jesse reached the log bridge something forced him off the path. Long narrow gashes marred the snowpack and led to the large hole in the creek ice. Shards of ice floated in the hole, the trail of blood leading from the sled and disappearing into the creek.

Jesse's rifle was still in its scabbard-like holster, and though his gear pack had been busted open, the items within appeared undamaged.

The leg was definitely Jesse's. Wyatt recognized the upturned lambskin boot and the dark snow pants with a white stripe running down the side. Wyatt could picture the man's red ski patrol jacket with its gold supervisor patch. Blood stained the snow around the leg, the severed end impaled in the drift.

Wyatt had never seen a sled broken in half, but judging by the position of the remains he figured Jesse had tried to slip around whatever blocked the path, caught an edge on the log bridge, flipped, and landed on the stack of logs that served as a guide rail. An impact of that magnitude would be more than enough to break a sled that was nothing more than lashed-together wood. The sled's GPS tracker was still affixed to the driving bow, its red-light blinking. The device was basic and recorded time verse milage to ensure the racer didn't cheat, and in the event the musher went missing the devices could be located via a satellite query. Wyatt didn't see Jesse's radio.

He didn't want to leave the scene, but he contemplated going back to Checkpoint Eight, which was the only spot the helicopter could land, and even there would be tight. Wyatt considered expanding his search, but his gut told him to wait for backup, so he contacted Jada again.

"Can you bring the dogs back to Checkpoint Eight with you?" Jada asked, static crackling below her voice.

Wyatt eyed the four dogs tied to the tree. The beasts were dejected, one was wounded, and the dogs lay in the snow, whimpering. If he tied the gangline to the snowmobile and went slow…

He said, "Yes, I'll have to go slowly, but I think I can handle it."

"Good," Jada said. "Meet me there. I've got Captain Udell and Trooper Simmons with me. The captain can catch a ride with you and Simmons and I will take Kim's machine. Did you see a transport stretcher or spare sled at the checkpoint?"

He searched his memory and recalled seeing a red plastic sled-like stretcher next to Kim's tent. "Yes, there is one, but…" There was no body to transport, but he let the thought go unspoken. Jada and his fellow Rabbit Rangers would see all there was to see soon enough.

Wyatt connected the sled dogs' gangline to the snowmobile via a carabiner, and though the beasts were spooked by the roar of the machine's engine, they settled down.

It took thirty-five minutes to travel the mile and a half back to Checkpoint Eight, and as he broke free of the woods a blue and white helicopter with TROOPER stenciled on its side was hovering a hundred feet above the clearing.

Landing on densely packed snow was a challenge. Landing on pristine snowpack was a nastier beast, even with the special extra wide pontoon-like landing skids. Unlike sand and dirt, snow was simply water, and though it wouldn't damage the aircraft, the swirling snow caused visibility to drop to zero. Since there was no way to know exactly how deep the snow was in a given spot without extensive investigation, the chopper's pilot decided not to set the bird down.

Wyatt was met by Kim, who took care of the dogs as he watched the helicopter slowly drop until it was thirty feet from the ground. There it hovered as the copter's rotors pounded the air, kicking up snow and ice, white clouds of frozen mist stirred from the snowpack swirling like miniature tornadoes.

A yellow line fell from the chopper and three people dropped to the ground like spiders. The entire operation took less than five minutes, and when all three new arrivals were safely on the ground the rope retracted, and the pilot dipped the copter's nose as the aircraft cycled up its engines and rose into the sky. The craft rotated a hundred and eighty degrees and darted back in the direction it had come, cutting through the white snowy haze.

"I guess they've decided a medivac isn't needed," Kim said.

Wyatt jumped at the sound of her voice because he hadn't realized she'd sidled up next to him. He rolled his shoulders, pushing away the tension, and said, "They can be back here in ten minutes. What was the pilot supposed to do? Hover for an hour?"

She shrugged.

Three figures worked their way across the snowpack.

Jada wore a blue one-piece snowsuit, and Wyatt's colleagues were attired in the standard wildlife trooper uniform: green jacket, orange tactical vest, black knit caps, and black snow pants covering deep green work uniform slacks. On their belts, they carried a range of tools and equipment, including a holster for a sidearm, a multi-tool, pepper spray, and handcuffs.

When the trio arrived, everyone ducted into Kim's heated tent.

Wyatt knew Jada and the troopers well—Udell was his supervisor, though he rarely saw the man in the flesh. The State Troopers were the main safety and security force for the Terimore 200, and extra troopers were on duty all over the racecourse.

Jada was tall, her black hair tucked under an orange knit cap. Her dark complexion was unique in a land where sunshine was a treasured commodity, and she wasn't a musher, just a volunteer.

Udell was a few years from retirement, his massive paunch hidden by his tent-like jacket.

Trooper Richard "Ned" Simmons was a ten-year vet, and Wyatt liked the guy. They'd hung out a few times because he and Wyatt shared responsibility for the Terror Lake district, and both men lived on the outskirts of Mount Aire.

"What've we got here, Wyatt?" Udell said. The captain's voice revealed no emotion. Everyone within a hundred miles knew how Wyatt's father and uncle had died, and when it came to wildlife attacking people, folks danced around his feelings like a child that's failed for the first time.

Wyatt handed over his phone and said, "It isn't pretty."

The captain scanned the photos Wyatt had taken and said, "We better go take a look."

Back outside, the chill wind nipping at every gap in the group's clothing, Jada said, "Do we need the stretcher?"

"Let's bring it just in case," Wyatt said, but he thought the odds of finding Jesse were somewhere between zero and oblivion.

Back at the scene the three troopers and Jada did a thorough search of the area, and they found no further signs of Jesse.

The group stood at the edge of the creek, staring at the water sloshing about in the hole in the frozen surface.

As Jada gave central command an update, her voice was sullen, tears building in her eyes as she looked from the blood-splattered snow to the destroyed sled. She said, "Yeah. Let me talk to the wildlife folks and get right back to you." She locked her eyes on the snowpack and said, "The committee wants to know if we should stop the race."

"Who is going to notify Jesse's wife, Ginny?" Wyatt said, and as soon as the words escaped his mouth, he wished he could have them back.

"You know her, right?" the captain said.

Wyatt nodded.

"Call her as soon as we get back to civilization," Captain Udell said. "Tell her he's missing, but until we know more, tell her the search is ongoing."

As the foursome stared at the blood slick that led to the ice hole the wind bitched and argued.

"Jada, as the lead race organizer I think it's your call," the captain said. "About the race, I mean."

The tall woman sighed, a cloud of condensed moisture jetting from her mouth. "There are currently seventy-eight sleds out on the course. Each has an emergency radio and a GPS beacon, so we can contact them."

"This is a no-brainer, right?" said Trooper Simmons, speaking for the first time. "Odds are we've got a fatality caused by a bear or some such, and the safety of the racers should be paramount."

"A bear?" Wyatt said. "Do you see any bear prints?"

Trooper Simmons said nothing.

"The racers have come from all over the world," Jada said. "As you know, the Terimore 200 is a qualifying even for the Iditarod, and if we stop, they won't be able to compete."

"They won't be able to compete if they're dead," Wyatt said.

"Come on," she said. "A bit of hyperbole, no? These folks are used to danger. Experienced woodsmen, and they're all armed."

Wyatt pointed to the rifle in its scabbard attached to the broken sled.

"Maybe you should contact the committee," Trooper Simmons said.

Jada shook her head. "Most of them are out on the course."

Wyatt wanted to remind the group that it was also a year of the beast, but given his history, he didn't think he should be the one to raise the specter of a mythical beast.

"The clock is ticking," Captain Udell said.

Jada bit her nails, her face twisting with tension.

"We have to send out a warning, right?" Wyatt said. "Let the racers know what's happened."

Jada nodded emphatically as her face muscles loosened. "Let each racer decide what they'd like to do."

"What's your recommendation going to be?" Captain Udell said.

Jada didn't answer. She pulled her radio, switched it to the emergency channel, and sent out an alarm.

Dog teams make a lot of noise as they drive through the snow, and Jada waited until she had acknowledgment from every racer before she spoke to the group. She explained what had happened and recommended that racers abandon the race and head back to the nearest Checkpoint, but if racers wanted to continue racing that would be permitted as long as said racers understood they were going against the organizing committee's recommendation.

When she was done, Captain Udell said, "Let's get a team of police dogs out here and make sure Jesse isn't lying half dead somewhere."

To that, nobody had anything to say.

3

Mount Aire, Alaska, ***7:23 PM AKST, February 8th, 2017***

The last light of the dying day bruised the western sky, and with the sun went all hope of warmth. A westerly wind swept through town, specks of ice biting Wyatt's face and burrowing into his open jacket collar.

In the end, all the remaining competitors decided to complete the race, and there were no further incidents. The results were announced at an awards presentation the prior day, and two single and three double sleds earned spots in the Iditarod. Jesse Ombridge was still officially a missing person, and his likely death overshadowed the completion of the annual Terimore 200 and any desire to celebrate.

The two missing dogs were found roaming the woods, starving and scared, and that gave the searchers some hope, but it was fleeting. The trail of blood that led to the hole in the creek ice left little doubt as to what had occurred, though Wyatt was having a hard time swallowing it.

All he'd done for the last two days was catch cat naps and search for Jesse. There had been no additional signs of the musher; no tracks, blood drips, nothing. The day's search had been called for the night, and a decision would be made overnight about tomorrow. It wasn't Wyatt's call, but he had nothing to do except patrol anyway, so he hoped the official search would continue for at least another day.

Wyatt would be looking for Jesse for the rest of his life, whether he wanted to be or not. The lake and the woods around Mount Aire would never be the same for him, and he'd already had a nightmare in which an old version of himself finds Jesse's skeleton out in the evergreens.

Captain Udell told him these feelings were normal, but Wyatt couldn't shake the idea that he was partly responsible for what had happened, though despite beating himself up for hours, he couldn't figure out what exactly he could've done to change the outcome.

Jesse had been in the wrong place at the wrong time, like his father and uncle and all he could do now was do his best to ensure nobody else suffered the same fate.

Wyatt sidestepped a puddle as he made his way down Main Street—AKA the only street —to meet Ian at his shop before the friends headed over to Buck's Tavern.

Calling Mount Aire a town was an insult to towns. A muddy pothole-ridden road ran through the center of a series of structures of varied architectural integrity. Most of the buildings had metal roofs and were dirty and covered in snow and ice. Dirt paths ran along both sides of the street that served as sidewalks, but none of the buildings along the road faced the street directly. It was as if the structures had been constructed in some random pattern and the street had been worked in between them. Wyatt knew from the old timers at Buck's that was exactly how the town had started. Trappers, hunters, fishermen, and adventurers had congregated at the head of Terror Lake for more than two hundred years, and the base camp grew and became permanent in 1969 when it was granted a U.S. postal stop, ten years after Alaska joined the American union as a state.

The laughter of a young child floated on the breeze and sorrow leaked through Wyatt as he recalled his meeting with Jesse's wife, Ginny. It had been brutal and handing off the dead musher's dogs to his oldest son had been even more difficult. The sullen look of hopelessness and despair dragging down the kid's face made Wyatt's heart hurt. Not only had the boy lost his father, but he'd also most likely lose all his friends. Without his old man's paycheck coming in Ginny would probably be forced to leave the area to find employment so she could support her children. An all too common and sad refrain heard in Mount Aire. No memorial service was planned because Ginny was holding out hope, though even she seemed to know that the thread holding that hope aloft was as thin as a magician's invisible string.

The Guns, Ammo, and Bait Shop was more of a general store than the hunting outpost its name portended, but Ian did carry guns, ammo, and bait, in addition to food stuffs, general supplies, clothing, and just about anything someone who lived beyond the edge of civilization might need. A corner of the store was reserved for tools, both of the manual and power variety, and there was a carport behind the shop where snowmobiles, ATVs, and the occasional vehicle were repaired.

If you had a problem or needed something, Ian was the fix-it-can-get man, and Wyatt often joked with his old high school friend about how well he'd do in prison. As boys, the duo had spent countless hours on the four-wheel-drive bus that transported the children of the peninsula to Ninilchik to the K-12 schoolhouse.

The bell attached to the door's retraction spring announced his arrival as Wyatt entered the store, and he was assailed by the sweet smell of tobacco, the deep rusty scent of meat, and the distant tang of cordite. The place was empty, and the rear of the store was dark.

"That you, Wyatt?" came a voice from the backroom.

A glass counter filled with merchandise ran along one wall, and light streamed from the open door behind the counter that led to the backroom.

"In the flesh," Wyatt said. The fluorescent light above Wyatt's head fizzed, popped, and went dark. He stared at the dark tube, the ancient light fixture's metal ballast covers rusted. He wondered how old the fixture was. Ian's great-grandfather had opened the store as a trading outpost in 1936, and his family had run the place for the last eighty-one years.

Ian appeared in the open doorway behind the counter, his head covered in a bright red knit cap, his ski jacket an obnoxious neon green. He wore round bifocals that matched his oval face, and his piercing blue eyes were always jovial, his thin lips twisted in a perpetual smirk. He was twenty pounds overweight, and like everyone in Mount Aire in the middle of winter, he was carrying extra seasonal weight. He flicked a light switch, and the rest of the shop went dark.

"Oh," Ian said. "I'm sorry, Wyatt. Did you need anything before we go?"

Wyatt had planned to pick up a few things, but he saw the cash register had been shut down and suddenly he didn't feel like lugging Cheerios and beef jerky around with him all night. He said, "I'll stop in tomorrow."

Ian hiked his shoulders. "You O.K.?"

Wyatt wasn't, but nobody in Mount Aire ever answered that question truthfully. Did people anywhere? Maybe California. He said, "You know. As best as can be expected."

His friend's eyes shifted to the worn pine board floor. "Ginny leaving?"

Wyatt hiked his shoulders. "Sure sounds like it, but who knows? I've heard tell of a couple of jobs being thrown her way, and that might change things."

As if he felt some overriding responsibility for everyone in the town—which in some strange last line of supply way he was—Ian said, "I might be able to give her a few hours."

It was a nice gesture, but not what the likely widow needed, so Wyatt said nothing.

"I need a cocktail," Ian said. "Let's go."

Ian locked up, Wyatt watching the few solitary folks on the street bundled in their jackets as they hurried about their business.

Buck's Tavern was named after the iconic sled dog in The Call of the Wild, and it was the longest continually operating business in Mount Aire. Shops, hotels, saloons, and even a coffee shop had come and gone, but Buck's had been around since 1843, though before 1918 it had been known simply as The Stop.

The old wooden door creaked as Wyatt pushed it open, and snow and ice cycled into the pub as the duo entered. The place was roughly half full, but by 9 PM all the seats would be taken, and folks would be standing between the tables and packed against the bar. That's what happened when you were the only show in town.

A huge trophy moose head protruded from the wall above the bar, which ran along one wall. Faint light danced off the bottles stacked behind the bar, and a few faces lifted their eyes from their liquid confessions to study the friends as they made their way to an empty table, waving and saying hello to those who acknowledged them.

Ian was popular, the can-get man.

Wyatt, not so much. He was a Rabbit Ranger, a Duck Detective, the Fish Fuzz, the guy wearing an orange vest you didn't want to see walking through the woods toward your hunting blind or fishing tent. Still, Wyatt was known as a fair man who cared about the peninsula and its people, and his family's history was well-known by most who called Mount Aire home.

The room was subdued. A musher was missing and feared dead, so no music blared from the old jukebox, and only the hum of chatter carried across the dimly lit bar.

"Yo," the bartender yelled as Wyatt and Ian sat.

"The usual, Tom," said Wyatt.

"Same," added Ian.

As the men shed their hats and jackets Tom brought a beer and a chaser of rotgut whiskey for Ian, and a Stolichnaya vodka martini straight up for Wyatt. After imbibing a couple of cocktails Wyatt would move on to beer and finish the night off with whiskey and decaf coffee. He was as predictable as the winter cold, and Wyatt frowned at the thought. Hopefully, the exotic tincture would help him forget, or failing that, at least help him fall asleep at the end of the night.

Ian said, "Why the long face?" Then his friend looked around, his eyes going wide. "Did you know Jesse well?"

He shook his head no. "It's just… Do you ever feel like everything you do is a waste of time and that nothing ever changes?" Wyatt said.

"Every day."

With that, the two men sipped their drinks, the friends eavesdropping on the over-loud conversation of two old-timers holding court at the bar.

"I don't know, Harry, it all seems a little farfetched," said an old guy with white hair and a long gray beard. The men were sharing a pitcher of beer and each of them cradled a whiskey glass in their paws.

"Farfetched? The cycle has been true, and the body count is getting a bit high for that, no?" Harry responded.

Beard-boy waved a hand. "You ever hear of how a bottle of cognac appears on Edgar Allan Poe's grave each year on his birthday? It's been happening… It did happen for a really long time. Every year right on schedule."

"I'm not following the connection to the Akhlut," Harry said.

"The guy who was doing it died, or at least that's what is believed, but for all those years he made the legend true, you follow?"

"So you're saying the Akhlut legend is a hoax and we've got a serial killer loose on the peninsula, and every six years he or she crawls out from under their rock and kills people?"

Beard-boy said nothing.

"There ain't been no evidence of that," Harry said.

"There ain't been no evidence? Don't you think someone would've seen the creature by now? I mean, what is the thing? Bigfoot?"

That got a roar of laughter, and the two men took a timeout to drink whiskey and hydrate with beer.

Harry said, "Maybe, but I've heard tell of other incidents."

"Like?"

"You saw what was left of Tarlonie's cow," Harry said.

Beard-boy harrumphed. "That ain't no proof. Could've been a bear."

"That what you believe?" Harry said. "Was that what it looked like to you? Those strange prints, and that smell. I don't think—" The old man went silent as his eyes strayed to Wyatt.

"Well, out with it," Beard-boy said. "Cat got your tongue?"

Harry thrust his chin out in Wyatt's direction.

Wyatt was used to the odd stares, the uneasy glances, and when the two old men moved on to another topic Wyatt said, "Some shit just never changes."

Ian took a long sip of beer, eyeing Wyatt over the rim of his glass. "Are you saying you believe the old legends?"

"I don't know what I believe, but I can tell you there were no bear tracks anywhere near where Jesse's sled and le… remains were discovered."

"Just like your dad and uncle," Ian said.

Wyatt took a long pull off his drink and nodded. An unidentified wild animal was what the official investigation report listed as his dad and uncle's likely cause of death. There was a description of the odd tracks, but no proposed explanation, and aside from a few body parts, the corpses were never found in the surrounding wildness, not even bones.

Now another person had been taken and all the evidence suggested Jesse Umbridge had been dragged beneath the surface of a creek that fed Terror Lake.

"And it's not like there haven't been other incidents since they were killed," Wyatt added. "To the contrary."

Ian finished his beer, downed the last of his whiskey, and held up both glasses until Tom saw him and raised a finger.

The two men sat in silence as if unable to speak without full cocktails sitting before both men like chess pieces.

Tom brought the fresh beer and whiskey, took Ian's empties, and said, "Wyatt?"

"Sure, but no rush," he said, holding up his glass which was still a quarter full. When Tom was gone, Wyatt said, "You remember last cycle, right? 2011. I was new to the Possum Cops, and I was working out of Anchorage when the call for the first one of the cycle came in. You remember?"

"Yeah, I remember," Ian said.

4

The year of the beast legend had been passed down for countless generations, the stories so ingrained that the children of the peninsula thought of the Akhlut as their own personal Boogeyman. In hushed voices and sullen tones, the Inuit people speak of an orca-wolf hybrid, an apex predator that dominates in the water but is equally as adept at killing on land. The tales go back to a time before the indigenous Alaskans arrived in the area via Greenland over a thousand years ago. Prior to the late 1800s actual evidence of the cycle was sketchy, but there had been at least one death during the year of the beast in the Terror Lake area for more than a hundred years.

In 2011 there had been three.

Wyatt shifted in his seat and downed the rest of his drink. The bar's chatter faded, and he felt heat rise in him. He hadn't been around during the last year of the beast, but he'd heard the stories, and seen the pictures.

Ian took a long pull of whiskey, chased it with beer, and then said, "I remember the Colif kid. That wound is still open."

Wyatt nodded. "Her mother still puts flowers on her grave every day, even when it's covered in two feet of snow."

"There were two others last time?" Ian said and sipped his whiskey.

"Depends on how you count," Wyatt said. "Captain Udell—a lieutenant at the time—showed me the case files because… well, you know."

Ian buried his nose in his beer and said nothing.

"The first death was a drowning out on the lake. Ray Tesco," Wyatt said. "Very similar to what happened with my dad and uncle. No full corpse, nothing but blood and some body parts, and the captain said the tracks in the snow were similar to prints they'd found at death scenes in the past."

"Like the ones you just found at the scene of Jesse's… crash."

"Exactly like those," Wyatt said. "I've never seen a beast make tracks like that." He paused and the men drank, the alcohol sending waves of comfortable heat leaking to Wyatt's extremities. He continued, "Because there was no definitive explanation or proof, the case was left open, but the Colif girl was next, and that made everyone rethink Tesco."

"Yeah." Ian hit his beer and slammed the rest of his whiskey as if numbing himself for what was to come.

"The child was pulled off her bicycle, disemboweled, and her remains were left like an empty bag in a pile of snow. No bear did that, even the most hardened skeptics knew that, but that didn't mean they accepted the legend," Wyatt said, and he heard his mother in his head telling him that he sounded like his father.

Ian shook his head. "The opposite. I remember all the crazy stories." His gaze shifted to the old codgers at the bar, and he lowered his voice. "Crazy shit like a killer on the loose, rabid polar bear, and lake sharks. And those were the semi-plausible ones."

"You'd think three deaths would spark suspicion, make people see things they might not normally see."

Ian nodded. "And none of that takes into account the numerous animal carcasses that we didn't find. How many beasts are killed in the wild? Their carcasses left to boil in the sun or freeze in the snowpack?" he said.

"And people die every year in Mount Aire. Some even of natural causes," Wyatt finished, but neither man chuckled.

"The last death of 2011 isn't even officially a death," Ian said. "Don Sayers is still a missing person. There was no murder scene, no blood, body parts, nothing. That made it easy, if not convenient, for the powers that be to blow off the cycle talk and sweep it all under the rug for another six years."

"What could we do anyway?" Wyatt said. "It's not like people haven't hunted the beast."

"If it's real the thing is a ghost."

The bar babble fell away, and two voices rose above the din. Two alphas were debating the existence of the creature, the chatter of the two older dudes at the bar having stirred the mob.

"You've got your head in the damn snow," said Billy-joe Tolliver, a local woodsman. The big man had pushed up from his stool and was invading the personal space of Juno Ikin, a trapper Wyatt hadn't seen in town in months. Wyatt didn't know which was more disconcerting, that Brett believed in the Akhlut, or that Juno didn't.

"Say you," Juno said. "I've walked every inch of this peninsula, paddled most of its lakes, and I've never seen a creature that resembles your mythical beast in any way. How is that possible?"

"The peninsula is a big place," Brett said.

"Not that big," said Juno.

"Then how do you explain what happened to Jesse? And if you say a polar bear killed him, I hope you've got a weapon on you."

Juno said nothing, but he stepped forward and the two men stood inches apart, a stationary game of chicken in which neither contestant was allowed to blink.

Tom brought Wyatt a fresh drink, and on his way back to the bar he stepped between the two arguing men. "Don't act the fools talking about things that are above your pay grade."

"You're saying we're too stupid to understand?" Brett said, a smirk spreading over his red windburned face.

"I wasn't," Tom said, his face going sour. "But maybe I should've."

Someone coughed, and the gentle push of air escaping the vent above Wyatt and Ian's table was like a gale in the stillness.

Tom's face softened, and Wyatt almost chuckled. Debate and opinions aside, Brett drank a lot of beer, and customers were, if not always right, at least given the benefit of the doubt. The barkeep said, "Look, all I'm saying is there's no way we can know everything, right? There are things that can't be explained. How you got Frida to marry you, for example."

That got a laugh, and the pressure in the room released as the bar chatter resumed.

"Are we ever going to get by this?" Ian said.

Wyatt hiked his shoulders. "Without a color picture of the creature—no, scratch that," he said. "Without verified video of the beast, there'll always be people who don't believe."

Ian said, "Even with that…"

"Yeah. It's a tall tale for sure." Wyatt sighed. A tall tale he'd always been skeptical of, but with each passing second that skepticism was getting harder to maintain.

February melted away, and the search for Jesse Ombridge was called. With money an issue, closure as to Jesse's legal status was essential, and Ginny didn't want her children walking around hoping their father was going to stroll through the door. Captain Udell, based on all the available facts and supported by the on-scene accounts of himself, Wyatt, Jada, and Trooper Simmons, was forced to conclude Jesse had been killed, his corpse taken from the scene, most likely to the lake.

Who or what had perpetrated the crime was unknown, and Jesse was classified as Missing, Presumed Dead. A remembrance ceremony was held at the lake's edge, and Jesse's leg was placed in a grave in the town cemetery.

Watching Jesse's family at the funeral had triggered so many memories Wyatt barely held himself together as the priest spoke about a good soul ascending to heaven. How Ginny and her children would see Jesse again someday, how we simple humans couldn't possibly understand God's plan.

Wyatt had wanted to spit. God's plan hadn't taken the Akhlut into account, and if he had, God was a bigger asshole than Wyatt had originally believed.

He was reliving past pains and thinking of his father as he tear-assed down a narrow path north of Terror Lake. His course constantly drifted to the area where Jesse's sled had been found, thoughts of the dead musher never far from his mind.

A burst of radio static made Wyatt bring the snow machine to a stop, and he killed the engine and pulled his radio.

"Wyatt, Ms. Shiply needs you at her place ASAP," dispatch said. "Do you copy?"

"I copy. What is the nature of the call?"

"Henhouse break-in and one of her husband's sled dogs are missing. And before you ask, Jed is in Anchorage working and won't be back for a few days."

"Do we have—"

"Just head over there, copy?"

"10-4." Wyatt's stomach dropped out his ass and suddenly he had to hit the head, cold sweat dripping down his back.

The Shiply homestead was on the western side of Terror Lake, nestled a hundred yards from the lake's edge surrounded by tall evergreens packed so tightly together they were like a wall. Wyatt had been up to the place a couple of times to take reports about wolves attacking livestock.

Jed Shiply was an ornery old dude, but he was reasonable and knew there wasn't much Wyatt could do. So the guy put up fencing and strung up two hundred feet of razor wire. The inner compound was like a prison, and any creature bigger than a chipmunk would have a difficult time getting through the various defenses unscathed.

Wyatt fired up the machine and made a three-point turn. The afternoon sun had started its fall to the horizon, and light angled through the forest canopy like mana from heaven, the specks of ice fluttering in the breeze sparkling like tiny rainbow starbursts.

The trail met Circle Road, the partly paved street that ran around Terror Lake and tracked through Mount Aire. Wyatt blew by the Shiply driveway and had to backtrack because there was no mailbox, no driveway marker, and only vehicle tracks filled with drifted snow wound into the trees. If Wyatt hadn't known where to look, he wouldn't have found it. All his other visits to the Shiply compound had been in the summer months when the peninsula was much different than its current wintery incarnation.

He went down the driveway slowly, the snowmobile's engine gurgling dully. Wyatt didn't want to spook the livestock. The evergreens were laden with snow, and they arced over the driveway, creating a tunnel filled with shadowy darkness. Vines as thick as rope crisscrossed overhead, and he recalled they were grapevines, and in the summer clusters of white grapes hung from the natural ceiling like light fixtures.

Wyatt broke free of the trees and saw Mrs. Shiply waiting for him on her front porch, arms crossed over her chest, her reflective sunglasses gleaming in the fading light. He didn't remember her name, and embarrassment heated his chilled face. He'd met the woman several times and he prided himself on remembering his constituents' names. If he had more time he could call dispatch, but it was too late because the woman was watching him like she was an eagle, and he was a three-legged mouse.

Her name came to him as he killed the snowmobile's engine and he smiled. "Candice, how are you?" he said as he dismounted the machine.

She eyed him like he was a bug she wanted to stomp, but as he approached her face softened, though her relaxed expression didn't match the ferocity of her words. "These damn wolves… It's hard enough living out here on the edge of nowhere, but to be harassed? Law or no law, if I see the damn thing, I'm gonna put so many pellets in its ass it'll leak like a colander when it drinks."

Wyatt had to chuckle. "What did it get? I heard one of your dogs?"

"Come on and take a look," she said as she grabbed a rifle propped against the porch swing.

The pair worked their way around the Shiply house, Wyatt following Candice as she stepped in the narrow path pounded into the snowpack. Behind the house, there was a barn, two smaller outbuildings, and a henhouse, and through the snow-laden evergreens, frozen Terror Lake shimmered in the late afternoon sun. A wire fence topped with razor wire surrounded it all.

A blood trail marred the snow. It led to a lump of flesh and continued through a gaping hole in the fence.

"Jesus," Wyatt said.

"I'm thinking he had nothing to do with it," Candice said.

5

A side of the henhouse was missing, and broken boards, splinters, and white and brown feathers stuck from the snow. Tiny pools of blood clotted in the hay-covered floor, and the remaining chickens cowered under their nesting shelves, cooing and chirping softly.

Wyatt didn't see any wolf tracks. Wolves have large, padded paws with well-arched toes, the middle toe being longer, and they leave distinct prints, especially in the snow. The beasts had webbed feet, and the temperature of their foot pads were regulated separately from the rest of the canine's body. The temperature of the footpads was maintained just above the tissue-freezing point where the wolf's feet came in contact with the ground.

Drips of blood dappled the snow between the henhouse and the dog kennel, and a series of odd slash-like tracks ran down the center of the blood trail.

The dog kennel was comprised of six separate compartments, and a section of the roof had been ripped off. Five of the sections were undisturbed, and the huskies therein whined and yipped as Wyatt got closer to the destruction. The sixth compartment was empty, and a tooth much bigger than a canine's stuck from where the roof had been torn off. A splotch of blood and guts was splattered on the kennel wall, and there was no sign of the dog that called the kennel home.

Blood painted the snow, and half a chicken lay amongst roof shingles and broken pieces of plywood.

Heat rolled off both damaged structures in waves, the surviving animals subdued as if in reverence of their fallen mates.

"How many chickens did it get?" Wyatt asked.

"Not sure," Candice said. "Four, maybe five. I heard the dogs braying and yelping, so I figure they disturbed the bastard's little feast."

"That's all you heard? The dogs barking?"

Her face scrunched in thought, and she said, "There was this odd yelp, and it wasn't no dog getting chomped."

Wyatt waited.

"It sounded like a… like a whale giving birth, then there was this gagging bark like nothing I've ever heard."

"No wolf howls? Snarls? Barking? You know wolves sound different than dogs."

"Do you take me for a fool?" Anger creased Candice's face, but then her eyes narrowed, and her features softened. "No," she said. "I didn't hear any wolf cries."

Wyatt glanced over his shoulder at the odd tracks and blood trail that led through the ripped-open fence into the woods. "How long ago did this happen?" he asked.

She waved a hand. "Middle of the night. Maybe 3 AM? I didn't come out here until this morning to feed the chickens. That damn rooster was shrieking before the sun came up. It takes all the patience I've got to keep from turning that annoying little pecker into a cloud of feathers."

Wyatt took some pictures and made some notes for his report, Candice watching him the entire time like he might steal a few eggs.

The wind gusted, spearing Wyatt's face with tiny ice shards, clouds of frozen mist swirling above the snowpack and winding through the forest. The blood trail beckoned, but he didn't want Candice following after him.

Wyatt drew his Glock, racked the slide, and chambered a round for effect. "Go wait inside while I track this thing."

"Thing?"

He said nothing.

"You think whatever did this might still be around?" she said, motioning toward her henhouse and dog kennel.

"Never know." He lifted his gun for show. "Is there someone you can call to button up this mess for you?"

Her head jerked back like she'd been punched.

"Not that you can't handle it yourself," he backtracked.

That got a smile. "I can call Jed's brother if I need the loser."

The lump of flesh between the henhouse and the hole in the fence was unidentifiable, but it looked like the innards of one of the chickens. The rusty scent of blood carried on the breeze… and something else, like garbage mixed with rotten fish. He'd heard tell of that scent.

Wyatt tried to push thoughts of the Akhlut from his mind as he climbed through the torn gap in the fence and followed the alligator-like slash prints into the evergreen forest. Drips and small pools of blood-stained snowpack, birds and chipmunks fleeing before him as they sniffed and licked at the crimson stains.

He felt Candice watching him, but didn't look back.

A hedgerow of dense bushes with stiletto-length prickers lined the edge of the lake, except for an opening that led to a path that ran to a rickety dock that looked like it might fall over. Most folks on Terror Lake used floating docks that could be stacked on land during the winter, but not Jed and Candice. Poles stuck from the frozen lake like rotten teeth, and the decking was missing several boards and was slanted at a thirty-degree angle.

The blood trail and tracks ran to the dock, but then veered sharply left and ran along the lake's edge, the trail easy to see in the pristine white snow.

Wyatt paused, his mind conjuring images of the lake in summer, when boats dotted the water, and animals drank and frolicked in the shallows. He and his father had fished Terror Lake when he was a boy. Shit, he and his friends had skinny-dipped in the clear cool water, though he'd never told his parents. He could almost smell the evergreens, the invigorating scent of fresh water wafting through the forest.

He hugged himself, but he got only colder, so he lurched into motion, following the tracks, his cheeks tingling.

Wind scoured Terror Lake, the sun's glare reflecting off the ice and snow destroying Wyatt's depth perception. Shadows writhed just within the tree break, and suddenly he felt the weight of the Glock in his hand, but didn't holster the weapon.

He'd gone about an eighth of a mile when the trail arced east, out toward the center of the lake. Sweat dripped down his back in rivulets, and an uncomfortable cold settled on him, an unexplainable burden weighing him down. Wyatt considered going back, but his job, history, and curiosity drove him on.

Ice cracked and popped, distant hollow booms flowing through the ice like an electrical charge as he stepped onto the lake. Tall snowdrifts rose like miniature mountain peaks, slick patches of ice in-between, the wind scouring and molding the pliable landscape.

He looked back and saw he was almost half a mile out on the lake, but he continued, following the slashes and drips of blood around a snowdrift that rose from the lake like K2. Wind swirled, the snow twisting and adding to the giant mound of snow and ice.

Wyatt stopped walking and brought up the Glock, moisture fleeing his mouth for his armpits, his stomach grumbling, heart pounding.

The trail led to an opening in the side of the snowdrift, the nasty scent of rotten fish mixed with rust flowing from the black maw and crawling up his nostrils. A searing heat washed through Wyatt as his chill fled, his bladder suddenly screaming for attention.

He inched forward, covering his nose with a gloved hand, the Glock aimed at the dark opening. The smell was so rank he gagged, bile creeping up his throat, his breakfast looking to make an encore.

The opening was roughly eight feet high by five feet wide, but its edges were smooth as if whatever had built the den had to squeeze through the entrance many times.

This wasn't unusual. Many animals on the peninsula build dens for the winter months, and not unlike a human bivouac, the beasts utilized their body heat to warm their living spaces, and as Wyatt inched into the opening the temperature rose and his face no longer pulsed with pain.

Bones and dark patches of blood and dried gristle stained the snowpack, and the odd prints ran on into the gloom. Wyatt didn't have a flashlight, but he had his phone, and the snowdrift glowed beneath the mid-day sun, pale light illuminating the den.

Wyatt took several hesitant steps, Glock up, eyes straining to see what lay ahead. It occurred to him that he should be taking more pictures, documenting the scene, but there was plenty of time for that.

The open space narrowed into a tunnel. The snow walls were rough, as if dug with an immense shovel, and pale blue light filtered through the snow and ice. Fish bones cracked underfoot, and the wind chanted and sang as it piped into the den.

He should go back. Wyatt knew this with a surety he could only chalk up to instinct. What did he hope to accomplish? It was clear the huskie that had been taken was dead, and Wyatt's thoughts drifted back to Jesse's leg sticking from a snowdrift. Was finding Jesse's corpse a reason to go on?

There was no answer, and though warning lights flashed all over his mental control panel, he pushed on through the gloom, his eyes adjusting to the dim light. He pictured his approach to the snowdrift in his mind's eye to gauge its size and concluded he was close to its center.

The cry of a wolf carried into the den, and it was answered by another.

Had he miscalculated? Was he in a wolf's den? But no, he knew that wasn't likely, and it wasn't only because he saw no paw prints. What he did see were slash marks. Plus, Wyatt had never seen a wolf make a burrow on a frozen lake. The beasts preferred more secluded places, like caves, hollow logs, beaver lodges, or underground tunnels, all of which would help the canines stay warm through the long winter.

The passage stayed level and opened into a second space that was twice the size of the area at the entrance. The smell was unbearable, and Wyatt covered his nose as he did his best to hold back a gag, but failed.

He coughed and spittle leaked from his mouth, but the eggs, bacon, and toast he'd had for breakfast stayed down.

Wind chanted, the stink of rotting flesh driving out the scent of fish. The space was filled with piles of bones, dried fat and gristle still clinging to many of them. The walls and ice floor were stained brown, and the crimson of fresh blood could be seen on every surface.

At the center of the den, there was a large hole in the ice the size of a massive hot tub, and water, chunks of ice, and a blood slick made up of gristle and fat gyrated therein.

Wyatt's breath caught, pain racing down his spine and settling in his lower back. His vision went blurry, his mind unable to process what he was seeing. Terror took hold, tiny starbursts dotting his field of vision, his knees threatening to come unhinged.

Next to the ice hole, lying at the center of a dried pool of blood, was a human finger adorned with a gold ring that looked like a wedding band.

Wyatt rocked back, swaying, mind spinning. Was it Jesse's finger? Had he worn a wedding ring? Wyatt didn't know.

He holstered the Glock and tapped at his phone. With the device's glaring light pushing away the gloom, he documented the den with a two-minute video and took several pictures of the finger before wrapping it in a tissue and stowing it in his jacket pocket. Wyatt knew tampering with evidence—and the finger was surely evidence—was against procedure, but given the situation, he was concerned that an animal might… That the digit would be gone when the chief came around to take a look.

The ice vibrated and boomed, and Wyatt put out his hands to steady himself, but there was nothing to hold on to.

Ribbons of black and white slithered through the water as something huge swam beneath the ice.

Wyatt pointed his cell phone at the frozen lake, but there was no contrast, and the camera couldn't pick up the details of what he was seeing. He stood transfixed, his feet frozen to the ice, his nerves dancing just beneath his skin as he put his phone away.

The water in the ice hole began to churn, mounds of whitewater and popping bubbles disturbing the floating chunks of ice.

The space grew dark, the sunlight illuminating the snowdrift dimming. Wyatt figured a cloud had floated across the sun, but that realization didn't make him feel any better about his situation.

With a gurgle, a fist of water surged from the hole, spilling over the ice, and for a heartbeat the frozen lake was clear.

A huge black eye rimmed in white stared up at Wyatt.

He double-timed it out of there, slipping and sliding, the sound of cracking ice and popping bubbles pursuing him.

6

Wyatt and Captain Udell sat in the chief's office at the back of Town Hall, which shared one of the village's few commercial office buildings with Mount Aire's two dentists. There was a dark sludge stain at the bottom of the coffee pot, and stacks of files and unopened mail covered in dust sat on every vertical surface. There were no windows, and the fluorescent light above hummed and buzzed, its life-sucking rays of pale light barely illuminating the space. Shadows danced on the walls as the men shifted position, and the office stank of disinfectant and clove oil from the dental offices.

The place had a distinctly unlived in feel because the captain rarely used the room. He had three other similar setups around the peninsula, but Udell spent most of his time shuttling from zone to zone, keeping an eye on the doings of the fifty-four other Wildlife Troopers that patrolled the Kenai Peninsula.

The captain cycled through printouts of the most pertinent photos of the Shiply compound and the den out on the lake, his face a mask of nonemotion. "No picture of this eye you saw beneath the ice?" he asked.

Anger welled in Wyatt. The captain's tone said he didn't fully believe what Wyatt had told him. He cleared his throat and cracked his neck to ease his tension, then said, "Like I mentioned before, the ice cleared for a second when the water washed over the packed snow. By the time I thought to take a picture the ice was white and whatever was moving about below was gone."

Captain Udell sighed and leaned back in his chair, and it screeched like someone had stepped on a cat's tail. "Did you speak with Ginny Ombridge?"

Wyatt nodded. The ring on the finger he'd found had left no doubts as to whose digit it was. The gold band was engraved with Ginny and Jesse's names and the date of their nuptials.

"How is she? Has she… accepted her reality?" he said. "I know a few people in Anchorage who might be able to help her find work, and there are a couple of positions she might be qualified for in the central trooper office."

"Yeah," Wyatt said. "I don't think she's told the children yet, but I can't see how she can stay."

"And the finding of the finger?"

Wyatt hiked his shoulders. "She's come to terms with his death. She was more upset and concerned about the logistics of how the finger was going to be added to the grave with the leg."

"As for the rest." The captain shook his head. "I have a meeting at central next week and I'll raise our concerns, but without any direct proof I don't see them ringing the alarm bell."

Wyatt sighed so loud he apologized. "Sorry, but no direct proof? What about the strange tracks? The holes in the ice? The fact we didn't find any corpses, animal or human. The strange den, and..." He wasn't going to be the one to bring up the year of the beast. "And what of that?" Wyatt pointed at the large broken tooth sitting on the desk before the captain.

Captain Udell said, "I'll send it to the FBI Quantico lab so the feds can check it out."

Wyatt didn't ask why the captain wasn't sending the tooth to the state crime lab because he knew why. His boss didn't want the senior brass to know Udell and his crew were chasing a ghost. Analyzation of the tooth would take longer, but at least the piece would get a thorough analysis, and there was nothing he could do to change the situation anyway, so Wyatt nodded.

"Anything else? That budget I sent you for the next two years O.K.?"

"I skimmed the stuff and the only issue I saw was putting off the purchase of the new snow equipment."

The captain nodded. "But you saw the extra repair money I allocated?"

Wyatt nodded.

"Alright," Captain Udell said as he pushed up from his chair and held out his hand. Wyatt was being dismissed. "Keep your gun at the ready, your eyes open, and call me if you see so much as a fieldmouse acting strange."

Wyatt nodded again as he shook his boss's hand, and said, "2017 has been a wicked bitch so far."

"Things will settle down. You'll see," Captain Udell said.

"I sure hope you're right."

The captain was right, things did settle down, and it wasn't until mid-April that things got stirred up again.

Wyatt got a call about a group of brown bears roughhousing and harassing livestock up on the northeastern slope of Lake Terror, which was the most sparsely populated side of the lake.

Brown bears, better known in Mount Aire as Grizzlies, aren't full hibernators and can be woken easily, and as winter waned both males and females left their dens in search of food. Not unlike wolves, brown bears spend the cold months in caves, crevices, or hollow logs.

Wyatt was relaxed and not expecting much of a problem as he drove one of three vehicles he shared with the other troopers in the area. ATVs and snowmobiles were the main modes of transport, but the resident that called in the bear activity house was along the road, which was plowed, so there was easy access.

The truck's radio crackled with static, then, "Wyatt. Do you copy?" It was the central dispatch station in Ninilchik.

Wyatt lifted the handset, opened a channel, and said, "I copy. Go ahead."

"We've got a situation," the trooper said. "What's your current position?"

"I'm five minutes out from the Lenard place?" Wyatt said, and he silently thanked Captain Udell for his budget cuts, which put an end to the idea of GPS locators on all trooper vehicles.

"O.K., good. I'll call Mrs. Lenard and tell her you'll be by another time. I need you to head to Kingman's Ranch. Apparently, our bears are on the move. Two males are fighting, and one of the beasts already took one of the sheep as—hold on a second."

With a snap of static, the channel closed and as he waited Wyatt took a long pull of coffee. Kingman's Ranch was nestled in the woods on the northeast corner of Terror Lake. A narrow valley protected the ranch from the elements, and the lamb, deer, cows, and chickens raised there supplied a large portion of the meat sold in Mount Aire. To get there Wyatt would have to cross the glacier, and suddenly he wished he'd taken one of the snowcats.

He was considering heading back to switch to a snowmobile when dispatch hailed him again.

"Things have escalated," the trooper said. "One of the cattle workers tried to shoo away the bears, and from what I can gather one of the beasts got the guy. I'm dispatching a medivac, but I need you there ASAP. Approach with extreme caution. Do you have your rifle with you?"

"I do."

"You have authorization to use deadly force should it be necessary."

Wyatt glanced over his shoulder at the black rifle where it sat in the backseat. He'd been on the job for over ten years, and he'd yet to shoot a single healthy animal. He said, "Copy that."

He drove as fast as the plowed, but ice-covered, road would allow, and when he came to the yellow security barrier blocking the road, he brought the truck to a stop and searched through his keys for the one that would unlock the master lock securing the chain between the barriers. For a horrifying moment he thought he didn't have the key, but he found it, and quickly slipped from the truck and unlocked the barrier.

Time was of the essence, so he didn't waste time relocking the chain. Locals knew not to come this way, not unless they wanted to risk getting stuck on the glacier that spilled down to Terror Lake like a frozen water slide.

Wyatt came around a bend in the road, the truck rattling and squeaking, and thin orange fiberglass poles marked the trail ahead. The road turned to dirt-covered snowpack, then to sand-covered ice. He put the vehicle in four-wheel low and slowly climbed up the side of the glacier, being careful to stay on the marked trail. The rubber tires popped as the thin coating of verglas covering the snowpack cracked and shrieked.

Nobody had been over the glacier in some time, and as Wyatt inched the truck forward, he tried to recall the last time he'd been up this way. Summer, he concluded. He liked sitting at the edge of the glacier when the heat of summer was baking the peninsula. There was nothing better than nature's AC. It was free and the scenery was better than where he lived.

Wyatt arrived at Kingman's Ranch to find organized chaos.

Gunshots echoed off the valley walls, and Wyatt pressed the SUV's gas pedal to the floor, the truck fishtailing as he sped down the dirt road that led through a thin barrier woods to the heart of the ranch.

The forest thinned, revealing the main house and several outbuildings, the snow-covered pastures of the valley beyond.

Wyatt wound his way through the buildings and found a cluster of men and women standing before the open doors of a large barn. He informed dispatch that he'd arrived as he killed the engine and turned on his hip radio. As he got out, he checked his Glock, then grabbed the rifle from the backseat.

The crowd before the barn parted like he was a human snowplow, and Wyatt saw a man lying on the ground, the front of his black winter jacket torn to shreds and glistening with fresh blood.

"Wyatt, thank God you're here. Is the medivac on the way?" Wyatt had met the woman before, but only once, and despite his continual effort to know the names of those in his patrol zone, and the fact that he ate her meats, he couldn't remember the woman's name.

"Yes," he said. "Who is firing that gun?"

“This way,” the woman said. She led him around the barn, between a chicken coop and a storage shed, and through a stone archway. Wind pushed clouds of snow over the valley floor, the steep gray mountains rising into the bright blue cloud-streaked sky.

A hundred yards off two men stood over two huge lumps of brown fur. Beyond them, out on the open pasture, two Grizzlies stood on their hindlegs as they fought toe to toe, swiping at each other with their massive paws like boxers, three-inch black claws glinting in the bright light. The neck of one of the beasts was drenched in blood, and both creatures screamed and howled at each other, spittle flying from their growling mouths, bloody teeth and raging black eyes distorting their otherwise tender faces.

Wyatt and the woman reached the two men and the carcasses of the two black bears they'd killed.

Upon seeing Wyatt's orange vest, one of the men said, “Now don't go writing any summons, Mr. Rabbit Ranger. Remember we called you. This one here…” The guy poked the dead bear to his left with the tip of his rifle. “He's the one who took a chunk out of Danny.”

“Shut it, Snacks,” the woman said before addressing Wyatt, “All Danny tried to do was chase the beasts away. We didn't want to shoot anything, but these little fuc—indigenous beasts—poach our livestock on a regular basis.”

“Did you try and scare them off with a few shots into the air?” Wyatt said as he stared at the two bears who were still pushing each other around and yelping, but they appeared to be tiring.

The ranch lady motioned toward the main event. “Ten shots. Then Danny tried to shoo them off and the dead male there charged him, and you know how fast these bastards can be.”

He did, and Wyatt's gaze strayed to the fighters who were only a hundred yards off.

Five minutes slipped away, and in the end, it was the thunder of the chopper that drove the remaining bears off. Wyatt kept his record of not shooting a healthy animal intact, though he cursed himself for not loading a tracker dart into the gun. He'd missed an excellent opportunity to tag one of the alphas to track his movements. It was always helpful knowing where the big boys lived and roamed.

Danny was taken away in the chopper, and word from the onboard paramedic was that he was going to make it, though he was going to be in the hospital for a long time. Per protocol, Wyatt was supposed to confiscate the two dead bears. The Wildlife Troopers did this to discourage illegal killings disguised as necessary shootings. If the killer didn't get the meat and fur, there was no reason to kill a bear unless it was truly harassing or threatening someone. Of course, people poached bears all the time, and it was his job to do his best to stop it.

Still, his plate was overflowing, the shooting appeared necessary, and if anyone would utilize the meat and fur properly it would be the ranch, so he let it slide.

Wyatt documented the scene, did a few brief interviews for his report, and headed back to the truck to update the captain.

"I agree about the carcasses," the captain said. "We've got better things to do. I'll get on the horn with central as soon as we hang up. You feel better about things?"

Wyatt wasn't sure what his boss meant. "Sir?"

"There's no strange monster running around. Nothing to see here except winter-starved bears," the captain said, though Wyatt knew from the tone of his voice he wasn't buying his own bullshit.

Wyatt let the turd float as he tried to embrace denial, but the tangle in his gut and the image of Jesse's finger adorned with his wedding ring reminded him it was a year of the beast, and it was only April.

7

Terimore Lake, Alaska, ***11:19 AM AKST, May 8th, 2017***

Spring sprouted in slow motion.

Wyatt drove along Circle Road on the east side of Terror Lake, tall shadows falling over the street, the road a patchwork of pavement, potholes, snow, and ice. Evergreens unburdened by snow encroached on the road, a faint tinge of green sprouting from the skeletal undergrowth, pinecones, dirt, stones, and bronze pine needles decorating the shrinking snowdrifts along the road's shoulder. An occasional gate or driveway marked the location of lake houses, and no trespassing and no hunting signs were prominently displayed on some of them.

He came upon a black pickup that had seen better days parked on the shoulder of the road. The vehicle tilted at a twenty-degree angle because the passenger side wheels were on a snowdrift. Wyatt slowed and took a picture of the license plate because he didn't recognize the truck. Not many people live in and around Mount Aire, and he recognized most of the local vehicles.

It wasn't that he didn't know whose truck it was that bothered him. That mystery could be solved with a two-minute call to dispatch. No, what concerned him was what was the driver of the pickup doing in the woods in May? There were currently no open hunting seasons, though there were exceptions. Alaskans could hunt any species that's considered overpopulated in the region, or if said hunter had no other reasonable means of sustenance. Currently, there were no such conditions locally that he was aware of.

Enforcing wildlife protections and taking down poachers was one of Wyatt's main responsibilities, but the person could be hiking, hunting with a camera, or scoping out a location for a future hunting blind. Most hunting seasons opened in late summer and ran through the winter, though there were instances where seasons of certain species were extended, though he'd never heard of any extensions that lasted into May.

An eighth of a mile down the road there were two more vehicles—a sedan of indeterminate make and year due to it being covered in mud and a white Jeep Wrangler—were nestled against the snowbank that ran along the shoulder like a protective wall, mist lifting from the snowpack within the forest beyond, snakes of moisture slithering onto the road.

Wyatt pulled in behind the Jeep and killed the car's engine. The Wrangler was Tommy Maddox's ride. He could tell by the gold eagle on the hood. Tommy was a standup guy, and Wyatt couldn't imagine the man was poaching, so with curiosity and boredom driving him on, Wyatt set out to investigate.

The air was a crisp fifty-eight degrees, the ground covered with the compressed remnants of the winter snowfall. Dirty trails spidered through the white snow like blood veins, the paths muddy and pocked with puddles. Spring on the peninsula was a wet, but fruitful time when the outline of summer emerged, and the wildlife rushed to pack in half a year of living in three short months. Birds sang, and chipmunks, marmots, and squirrels darted about, their prints in the melting snow cycling through the trees.

Wyatt hit a fork in the path, the faint rumble of water filtering through the forest. He followed the soothing sound of water falling over stones, and he thought of something that he should've considered. Perhaps the folks parked on Circle Road were fishing?

With the proper permit, fishing was permitted on the Kenai Peninsula all year round, and rainbow trout and Dolly Varden char were common staples of the local fishermen. There was nothing better than a whole trout wrapped in foil with butter and herbs and steamed to perfection. Wyatt took his quota of the tasty beasts every year if he could.

He looked right, then left, but didn't see any houses, yet he knew he was on somebody's land. That meant, at a minimum, that Tommy and the other two mystery people had trespassed, though he'd yet to see any private property signs posted along the trail.

The path ended at a pond with three men standing in its shallow water. The men were waist deep, tiny waves lapping against their hip waders, the snap and zing of the fishing lines and spinning reels carrying over the rumble of the stream.

No outdoorsman, no matter how environmentally conscious and law-abiding, looks forward to the Fish Fuzz strolling from the forest wearing their orange vests like medieval armor. The river itself couldn't be privately owned, so technically the trio wasn't trespassing, but despite this, all three men froze when they saw Wyatt.

"Afternoon," Wyatt said. "You doing well, Tommy?"

"Meh," the big man answered. He wore reflective sunglasses, no hat or jacket, and an unlit cigar dangled from between his lips. "I've got a couple of rainbows. They're in the bucket over here if you want to take a look. They're all of legal size and I'm well below my limit."

"No worries," Wyatt said. There were three fishing pails with tacklebox jackets, and he casually strolled by them and examined the fishing licenses in the clear plastic holders affixed to the side of the pails. He did his best not to be obvious, but one of the two men Wyatt didn't know said, "All our licenses are up-to-date."

"I see that. Good," Wyatt said. "The names on the tags say Greg and TJ, which is which?"

The 'our licenses are current' guy lifted a hand and said, "Greg Knapp."

"Pleased to meet you," Wyatt said. "How is it you and I never met before? I know most of the anglers out this way."

"New to town, and TJ here is showing me the spots."

TJ was casting and had yet to speak.

The pond was nothing more than a notch in the stream where a series of large boulders had impeded the river's flow, and from his elevated position Wyatt saw Terror Lake shimmering, its surface covered in melted ice, a layer of solid ice beneath. The snowdrifts were gone, and Wyatt's gaze strayed to the center of the lake as he searched for the den he'd investigated, but it had either melted, or it was hiding within the shadowy glare.

Wyatt looked in the fishing pails, and as Tommy had said, all the fish looked of legal length. He could measure the fish, but he could tell by the red and blue coloring and dark speckles covering the pale scales that the fish weren't young.

"Not to be a pest, but do you guys have permission to trek in here? I don't know whose land you walked through, and nobody complained, but there can be—"

A strangled roar, followed by a staccato cackle-bark pierced the day.

The sound had come from the lake, and all four men stared in that direction.

"Tommy," Wyatt said. "Have you heard that call out here before?"

Wind gusted and sang as Tommy shook his head no.

TJ found his voice. "You gonna check it out? Or just continue to bust our peanuts?"

"Hey, now," said Tommy. "Wyatt's doing his job, and we're all better for it or there ain't going to be no more fish to catch."

TJ licked his lips and nodded. "Yeah, I didn't mean anything by it." Yet the tone of the man's voice said he had.

Sweat dripped down Wyatt's back. He had heard that cry before. More times than he'd like to admit. He drew his Glock and said, "Keep an eye out. I'm sure you heard about Jesse Ombridge?"

All three fishermen nodded.

Wyatt picked his way along the stream, leaving the pond and the anglers behind. Evergreens and underbrush encroached on the edge of the river, and he had to walk in the shallow water, his rubber boots squeaking on stones, a steady unease growing in him like a sickness.

Another cry, but this one was closer and sounded more ferocious. Ahead, branches creaked and cracked, the huff of breathing and the crunch of approaching footsteps rising above the wind.

The river plunged downward and a thicket of pricker vines and scrub pines filled the escarpment that ran to the lake's edge. There was no path, and Wyatt paused, trying to see through the undergrowth and evergreens, the Glock cold in his ungloved hand.

A flash of black against snow, a growl, harsh panting.

Wyatt felt an overwhelming urge to hide, but instead went on, picking his way through the melting snow, slipping and sliding in mud. He almost fell twice, but when he reached the lake's edge his heart rattled in his chest.

Two white-rimmed eyes stared at him from behind a tangle of vines with little green buds running along their branches like ants.

His feet were glued to the ground, his head a fog of wonder, fear, and confusion. Wyatt remembered the gun in his hand, and he lifted it and aimed the weapon at the eyes.

The eyes winked out, shadows dancing beneath the tangle of vines.

Breaking branches, chuffing, cracking ice, and the slosh of water echoed up the slope, but Wyatt didn't move. Couldn't move.

The creature that pushed from the vegetation didn't look of this world. It was the size of a baby elephant, and it pressed itself to the ground like a stalking cat. Dark, white-rimmed eyes blinked in the sunlight, the beast's slick black and white skin glistening. The beast inched forward on all fours, muscles knotting its… legs? Pectoral fin-like legs with flat black talons moved in perfect coordination, and the tall dorsal fin that protruded from the creature's back cast a long shadow over the underbrush. Its thick, muscular tail ended with two flukes, and the creature's head could only be described as wolf-like. A narrow snout ended in a mouth full of three-inch teeth, its long ears pressed to its head, its eyes black pools above a slit of a nose.

The Akhlut.

Even as he stared he didn't believe, couldn't believe. If what his eyes were telling his brain was true, reality as he knew had been forever altered.

The Akhlut came forward, eyes fixed on Wyatt as it wormed its way around trees and through the underbrush.

Wyatt pulled his phone. This time there would be proof the bigwigs couldn't deny. The warmth of fear filled his stomach as he fumbled with his cell, trying to unlock the screen. But his hands were wet, sweat was dripping into his eyes, and the growl of the beast as it came forward made him give-up on the phone and focus his attention on the Glock.

He squeezed off a shot and the beast stopped coming at him, its dark eyes surveying Wyatt through the trees.

A branch cracked and Wyatt twisted around, swinging the gun.

Yellow eyes peered from the foliage as a large lynx stalked him.

The Akhlut screamed with rage, and the lynx sprang at Wyatt.

He tried to aim the gun at the cat, but it was too fast and he too slow. The beast hissed, its claws out and looking for flesh. Wyatt stepped back to avoid getting gashed and tumbled down the embankment toward the lake… and the Akhlut.

Wyatt felt oddly relaxed as the pricker vines tore at his jacket, blurs of green, white, brown, and blue spinning before him. He was too young for this, and to lose to the creature like this? Like his father and uncle? The irony hurt his brain, and when he smacked into a stone, pain spidering out from his midsection, an alarm klaxon ringing in his head, he saw his mother and his dead father in his mind's eye.

Then the world slowly lost color and faded to black.

When he came awake Wyatt was lying on his back, clouds streaming across a blue sky, the faces of Tommy, TJ, and Greg staring down at him. He checked his jacket pocket for his father's knife, and when he felt it beneath the fabric he closed his eyes, an image of the Akhlut painted on the insides of his eyelids.

8

Aside from having to spend the rest of his career dealing with the practical jokes, jabs, and the constant snickers of his fellow troopers for having been found unconscious by three anglers while on duty, Captain Udell wasn't pleased.

Wyatt sat on the examination table, his legs dangling over the side, the sheet of paper covering the table's gray pleather cushion crackling each time he shifted position. The air was heavy with the scent of disinfectant and body odor.

Captain Udell sat in a chair off to the side, gazing out the room's only window.

The doctor, Janet Riole, was a Mount Aire lifer and had only left town to follow in her father's footsteps and go to medical school. Her hand was beneath Wyatt's shirt, and she ranged a stethoscope across his chest for what felt like the thousandth time.

She said, "You passed the concussion test and I think you're O.K. to go home. The knot on your head is pretty nasty, though, and the laceration on your left side is going to be black as night come tomorrow. Do you live with anyone that can keep half an eye on you? Just in case?"

"I'll be fine," Wyatt said.

"That wasn't the question." The doctor looked at the captain, who sighed.

"Can Ian drop by tonight and check in on you?" Captain Udell said with an 'I'm not doing it' tone.

Wyatt knew Ian would use any excuse to get a break from his constantly bickering children, so he nodded and said, "I can ask."

"Good. Rest up," Dr. Riole said. Then she addressed the captain. "Nothing for him but light duty for the next week or so, and I'll expect to see him again before he returns to full duty."

"Got it," said the captain.

The doctor nodded and headed for the door.

When she was gone Captain Udell asked, "Now can you tell me exactly what the hell happened out there?"

He hadn't said much because he was being cautious, but now that he'd had a couple of hours to ruminate, he wasn't sure what he'd seen.

No, correction, came that little voice from the back of his mind that didn't allow him to bullshit himself. He knew exactly what he'd seen, and the only question was could he admit it to himself?

Wyatt was the guy who had lost his father and uncle under mysterious circumstances. Anything he said, any opinion he expressed, no matter how mainstream or off-the-charts strange, would be viewed through the lens of his loss. He'd never lied to the captain, but what was he supposed to say? I saw the Akhlut. A beast that almost every inhabitant of the peninsula had been doing their best to deny the existence of for more than a hundred years? He said, "I... don't really remember. I was checking licenses, as you know, and the four of us heard this strange call, so I checked it out."

"And?"

Wyatt hiked his shoulders. "A lynx came at me."

"And your sidearm?" the captain said. "Tommy and the other two said they heard a gunshot, and that when they found you the Glock was lying on the ground beside you. I checked your weapon, and it had been fired once. There was a round in the firing chamber and thirteen in the magazine."

Shit. The gun. He'd forgotten all about that in his fogged state. "Right... right, it's coming back to me now, sorry," he said as he rubbed his forehead. "My head is still pounding."

Captain Udell hoisted his eyebrows.

"I saw the lynx in the underbrush, and I fired one shot into the air to scare the thing off."

"Did you?"

Wyatt said nothing. Now his head was ringing for real.

"Scare the beast away?"

Cold sweat dripped down his back and Wyatt did his best to keep his face expressionless. He was a horrible poker player and he hated lying.

Air whistled through the ceiling vent, the tinkle of ice pellets hitting glass filling the room as the wind gusted.

The captain got to his feet with a groan.

Wyatt had to say something. "The creature took off," he finally said. "I'm fuzzy after that." The more information he provided, the greater chance he'd trip up. As a trooper, he'd learned all about that at the academy. He'd also learned that if you stayed silent, people talked. They just couldn't help themselves.

Problem was the captain had been through the same training and he could smell dishonesty a mile away and closer on Sundays. "Do you have anything to add?" he asked.

Wyatt said nothing.

"Were you thinking about your dad and uncle when you were out there?"

"I don't recall," Wyatt said, and that was the truth. Then he lied. "As I said, things got a little fuzzy."

The captain eyed him, and Wyatt felt the pressure of that stare. Captain Udell knew he wasn't telling the whole truth, but as he exhaled a long breath Wyatt got the feeling he was being taken down off the hook. "Take tomorrow off. Then I want you to spend a few days getting the boats and ATVs ready. The trails will be clear, and the lake will be navigable soon."

Wyatt licked his lips and rolled his eyes.

"Do you have something to say, Trooper?"

Like when his mother called him by his full name, when the boss slung trooper around it meant he wasn't in the mood for a debate.

"I keep the equipment in tip-top shape," Wyatt said. "You know that. Why can't I patrol? How much lighter duty is there than that? If I come across anything, I'll call for assistance."

"You'll do what you've been told, Trooper Wyatt. That's an order. You're banned from even taking a walk in the woods until further notice. I find out you're not obeying my orders... Well, as you know I don't make threats."

Only promises. Wyatt had to stifle a groan. "Understood, sir."

"Do you have someone to give you a ride home?"

"Naw, I can walk it, and I want to stop by Ian's store anyway and it's not far," Wyatt said.

The captain nodded. "Keep in touch, and..." He pulled open the room's door and paused. "And I'll be by the boat shack the day after tomorrow, so have a list of parts ready. And make sure you have a draft of your report documenting today's... incident ready for my review."

Wyatt nodded. "We won't need any parts." But you're not coming for the parts list, are you, boss? And Wyatt knew he had more than forty-eight hours to complete his report, but he would follow orders.

Captain Udell licked his lips, turned on a heel, and left Wyatt alone with his thoughts.

Mount Aire was subdued. It was the quiet hour between the end of the workday and dinner. It was a time of errands and tasks, so Wyatt wasn't surprised when he arrived at Ian's store and found a line at the counter.

All heads turned his way as he entered, the bell jingling, snow cycling into the shop. He quickly closed the door behind him and stomped his feet, shaking off the dirty snow and mud.

Ian said, "Hey Wyatt, wh—" Concern melted away his friend's smile. "Are you O.K.? You look like you've seen a ghost."

Wyatt shrugged. "Need a hand?" He'd helped at the store many times.

"If you feel up to it," Ian said. "I heard you took a tumble."

The chatter of the customers had died away and everyone was listening to the conversation while trying to look like they weren't listening.

"You really shouldn't listen to the little birdies," Wyatt said.

"But their songs are usually true and so entertaining."

Wyatt didn't respond as he worked his way past the customers and behind the counter, where he took up position next to the second cash register.

Ian leaned over and tapped a few buttons, and Wyatt's register came to life.

It took almost half an hour, but when the doorbell rang and the last customer pushed out into the growing darkness, Ian sighed and pulled a bottle of whiskey from below the counter along with two coffee mugs.

"Would you like a nip?" Ian said.

Wyatt wanted a nip more than he had in a long time, but he shook his head no. "Later."

"Suit yourself." Ian poured himself a shot and tossed it back. Then he poured another before putting away the bottle. "What can I get you?"

"The doctor says I need a chaperone. Can you break away for the night? Beers and burgers on me?"

"That depends," his friend said. "Are you going to tell me the whole truth and nothing but the truth?"

Wyatt chuckled and said, "We'll see."

Moonlight splashed over the muddy street, and Wyatt returned a couple of waves and a few hellos as he threaded along the dirt path that ran alongside Main Street. The diner was already humming, the intoxicating scent of charred meat washing over the town. Light streamed from windows, and beneath the gentle push of the wind the undercurrent of humanity could be heard; music, televisions, rumbling generators, and car engines.

He lived in a house at the edge of town that had once belonged to a prominent member of the Mount Aire community, but modern times being what they were the two-story house had been converted into four apartments. The facade was dirty and worn, and two rickety-looking staircases climbed up the sides of the building like an afterthought.

There were interior entrances to all the apartments, but the two on the upper levels required a fire escape, and Wyatt used his as an entrance. His PD snowmobile sat protected beneath the steps where he'd left it two days prior, and it was covered in a light sheen of wind-blown snow.

The metal stairs rang as he climbed, his bag of groceries weighing him down. He was tired, more tired than he should be, and when he got to his apartment, he was winded.

There was a covered grill and a locked storage box on the stair landing outside his door, and as he unlocked the apartment a chill tiptoed down his spine. Wyatt swayed on his feet. He might not have a concussion, but that didn't mean he hadn't been concussed.

Heat spilled from the dark room beyond as he pushed into his living room, the scent of onions and carpet freshener tickling his nose. Wyatt went into the closet-like kitchen, put away the groceries, and hit the shower. He stood under the stream until the hot water ran out, and as he was drying himself off, he heard a knock at the door.

"Come in," he yelled. "It's open."

"Do you want me to get the grill started? I'm starving," Ian said.

"Knock yourself out."

Ten minutes later Wyatt emerged wearing a light knit cap, sweatpants, and a sweatshirt with the head of a snarling brown bear eating a red fish on its front, the logo of the minor league hockey team the Kenai River Brown Bears.

Ian was making hamburger paddies from the ground beef he'd sold Wyatt an hour earlier, and he had a whiskey at his elbow.

The men grilled, ate, and drank, and with a full stomach, Wyatt felt much better.

"Do you need me to stay the night?" Ian sipped his drink as he watched Wyatt over the rim of his glass.

Wyatt took a pull off his beer as he shook his head no. "I think I'll survive alone."

Ian nodded, but said nothing.

The rumble of voices could be heard in the hallway outside the apartment. Wyatt and Ian both glanced at the apartment's main entrance. Wyatt didn't recall the last time the door was open because he always used the fire escape. Music filtered under the door as people chatted, their voices falling silent as they retreated down the hallway.

With the alcohol greasing his lips and settling his stomach, Wyatt told Ian what had happened. How he'd seen the three vehicles on the side of the road, how he'd found Tommy and the others. The strangled cry they'd heard.

"You recognized the call?" Ian asked.

Wyatt nodded. "Not that I could tell you exactly what beast made the sound, but it had a certain whale song quality to it."

"It?"

When Wyatt was done describing the beast, Ian downed the rest of his drink and poured another. "What did the captain have to say?"

Wyatt sucked on his lips and said nothing.

"You didn't tell him?"

"Not the last part."

Ian rocked back, but as understanding smoothed his facial features he said, "I guess I understand. You… are you sure, I mean… Shit." Ian took a long pull of whiskey.

"The thing is… I… I felt it appraising me. There was intelligence behind those eyes. Maybe even wisdom, and I felt helpless."

With his burden passed on the two men drank in silence until Ian declared he needed to get home to the dependents.

"I know this goes without saying, but what I told you is on a need-to-know basis, and even you don't need to know."

Ian pushed to his feet, staggered, then steadied himself. "Good thing I'm walking tonight," he said.

"We understand each other, yes?"

Ian locked his mouth and threw away the imaginary key.

But secrecy is a funny thing and means different things to different people. Married couples have few secrets—at least when it doesn't involve their own doings.

That night, with the whiskey flowing through him and loosening his tongue, Ian told his wife, who told her friend, and by the time Wyatt emerged from his cocoon twenty-four hours later most of Mount Aire knew what had happened.

People averted their eyes when they saw him and asked him how he was in hushed tones like he'd almost died. The sympathy and pity revealed in their faces twisted his stomach and set his anger ablaze.

Once again Wyatt was a ghost in his town, but with a strange sense of relief, he didn't mind.

9

Terimore Lake, Alaska, ***11:19 AM AKST, June 6th, 2017***

Memories fade, time marches on, and sometimes ghosts become less opaque. Slowly the hellos returned, conversations at Buck's resumed, and Wyatt's life shifted back into gear. The knot on his head subsided, and the black bruise on his side faded to yellow even as the world sprouted green.

Miniature icebergs smacked and popped as they floated in the meltwater, bumping into each other as the wake of Wyatt's patrol boat stirred the thawing lake. The sixteen-foot Zodiac's rubber gunnel squeaked as it rubbed ice, the 50 hp Johnson pushing the boat forward. Terror Lake was more than half-thawed, but it would take another couple of weeks before the lake was fully free of ice obstacles. Logs and debris dragged down from the mountains with the snowmelt was another matter altogether. It had been a warm spring and summer was coming on at full throttle, the humidity rising as the forest bloomed with color, formed texture, and created nature's perfume.

Wyatt eased back on the throttle and snapped the control handle into neutral, the engine gurgling faintly. He lifted his binoculars and scanned the northern edge of the lake where the glacier met the water. Thick brown rivulets spilled down the front of the glacier like dirty tears, mixing with the clean lake water.

Thick clouds of vapor rose from the glacier and chunks of ice in the flowing water. The temperature of the lake was cold, but still warmer than the water coming off the glacier. Fingers of mist massaged the edges of the forest, and it looked like molten lava was spewing into the lake, the points where the brown streams entered the water obscured by billowing fog.

Wyatt let the binoculars drop to his chest, and they swung on a lanyard as he tapped the control arm and nudged the outboard into gear. He leaned back on the bench seat behind the control console, the middle finger of his right hand wrapped around the ship's wheel. The basic Garmin depth finder showed seventy-six feet, and the SONAR was clear.

It was quiet out on the lake. Shiners darted about just below the surface, waterfowl bathed, and birds streamed in from the south, their distant cries comforting. Few boats moved around the lake, folks looking to beat the rush and grab some early fish. He didn't feel like checking permits. Most locals wouldn't venture out on the lake for another week or two, and none of the floating docks had been deployed, and no lawn chairs sat on the manmade beaches. Summer had almost arrived, but the peninsula's human inhabitants were still in wake-up mode.

He adjusted course and headed for the center of the lake. The glare of the sun on the ice and water made it difficult to see, and Wyatt struggled to find the huge snowdrift where he'd found the… He couldn't lie to himself anymore. Where he found the Akhlut's den.

The use of the singular—the Akhlut. It jarred a school lesson so far back in his memory that the teacher's face was a blur. Was there more than one beast? Reproductive and habitat issues aside, was it possible the creature was a singular freak of nature with an incredibly long lifespan or had some unknown method of renewal? Could that explain its behavior? He thought not. Odds were there was a family—maybe more than one, that called the Terror Lake home.

That the beast hadn't been seen anywhere else in the world was less of an issue for Wyatt, though it did twist his mental pretzel. There were many species unique to specific environments, and sometimes the location of the habitat is as crucial as the make-up of the habitat itself. Could the Akhlut live in the Amazon Basin? Maybe, but it somehow seemed unlikely. This fish… whatever the hell it was, appeared to like the cold.

Wyatt had heard talk of tunnels at the bottom of Lake Terror his entire life, and underwater drones had been used to map sections of the lake bottom. No tunnels or pits in the lake floor were discovered, though only a fraction of the total area was surveyed.

All that was left of the giant snowdrift den was an igloo-like mound of ice, its entrance having dwindled to doghouse size. The ice was scoured and smooth all around the diminished den, and there was no sign of tracks on the slick ice.

He angled up the Johnson, the hum of hydraulics and gurgling water carrying over the lake. Wyatt gunned the throttle and drove the bow of the Zodiac onto the remnants of the snowdrift, the hard plastic hull shrieking as it bumped up onto the ice. With the boat stationary, Wyatt killed the motor, leaned back, and closed his eyes, the sun's heat warming his face and rejuvenating him like an electrical current charged a battery.

Water lapped against the boat's transom, and the wind whispered and sighed, the uneven breeze a swirling mix of cold from the glacier and warmth from the surrounding forest.

Wyatt didn't know how long he'd been daydreaming and sucking in sunrays before a roar roused him. His first thought was the bow of the boat had slid off the ice and screeched, but as his eyes adjusted to the bright daylight, he saw that wasn't the case.

Splashes and an uneven rhythmic tapping reverberated over Terror Lake, like a hammer smacking ice. Thin ripples spread over the lake as something darted along the western shoreline.

Wyatt fumbled for the binoculars.

A fishing pole surged through the water, and as Wyatt focused the field glasses he saw a huge Arctic char streaking through the water, its red scales glistening, the pole dragging behind the creature as it fought to escape the hook set in its mouth.

Wyatt laughed. The big fish had jerked the pole right out of its owner's hands.

He sighed, lowered the outboard, and fired it up.

Rubber squealed and plastic screamed as the boat slid off the ice. Wyatt spun the wheel and dropped the hammer. The Zodiac leaped from the water, spitting a rooster tail of dirty slush, ice, and water. He set a course for the pole, which was moving fast through an obstacle course of logs and ice.

The sun disappeared behind a cloud and the bright glare faded.

A boat floated listlessly along the western shore.

Working the ship's wheel with one hand, Wyatt stared through the binoculars as he changed course.

The boat was a ten-foot aluminum scow with a squared-off hull and an electric motor, which was in the down position but appeared to be off. The craft was empty. Wyatt could see inside the small vessel. The boat rocked in the gentle waves churned up by the wind, floating ice, and debris.

A pang of worry crawled down Wyatt's spine and intense pain settled in his lower back.

He arced the Zodiac toward the scow, and the vessel sliced through the water, the bow hardly bouncing and barely throwing spray.

There was nobody in the water around the boat and with a growing sense of apprehension that quickly transformed into action he brought the boat in closer. Was that a blood slick in the water?

As he approached, he cut the engine and let the boat glide, the bow bumping the aluminum fishing boat.

He threw a line around the abandoned scow's front cleat and tied the rope off on the Zodiac.

There was a fishing pail in the boat, a cooler, and a half-frozen lump of bait sat on the forward bench seat. The electric motor's throttle control was in neutral, and a large orange switch that controlled the battery was in the off position. He saw no radio, no life jackets, but there was a first aid kit and an emergency whistle. There were no registration numbers on the vessel because none were required. Boats under twelve feet without a gasoline engine were in the same class as kayaks and row boats. Lifejackets and related safety equipment were still mandatory and subject to verification, but there were no other requirements.

Wyatt surveyed the area again, searching for the bright colors of a life jacket, but all he saw was the silvery glare of sunlight dancing on the mix of water and ice. Thermals of heat hung over the portions of the lake that were still frozen, and clouds of vaper settled over the free-flowing water, blocking his view.

He opened a channel to dispatch and reported what he'd found.

"Can you mark the area with a buoy and secure the boat?"

"I can manage something," Wyatt said.

"Any idea how long ago all this went down?"

Wyatt glanced at the oily slick, fragments of a sandwich floating on the surface. Then he remembered the fishing pole and the escaping fish. "I'd guess in the last hour or so," he said. While I was chilling at the center of the lake. "Although I guess the fish could've been dragging that pole around for hours."

"Can you see the shoreline clearly from where you are?"

"A little," he said. "I'll check it out."

"And I'll get on the horn to the captain. Keep your radio on."

"10-4."

Wyatt set out a marker buoy and tied the small boat to it. When he peered through the binoculars at the eastern shoreline he started.

A fist of rolling whitewater surged across the lake, pushing aside chunks of ice like an underwater snowplow. A tall black dorsal fin rose above the white mound and scythed through the water, leaving a wake, streaks of black appearing and disappearing in the churning water and clouds of mist.

The knot of water was moving at an incredible speed as it zipped through the shallows along the lake's western shoreline. Wyatt cycled up the outboard and went to investigate.

Thoughts of the Akhlut and his recent incident crushed the tiny remaining seed of denial. Nothing that big lived in Terror Lake. There was only one explanation. Wyatt pulled his phone and wedged it between the SONAR and depth finder. He wasn't going to miss his opportunity this time.

Ahead, the Akhlut rose like a leviathan from the lake, chunks of ice cresting and breaking on its wolf-like head as it changed direction and headed straight at the Zodiac.

The rumble of the motor echoed off the lake like thunder, and for the first time, Wyatt considered why he was racing toward danger, not away from it. He saw no other boats in the area, and there was nobody to protect.

Flashes of black appeared in the whitewater, teeth glinting through the foam, two dark white-rimmed eyes aglow with malevolence. The tall dorsal fin swayed, the creature's pectoral fin-like legs pounding the water.

Fear cascaded through Wyatt, and he let the binoculars dangle as he reached into his jacket and felt the butt of his Glock. What good would the pistol be against the beast?

A log floated in the water before the boat, and Wyatt jerked hard on the ship's wheel, the outboard screaming as the vessel zigzagged around the debris.

When Wyatt refocused on the lake ahead, the Akhlut was gone and only a whirlpool of spinning water remained. He put the boat in neutral when he reached the vortex and the boat was pulled in a circle.

Patches of black and white streaked beneath the boat, Wyatt's nerves pulsating with fear and indecision. There wasn't a training class that covered mythical beasts.

The Zodiac shuddered as its bottom was pushed and shoved, and the boat was forced out of the water as it listed hard to port, the outboard screaming as it was lifted from the water.

He gripped the steering wheel, and his phone, water, and logbook slid off the command console and hit the deck.

A massive pucker resounded over the lake, and the Zodiac came down with a crash, water surging over the gunnel and swamping the boat. Though the Zodiac had a small bilge, the craft was self-bailing thanks to the gap between the boat's sides and deck. This allowed the water to drain fast, and the eight separate inflated sections that made up the vessel's sides made it very hard to sink.

As the lake settled and the floodwater drained away, Wyatt pulled the Glock.

Bubbles popped and snapped on the surface, the whitewater faded, and the stench of rotten fish and garbage baking in the sun wafted over the lake. He rolled his shoulders, his chest heaving with a pain that threatened to take his breath away.

10

Wyatt ranged the Glock around, aiming it at the surface of the lake as he searched for black and white spots sliding through the water. Shiners darted about, insects alighting on the calm surface, Wyatt's harried reflection staring back at him from the settled water.

Of the Akhlut there was no sign.

He holstered the Glock and grabbed his water bottle. Wyatt's heart raced like he'd just sprinted a mile, and tiny stars danced before his eyes. The ringing filling his head dropped in pitch and tone then fell away, and the outboard rumbling faintly and water slapping against the boat filled the stillness. A gentle breeze brought the natural perfume of evergreens, and he sniffed, but couldn't pick up the scent of rotten fish or garbage.

Nausea crept through him as the adrenaline fled and he drank water.

A male Bufflehead duck landed in the water beside the boat. The bird's iridescent purple-green plumage was slick with water and stood out against the beast's white chest and dark back. The duck squawked at him as if to say, "Get on with it. You've got a job to do."

His job. Wyatt steadied himself as he lifted the radio handset, but he didn't open a channel.

Wyatt had been ordered to check-out the shoreline and he had yet to do that. What did he have to report? Another surreal undocumented encounter with a mythical beast? He recalled the cold shoulders, the days of unease when those he knew well were uncomfortable around him, looking at him with eyes that asked if he was going down the same road his father had.

The Bufflehead yelled and surged into the air, pumping its wings as it rose into the sky and glided east toward the shoreline, leading the way.

He sighed, put the handset back in its cradle, nudged the control lever, and put the engine in gear. The Zodiac eased through the water, pushing aside chunks of ice, ripples running away from the bow.

Terror Lake was three miles wide and six miles long, and Wyatt was a quarter mile off the eastern shore, the dirty glacier looming on the northern horizon. Evergreens packed the eastern shoreline, broken occasionally by a pseudo beach or a boat house. Docks were stacked under colorful tarps, and the outlines of houses could be seen beneath the shadowy tree canopy. There weren't many homesteads up this way, and the wilderness surrounding the lake was vast, untamed, and unforgiving.

Intense chirping erupted from above and two tiny brown birds landed on the lake. They watched the boat as they bathed, their tiny beaks pecking insects off the surface of the lake.

A flash of silver scales knifed from the water, a two-foot white missile speckled green, narrow jaws flexed open revealing rows of needle-like teeth. The pike's mouth clamped down on one of the birds as it breached, the sound of cracking bones and the bird's shrill cry echoing over the lake. The fish thrashed, blood splattering the water, feathers floating in the air.

Pike fish are insatiable predators who often hunt small birds and mammals along shorelines, but Wyatt was still entranced as he watched the snake-like jackfish drag the struggling bird beneath the surface and disappear into the depths.

Blood bubbles popped on the surface amidst the feathers, and the wind picked up, creating tiny waves in the gore.

A yelling voice snapped him from his ruminating. "*Sunaaga! Sunaaga!*" came a voice from behind him.

Wyatt turned and saw a man paddling a long wooden kayak. The newcomer wore a blue life jacket over a deerskin tunic, a fur hat with its ear flaps up, and wraparound reflective sunglasses. The juxtaposition of the natural and modern looked odd, but as the guy raised his hand and waved, Wyatt's concern slipped away. He knew there were several Inuit language dialects, but he thought sunaaga meant something like friend. There was a shotgun strapped to the deck of the kayak along with a fishing pole.

"Hello," Wyatt said. "Did you see that?"

The man nodded. "Nature in its purest form." The guy leaned forward as if staring. "You are Terry Wyatt?"

A pang of anxiety trickled through him as he nodded.

"I am Renne Kalvak, but please call me Kal."

"How is it you know me, and I don't know you?" It sounded odd as he said it, and Wyatt wanted to take the words back. More than a thousand people lived in and around Mount Aire.

"You're the local Fish Fuzz, no?"

Wyatt chuckled despite himself. "Yup." Awkward silence. "Are you familiar with that boat over there? Do you have any idea who the owner is?"

Kal lifted binoculars and gazed toward the center of the lake, then shook his head no.

"That boat was abandoned, and its owner is missing."

Kal made no sign.

"Do you live around here?"

"I'm visiting my brother," Kal said. "Perhaps you know him? Adamee?"

The name did ring a bell, but he couldn't picture the man's face. "Sorry, but no."

"I'm from Ninilchik."

Wyatt nodded. "No luck, huh?" He pointed at the fishing pole. Wyatt didn't see a line of fish hanging from the kayak, so he assumed the man hadn't caught anything, but Alaskans were nothing if not polite. A sense of urgency strummed Wyatt's spine, an innate sense reminding him the owner of the scow had been taken, and he needed to get on with the search.

"Haven't tried," Kal said. "I'm just enjoying the weather and the lake before it gets…"

"Crowded?"

Kal nodded.

"You don't need to be embarrassed. I feel the same way," Wyatt said.

Silver scales flashed in the water and a lump of bloody bones and innards floated to the surface.

Wyatt thought of the beast and said, "Have you seen anything odd over this way?"

Kal shook his head no. "I've seen nobody except you, but…"

"But?"

"I'm sorry," Kal said. "I don't mean to insult… But surely you know the legend of the Akhlut?"

"Doesn't everyone in these parts?" Wyatt said, a bit too harshly. "A wolf-orca hybrid freak that appears every six years." Wyatt felt bad for getting aggravated, but heat rose in him like a tide, and he put his hand on the throttle control, the western shore beckoning.

"But do you know why the beast comes?"

"To feed its young."

"Yes, that is the plausible explanation, but my ancestors believed there was much more to it than simply predator and prey. Have you not heard of the curse?"

Wyatt thought he'd heard all the Inuit legends, but he said nothing.

"Let me say that I would not swim in these waters, and I would not venture out here without this." He pointed at his gun.

A breeze dusted Wyatt's face with mist as his eyes ranged over the western shoreline. Nothing moved except the swaying branches of the evergreens. He waited, his nerves jackhammering his spine with urgency.

"Have you heard the tale of the lady of the lake?"

Wyatt's face scrunched. "You mean the woman who gave Excalibur to King Arthur?"

Kal laughed hard and loud, the sound carrying over the water and echoing off the mountains. "My people believe Terror Lake contains an untold number of lost souls. The victims of the Akhlut, a beast created from stardust and dirt by the ghost of a young Inuit princess named Madeleine. Legend says that sometime in the 1700s, Madeleine fell madly in love with a white fisherman she spotted on Terror Lake."

"I do remember some of this now," Wyatt said.

Kal nodded. "It is said that the man saw Madeleine one day as she frolicked in the shallows, watching him, and he came to love her as well. The two lovers hid their relationship and used the lake as their meeting place. This went on for some time, but when the chief discovered his daughter was seeing the fisherman, he forbid her from seeing him."

Wyatt felt time growing short. He needed to get going, but something about the man's methodic voice, and the relevance of the myth held him in place.

"The princess tried to send her love messages, tried to run away to see him, and when no other options were left to the princess, she began floating notes across the lake on boats made of leaves and twigs."

"Right," Wyatt said. He needed to end this conversation and be on his way. "I do remember now. She came to a nasty end, right?"

Kal nodded. "She got no response from her lover, so she rowed out to the middle of the lake and stabbed herself in the heart. Her lingering ghost created the Akhlut, and every six years the lady of the lake commands the beast to bring a young man to her watery grave to replace her lost love."

"Is that what you believe?" Wyatt said.

"It is… how do the kids say it? It's a Boogeyman, no?"

No. "That's what many folks think," Wyatt said. "Listen, I'm sorry, but I've got to check the shoreline. Do you have an emergency radio?"

Kal said nothing.

"If you see anything unusual, call the office when you get off the lake, O.K.?"

"I will, and you be careful Wildlife Trooper Wyatt."

Something in the man's voice told Wyatt Kal knew more about Terror Lake and its secrets than he had revealed. He said, "Actually, you really shouldn't be out here. We've got a missing person and no idea what happened. Why don't you head in for the day?" It was his 'it's a question but not really a question' tone.

Kal frowned, daggers of multicolored light reflecting off his wraparound shades.

Folks that lived on the peninsula were a tough breed, and little ruffled their feathers or scared them from their preferred habitat. He added some sugar. "It would make me feel better," Wyatt coaxed. "Just for today. And I'll owe you a beverage at Buck's."

"As you wish," said Kal as he braced his kayak and spun the boat around.

Wyatt cycled up the motor and got going, the bow bouncing and throwing spray. He headed southwest, angling away from the glacier, and increasing the size of the search area.

A patch of water reeds packed the shoreline ahead and Wyatt brought the Zodiac to a crawl.

The reeds were undisturbed and the forest beyond was filled with life. A deer stood drinking in the shallows, birds were perched in trees, and clouds of gnats and skeeters filled the air. If there was one surety in this world that Wyatt could count on it was nature's alarm. The wildlife he saw were undisturbed and calm. If the creature had come this way dragging a victim, the forest would have cleared out faster than a restaurant after the state roach detectives show up.

He moved the boat in as close to shore as he dared, the depth finder cycling back and forth between one and two feet as Wyatt angled the outboard up, the sound of servos rising above the humming wind. With bird song easing his racing mind, he guided the Zodiac along the shore, binoculars pressed to his eyes.

When he reached the glacier, he'd found nothing of note, and his thoughts shifted back to the abandoned scow. He spun the ship's wheel, pushed down the throttle, and the boat jumped from the lake, spitting dirty water.

The buoy had drifted, but the aluminum boat and its contents were still tied to it. He turned three hundred and sixty degrees, struggling to see through the haze and glare as he scanned the surface of the lake once more. He saw no life jackets or flaying arms. No flashes of black and white streaking through the water. No clues at all.

He radioed dispatch.

"That sure is strange, Wyatt," was dispatch's response.

Understatement of the year, so he said nothing.

"The captain wants you to bring the scow in. He'd like to see it."

"10-4," he said. "I'll leave it with my patrol boat until he tells me what to do with it. Has anyone been reported missing?"

"That's a negative."

Wyatt sighed. It could be days… depending on who it was maybe weeks before the identity of the missing person was discovered. People lived on the peninsula for various reasons, but if Wyatt had to choose a main reason it would be the endless solitude. Alaskans in general minded their own Ps and Qs, but those who lived on the Kenai Peninsula were often loners, and many folks who called the outskirts of the wilderness home went weeks without venturing into town.

"I think we need to canvas all the houses around the lake and see if anyone is missing or saw anything," Wyatt said.

"I'll pass that on to the captain, but as you know we're a little shorthanded."

"Copy that," Wyatt said. "I'll see what I can do about putting the word out around town, and I'll call Ned—Trooper Simmons—and get him involved. Is there anything else we can do?"

"Check in with the captain when you're on land."

"Copy that. Wyatt out." He closed the connection and set about tying the scow to the Zodiac via a tow line. Maybe the boat had broken loose of a mooring and its owner was hiking in the woods, or poaching?

Wyatt stared out across the lake, searching for Kal and his kayak, but he saw nothing but invisible waves of heat gliding over the melting ice and frosty water.

11

Wyatt goosed the throttle and the Honda ATV churned through the mud as it passed Mom's old wagon and climbed the dirt and pebble-covered snowbank at the head of her driveway. He killed the engine and took off his helmet, the cool night breeze invigorating.

Wellwood Court was one of four streets in the suburb of Mount Aire lovingly referred to by locals as The Flats. It was the only area that could be called a neighborhood, its houses standard prefabs, the paved streets relatively straight, though they were cracked and mounded from winter frost-heaves. Wyatt had grown up on this road. Had his first kiss here.

He felt his mother watching him through the curtains shielding the front window, and the heat of sorrow and regret spread through him.

Helen Caster Wyatt had never remarried, or even dated, but that was because of her reclusiveness and shyness more than a commitment or love for his dead father. Unlike most widows in Mount Aire, she'd struggled and fought to stay. She always claimed she'd done it for Wyatt, but he knew the real reason. His mother was scared to leave the peninsula because that was all she knew.

He dismounted, opened his saddlebag, and grabbed the bottle of wine he'd brought, but the barking and braying emanating from behind Mom's house made him pause. Some of the neighbors had dogs, but the commotion sounded too close for that.

With the snowpack newly melted, the ground around his mother's place was a mix of quicksand-like mud and patches of sprouting vegetation. There were no lawns in The Flats. Though water was cheap and plentiful, folks who lived on the peninsula didn't usually take the road more heavily traveled. Lawns were a waste of resources, and the pesticides and fertilizers used to keep them perfectly green and full had done more to damage Earth's environment than strip mining.

Folks who lived in The Flats planted gardens and flowers, never useless grass.

With these inconsequential landscaping issues clogging his mental slate, he decided he didn't want to walk around the house and get his boots caked with mud, but…

Recent events had Wyatt walking on eggshells, so he decided he had to see what was making all the racket, muddy shoes or not, but then his mother saved him the trouble.

"Hi, sweetie," came his mother's smoke-ravaged voice. She sounded like a taxicab dispatcher.

He lifted a hand and yelled, "What's all that barking?" After he asked, Wyatt realized the braying had ceased.

"Come on in and I'll show you."

Wyatt didn't like the sound of that at all, but as it turned out the stray huskie his mother had adopted wasn't the biggest surprise waiting for him inside Casa Wyatt.

Kim Farret sat on the couch in the living room, her blonde hair tied back, her yellow jacket on as if she'd just come in from outside. A dog sat on the floor before her.

"Kim?" Wyatt said, and he couldn't keep the surprise and disdain from his voice. The surprise he understood, but the disdain… She looked great. He turned to his mother and lifted his eyebrows.

"Don't look at me like that," his mother said. She was always trying to set him up with somebody, and she knew Wyatt and Kim already had a history. Plus, Kim lived in The Flats now, though she hadn't when Wyatt was a boy. "She's helping me with Coco."

Wyatt stared down at the huskie. The poor thing was missing patches of fur and it looked old, like three legs in the grave old, but his hazel eyes were bright. "I was going to ask… about Coco."

Kim vaulted to her feet and pecked Wyatt on the cheek. "Don't be upset. Your mom is saving this guy's life."

"This is your doing?" But he was smiling.

"No!" said his mother, her voice cracking. "I had already made up my mind. Kim here saw me walking him and offered to give me a hand. It's not like I get any help out here."

Wyatt sighed. The old refrain was so ingrained he said nothing, and words made no difference anyway. No matter what he did or how often he did it, Wyatt would never be able to do enough for his mother.

"That's not fair, Helen," Kim said. "I told you what Wyatt has been dealing with." She looked at Wyatt, then at the floor as if she'd spoken out of turn.

The anger that rose in Wyatt told him she had, but the entire town knew about Jesse and all the odd happenings recently, so he didn't understand his frustration. Was it because he cared for Kim more than he'd thought?

Silence filled the house, the intense smell of stale smoke worse than in Buck's.

Wyatt found his words. "I like that you have some companionship, Mom, but do you need more responsibilities? Expenses?"

His mother looked at the floor, and Coco looked up at Wyatt, the beast's sorrowful eyes sucking him in.

"Fine," he said. "I'll speak with Ian and have dog food delivered on a schedule, so you don't need to worry about it. Where did this guy come from?" Wyatt put out his hand as he knelt, and Coco warmed right up to him.

As Wyatt stroked the animal his mother said, "You know me. I read an ad, and when I saw his face… He was a sled dog before he blew out his MCL, and his owner just let him loose. The poor thing was found freezing, skin and bones starving. If you had seen him…"

The dog looked skinny, but he didn't look too bad, and Wyatt felt guilty for not having visited his mother.

Perhaps sensing his guilt his mother fired another manipulation missile. "I've had him for almost two weeks."

Wyatt and Kim said nothing.

With Coco's arrival in the rearview, his mother moved on to matchmaking. "Kim, why don't you stay for dinner? I've got a whole chicken in the oven and there's plenty."

Kim said, "No. No, thank you. I should be going."

Coco whined.

"Wyatt, I hope you don't mind that I'm giving your mother a hand," Kim said.

He didn't know if he did or he didn't, but either way, he had no right to be angry. "No. Not at all. I meant to call you after I saw you out on the racecourse, but things have been…"

She put a hand on his shoulder, his mother beaming as Kim said, "I know."

"Don't not stay for dinner because of me," he said.

"I've got plans. No worries," she said as she shot him a mischievous grin that said I'm not going to wait around forever. "Bye Mrs. Wyatt. I'll be by tomorrow." Then she was gone like a fresh breeze, the front door clicking shut behind her.

Coco whined.

"I'm with you," his mother said as she gave Wyatt the hairy eyeball. "You could have been more…" Her lips pursed like she'd taken a bite out of a lemon.

"What? What should I have been? You sandbag me and wonder why I'm not thrilled?"

"Stop being so dramatic. You didn't seem too upset to me," she said. "You're not getting any younger."

He lifted the bottle of wine and said, "Want a glass?"

She waved a hand dismissively.

As Wyatt poured two glasses of the climate-chilled Pinot Grigio he thought about Kim. He did like her, but he wasn't bowled over, whatever the hell that meant. The singles scene in Mount Aire was a notch above nothing, and Kim was pretty, smart, had a good job, and most importantly, she seemed to like him despite the solitary nature he'd inherited from his mother and the fact that he worked most of his waking life. Maybe that would change if there was something more important in his life than the beasts of the peninsula.

The truth was he was manufacturing excuses to push Kim away. He'd done this his entire life. When someone got too close, he got uncomfortable and started putting up walls. Kim had tried to climb and tear down those barriers, but admittedly he was a pain in the ass when it came to his privacy and feelings. Ian joked that he was closed off and emotionally stunted, and as Wyatt got older, he wondered how close his friend's joking was to a warning.

With Coco eyeballing him like he was a T-bone, Wyatt and his mother sat at the kitchen table and ate chicken, potatoes, steamed kale, and drank wine.

The two-way radio clipped to Wyatt's belt squawked with static, then fell silent.

Wyatt's mother jumped like a shotgun blast had blown out the kitchen window, even though he always wore the radio and bursts of static were common.

"Can't you turn that thing off while we eat?" she attacked.

He could, but he wouldn't. "Mom, Kim updated you on all the goings-on, right?"

She harrumphed. "Not that I heard it from my trooper son," she scolded. "Did you ever think maybe I was afraid out here alone?"

Wyatt stifled a chuckle. This guilt trail was well trodden, so he said nothing.

His nonresponse twisted her face, her sagging jowls jiggling, unfounded anger painting her face red. "It was bad enough that your father left me out on the barren wasteland by myself, with a thirteen-year-old boy, who I gave up my life for and now doesn't even have the courtesy to tell me when a dangerous beast is lurking around my house."

Wyatt was tired of thinking and talking about the year of the beast, but his mother just wouldn't let it go. She was like a tiger that had gotten its teeth into a gazelle.

She put down her fork and lowered her voice for emphasis. "I can't lose you too." It wasn't a bad act, and he knew on some level his mother meant what she was saying, but everything she said and did was a move in the great chess game of her manipulation.

Wyatt said nothing as he did his best to contain his anger and remind himself this woman gave birth to him, and she was old, scared, and felt the world owed her something because of the cards life had dealt her. He knew she would go to her grave never understanding that every living person on Earth was continually bombarded with obstacles, and she was no different than everyone else.

When they were done eating Wyatt cleaned the dishes, took out the garbage, and when his mother complained that the end table next to her recliner was wobbly, he pulled his father's utility knife, slipped out the screwdriver, and went to work with his mother hovering over him.

The house was hot, and his mother cracked open a window, the buzz of the growing night symphony reminding Wyatt that summer was right around the corner.

He wanted to tell his mother about everything that had happened. The encounters with the beast. The ice den at the center of the lake, the missing person, and his meeting with Kal. He needed to unload it all again and hear a different opinion than Ian's, but he knew he couldn't have a serious conversation with his mother. That road only led to more anger, frustration, and worry. The sense that he had nobody to talk to weighed on him, and he thought of Kim.

His radio wailed. "Wyatt, do you copy?"

"Copy. What's up?"

"Thank god you have your radio on."

"Isn't Ned—Trooper Simmons—on duty?" Wyatt said.

"Why is your radio on then?" his mother interrupted.

Dispatch said, "He is but he's not answering."

Wyatt's dinner settled in his stomach like a cold stone, and he downed the last of his wine. "O.K.," he said. "What've you got?"

"Not sure. A panicked call from Sissie London. She and her boyfriend… one second… Darrel were, and I'm quoting now, 'We were hanging out at The Hole and now Darrel is gone, and everyone is panicking, and she's scared and would we please send help'."

"That's all you could get out of her?"

"She was terrified and kept repeating the same thing over and over."

Wyatt said, "I have to assume she meant the swimming hole? It is polar swim time."

"Copy that."

His mother sighed and said, "You should make them put an electric fence around that place."

Wyatt almost laughed. The Hole was where the local teens swam. Sometimes with clothes on and sometimes not. Wyatt had skinny-dipped there in his youth, and it was certainly time for the annual youth polar bear ritual of swimming in the freezing water. Heat spread over his face. But that was then, and this was a year of the beast. He said into the radio, "Has the ambulance been called?"

"Affirmative."

"O.K., on my way."

"Thanks, Wyatt. Report in as soon as you're able."

"10-4." Wyatt pressed to his feet.

"That was a fast visit," his mother prodded.

Anger stretched the boundaries of Wyatt's patience. She'd heard the message and chose to make his life more difficult, and Wyatt knew that's not what mothers are supposed to do. He said nothing as he put on his jacket, kissed her on the forehead, and headed for the door.

Coco whined and Wyatt stopped to stroke the beast.

"Call Kim," his mother said as she lit a cigarette. "Have a couple of cocktails. Maybe things have changed." She blew a stream of smoke in Wyatt's direction.

He said nothing.

"Promise me?"

Wyatt pushed out into the night without another word.

The buzz of crickets carried over The Flats as he mounted the ATV and fired it up. Maybe he would call Kim. What could it hurt?

Moonlight cut through the thin cloud cover and stars blinked in the blackness. It was a beautiful night, but Wyatt's knotted gut and stinging fingertips told him things were about to go south.

12

The ATV's headlights cut through the blackness and shadows gyrated at the edges of the muddy trail. Moonlight lit the forest with an unearthly glow, and the glowing eyes of animals streaked through the darkness as the beasts fled the growl of the ATV. The chicken Wyatt's mother had cooked sat in his stomach like rancid butter, and he already felt pressure in his bowels. Three glasses of wine had him comfortably numb, but he was alert, and his rifle was in its scabbard, the Glock on his hip.

He cut over Circle Road and headed southwest, the land falling away to marshland and a series of ponds, most of which were nothing more than big puddles. The Hole was a different beast.

Nobody knew how deep The Hole was because its bottom was comprised of thick black mud of indeterminate thickness, millennia worth of vegetation having broken down and filtered through the water, settling on the bottom. When he, Ian, and their crew had their polar plunge keggers, they'd been careful not to touch the bottom of The Hole and stir up the sludge.

Warmth spread through Wyatt as he drove the ATV, memories of those teenage summer nights so clear in his mind it felt like yesterday.

He jerked the ATV's handlebars, the machine fishtailing as Wyatt avoided a huge puddle.

Ahead the glow of car headlights was a beacon on the blackness, clouds of misty light filtering through the forest. Wyatt squeezed the brake handle and eased up on the throttle as he picked his way down the slope, avoiding dips in the path filled with meltwater, and evergreen branches sagging over the trail.

Starlight shimmered on the surface of the pond, and an array of trucks, ATVs, dirt bikes, and mountain bicycles were scattered around The Hole's shoreline. Headlight beams spilled over the area, and a group of teenagers stood at the edge of the pond, bunched together like a flock of birds protecting one of their injured mates.

When Wyatt broke free of the vegetation all heads swung in his direction. He stopped the ATV ten feet from the crowd and killed the engine as one of the kids stepped forward. Wyatt recognized the girl as Sissie London, one of Mount Aire's few teenagers, and the kid who'd called in the emergency. If the dating pool for Wyatt seemed slim, teenagers that lived on the peninsula had it worse. They gathered for school and events, but the school in Ninilchik educated kids that lived all around the western zone of the Kanai Peninsula.

"Wyatt, thank God," Sissie said. She was wearing shorts and a bikini top, but she'd donned a fleece jacket to ward off spring's nightly chill.

"Don't know about that," he said.

Wyatt counted eleven teenagers in all, and he recognized most of them. The kids pressed in around Sissie and Wyatt, eyes wide, wet heads covered with knit caps, towels draped over shoulders. There was a keg of beer in an ice tub sitting on the tailgate of a pick-up, and he thought he caught the tangy-sweet smell of marijuana. All the teenagers appeared genuinely shaken. Even Big Bear Fred, a thirteen-year-old boy who could pass for a thirty-year-old man.

"What's happened? Still no sign of Darrel?" Wyatt said.

Sissie was normally an attractive young lady, but she'd been crying, and her waterproof mascara failed to live up to the hype. Her hair was tied back in a swim knot, her eyes were wide, and carelines creased her face. "I don't know," she finally forced out.

The crowd sighed and mumbled, but no one spoke.

Wyatt waited as the girl got herself together.

"Everyone was partying, and…" She glanced over at the beer keg. None of the kids were of drinking age.

"Don't worry about that," Wyatt said, waving a hand toward the keg. "Go on. Time is of the essence."

"Everyone was partying, taking their polar plunge. You must have gone to the polar kegger when you were…" She paused as she searched for a word that wouldn't insult him and Wyatt almost laughed. "When you were young, right?"

He nodded to urge her on.

"Darrel and I wanted a little privacy," she looked at the ground, her cheeks blossoming red. "We swam off to the corner over there, and…"

Wyatt could guess what the "and" was, but he needed to hear it from Sissie. He said, "Don't worry. Nobody is going to crucify you for making out."

She smiled and said, "My mom might."

Wyatt sighed and waited, and when the teenager didn't continue, he said, "What happens at the polar plunge kegger stays at the polar plunge kegger."

That got a spattering of chuckles, and Wyatt felt the tension drain from the group.

"We took off our suits, and we were playing around. You know, splashing each other, trying to get close but… I don't know," Sissie stumbled. "He went under and didn't come back up."

Sissie paused as if that was it and Darrel had disappeared into the depths like a fish.

"Did you see anything else?"

She nodded, tears building in her eyes. "I saw him swimming toward me just below the surface. Then there was a flash of white in the water, some splashing, and I felt something brush against my leg. I freaked a little, but when I looked for Darrel all I saw was swirling water and popping bubbles."

"Then what?"

"She screamed like Jaws had hold of her leg," came a voice from the crowd.

Sissie hung her head and said, "I did. I was… in shock, I think. I just couldn't believe it. We all panicked, and everyone got out of the water and I called the police."

"How long ago did all this happen?" Wyatt asked. It had been twenty minutes since he'd been dispatched to the scene.

Sissie looked around for help, and the wiseass who'd made note of her scream said, "About an hour ago."

"Have you seen Trooper Simmons tonight?" Wyatt and his fellow Wildlife Trooper checked all the teenage hangouts at certain times of the year when they knew there'd be a presence.

"He was here earlier and told us to behave, be safe, and have fun. Then he left," Sissie said.

"Which way did he go?"

All the teenagers turned and pointed as one toward the northeast corner of the pond, where moonlight illuminated a thin trail that ran into a thicket of scrub pine and junipers that encroached to The Hole's edge.

Wyatt stared into the forest, willing Ned to emerge with Darrel sitting behind him on the ATV.

An owl hooted, and a gentle breeze stirred the evergreens, pine needles clicking and tapping as branches creaked and moaned.

"Clean up your mess while I take a look," Wyatt said as he pulled his flashlight. "The polar plunge kegger is officially over."

None of the teenagers protested.

Wyatt made his way around The Hole, examining the shoreline, but found nothing of note except footprints in the wet mud.

The faint sound of a siren cutting through the night echoed over the peninsula, red spinning light cutting through the forest like a lighthouse beacon.

Wyatt updated dispatch, and with no injuries, there was no reason for the ambulance and the unit was called off.

Leaves, lily pads, and other debris floated on the surface of The Hole, but there was no blood slick, nothing that would indicate an injured human. Darrel had disappeared, but as an unreal heat spread through Wyatt, he knew what had happened, though there was no proof to support his conclusion.

Documenting the scene in the dark was difficult, and Wyatt would have to come back in the daylight, but with the day fading he took pictures, made a list of every kid at the kegger, and made sure no one had left after the incident. None had, and when the area had been cleaned, and Wyatt had done everything he could, he told the kids to go home. He knew they would just find another place to drink, but he didn't care if they went home, as long as they didn't stay at The Hole.

As he stared at the pond, willing himself to see something that wasn't there, Wyatt saw himself, Ian, and their friends swimming naked under the starlight. Nothing moved in the pond and after ten minutes of staring at the water, he wasn't sure what to do next.

He pulled his radio and called dispatch.

"We'll have to get out there tomorrow," said dispatch. "Get someone down there in a frog suit."

"You think he drowned?" Wyatt said, though he knew of no other plausible explanation, and yet dead bodies usually float.

"Maybe he got caught up on something when he was swimming underwater and he couldn't break free," came the voice over a gentle track of static.

Understatement of the year. Wyatt said nothing and didn't point out how clear The Hole's water was.

"Did you see any sign of the kid crawling from the pond? Footprints leading into the forest? No," said the dispatcher as she answered her own questions. "And none of the kids saw him after he went under, so we have to assume he's in the pond."

Wyatt couldn't argue with that.

"Let's see what the daylight brings. We might have a floater by then."

The robotic manner of the dispatcher irked him, but then he had a horrible thought. Maybe a piece of the kid might float. Wyatt pointed the flashlight across The Hole in the direction the teenagers said Ned had gone. He asked, "Any word from Trooper Simmons?"

"Negative."

"He stopped here tonight," Wyatt said.

"How long ago?"

"A couple of hours, I'd guess. I found the tracks of his ATV heading into the forest."

"Are you prepared to track him? Over."

A chill spread through Wyatt, his head pounding. He said, "Yeah… but…" What did he want to say? He wasn't comfortable leaving the scene. But what could he do in the dark without the ability to check beneath The Hole's surface?

"Are you there, Trooper?"

"Yes, I'm prepared to track him, it's just…"

"Do you have a trail camera handy?"

A spark energized Wyatt. He did have a trail camera. It wouldn't provide a live feed, but it could record the comings and goings at The Hole for the next twelve hours.

"That's a 10-4," he said. "I'll get it set up and see if I can find Trooper Simmons. Has the captain been notified?"

"Yes, Wyatt. He said to let him know if he's needed."

If there was nothing Wyatt could do, there certainly wasn't anything Captain Udell could do, except maybe provide another set of eyes. "Got it. I'll be in touch."

"Dispatch out."

Silence crept over The Hole, the slosh of water and the arguing trees the only sounds.

Wyatt panned the flashlight around and fished out the camera from his saddlebag. He mounted the camouflage-colored Coleman Xtreme 500 on a thick tree trunk and adjusted the angle and zoom so the entire pond was in the frame. The trail camera was equipped with night vision, and as Wyatt mounted the ATV and slipped on his helmet, he felt better about leaving the scene.

He fired up the machine and slowly worked his way around The Hole to where Trooper Simmons's ATV tracks plunged into the woods. The tracks of Ned's quad were easy to see on the muddy trail, the glare of headlights reflecting off the puddles and driving the shadows into the forest.

Wyatt worked the handlebars and throttle, his skin crawling with the knowledge that the Akhlut had taken another life. This was turning into a nightmare, and shame filled him as he pitied himself for having been chosen to be part of what was becoming one of the deadliest years of the beast in the last hundred years.

Ahead, a faint light, like a dying flame, cycled through the woods. As Wyatt got closer, he saw two pinpricks of red in the darkness, the faint glow beyond.

It was Ned's ATV. The engine had been shut down, and the lights were on, but fading as the battery drained. The rifle wasn't in its scabbard, and the machine looked undamaged.

With a shaking hand, Wyatt pulled his radio and hailed dispatch.

"Go ahead, Wyatt."

"I've found Trooper Simmons's ATV, but he's not here, and there are tracks leading on into the forest."

"What are you saying, Trooper Wyatt?"

"I'm saying Ned is missing."

13

Static crackled over the radio, but for the first time in Wyatt's career dispatch didn't parrot out an immediate response. He shut down the ATV, took off his helmet, and dismounted as he fiddled with the volume on his radio.

Moonlight painted the scene in lurid black and white, the wall of shadows beyond the cloud of the ATV's headlights forcing itself on Wyatt, suffocating him. His heart pounded in his chest, and he felt cold, yet perspiration glided down his back and moistened his forehead. He pulled the rifle from its scabbard and chambered a round as he eased toward Ned's ATV.

A gust of wind rustled the trees, and a low wheezing cycled through the forest as mist twisted between the evergreens.

Wyatt turned Ned's ATV's ignition key to the off position, and the dimmed headlights went dark. He grabbed Ned's keys and looked back at his ride. The ATV's headlights would stay lit for about two hours before the battery went dead if he didn't start the engine. He had plenty of gas in the tank and he had a full emergency container strapped to the ATV.

He killed the lights on his ATV and pocketed the keys along with Ned's. Then he fired up his flashlight and examined the ground around the missing trooper's ride. There were clear boot prints in the soft mud that showed the trooper dismounting, and a single line of tracks leading into the forest.

What was that saying about doing the same thing but expecting a different result? He wasn't insane, or maybe he was? He was the one who had seen the Akhlut, and knew what it could do, yet here he was, by himself, trekking into the forest in the dark. He should call for backup.

But there was no backup. No help. If he didn't do something now, when help did finally arrive it could be too late. Wyatt rolled his shoulders as he marshaled his courage, the cold steel of the rifle in his hands reassuring, so he pressed on.

The forest floor was damp and muddy, and bronze pine needles covered the ground, but Ned's boot prints were easy to see.

Static burst from his hip radio and Wyatt jumped.

"Wyatt, do you have any new information?" asked dispatch.

When dealing with command all communication had to be put through the filter of one's personal ambitions, career-wise and safety-wise. Politics and risk assessment also influenced the decision of when to push and be a wise ass, and when to stand at attention and take orders. Wyatt wanted to say, "I've been standing by awaiting instructions." What he said was "yes", and he relayed what he'd found.

Cold silence. A chopped word. The seconds dripped away, an owl hooted, and the sound of snapping branches echoed through the evergreens.

"Dispatch, you still there?"

"10-4, Wyatt. Sorry. We're communicating with the captain."

Wyatt saw no reason to stop now. He lurched forward, ducking under tree branches and easing around thickets of pricker bushes as he followed Ned's trail and waited on dispatch.

He hadn't gone far when he discovered a dime-sized black dot in the snow. Wyatt's stomach dropped. He'd seen enough blood recently to know crimson turned dark under the harsh gaze of an LED torch.

To Wyatt's surprise, the black dot wasn't blood. It was a button. He picked it up and placed it in his palm as he examined it under the flashlight's beam. Four holes, no thread. Wyatt looked down at himself, searching for a similar button, and found copies running down the front of his orange safety vest.

"Wyatt?" came a voice from his radio.

"I'm here."

"I'm linking in the captain."

He waited.

"Wyatt, it's Udell. Are you alright?"

He didn't know, but Wyatt said, "As far as I know." He told the captain about the tracks and the button and Wyatt could sense the tension and unease sizzle through the invisible radio waves.

"I've got backup coming your way, but they're at least twenty minutes out," the captain said.

"Twenty minutes?" Wyatt stared at the footprints in the snow and rubbed the button between his fingers. Trooper Simmons didn't have half an hour. Wyatt didn't think the man had any time at all.

The captain said nothing.

Wyatt understood his boss's predicament. He didn't want to send one of his troopers into an unknown situation alone. Especially given what had gone down recently. It didn't matter to the captain what was killing people. Bear, wolf, Akhlut… it was all the same to him.

Thing was, Ned wasn't some stranger, and even if he was, this was Wyatt's job. It's what he'd signed up for. He said, "Stay close to the radio. I'm going to continue my search."

"Copy that, Wyatt. Please call in every couple of minutes with a status report," the captain said. "Is The Hole the best place to send the backup?"

"Yes, sir. I'm tracking toward Terror Lake and they'll be able to follow me easily."

"Be careful, Trooper Wyatt."

He said nothing. If he hadn't found Ned's ATV and footprints, Wyatt would've asked for Ned's last known location and his last call, but the information meant nothing. All that mattered was the footprints.

The rumble of a river gurgling over stones leaked through the forest. It was June, and though the ferocity of the winter melt had decreased, most of the peninsula's rivers and streams were still running strong, and many of them would continue to flow well into fall. Varmints scampered in the undergrowth, all of which was sprouting with life, and birds cooed faintly in the blackness beneath the thick tree canopy.

A grumble, almost a growl, carried through the forest and Wyatt put the stock of the rifle to his shoulder, using the flashlight as a scope. The wind died away, the gurgle of the stream fading, and an unreal silence filled the woods.

The footprints ended, and the forest floor was dug up and disturbed. It was hard to see in the dark, and the wet ground made things more difficult, but Wyatt believed he saw the slash prints of the Akhlut's pectoral fin-like legs. There was no blood, but as he scanned the area he saw an orb of light to the east, daggers of white cutting through the evergreens.

He headed for the light, tree branches whipping his face, pricker vines tearing at his clothes.

The source of the white cloud was Ned's flashlight. It was propped against a tree trunk, lens pointed down into a pile of pine needles. The tracks continued, and judging by the position of the flashlight it looked as though the torch had been tossed away or dropped because there were no footprints in the mud around it.

Wyatt picked up the light and turned it off. As he did so he noticed a splotch of blood on the handle, and he had to remind himself a little blood didn't mean… He was kidding himself, and this wasn't the time for self-delusion. He reached into his jacket and felt his father's knife.

He updated the captain, and slowly followed the tracks, scanning the woods, rifle stock pressed to his shoulder, the flashlight held to the gun's forestock, his heart threatening to break through his ribs and escape his chest.

A bestial roar froze him in his tracks.

Wolf cries answered the odd call and an owl hooted incessantly as if complaining that all the commotion was ruining its evening. Wyatt knew the feeling. He was supposed to be at his mother's watching T.V.

Two glowing white-rimmed eyes appeared in the vegetation ahead.

Wyatt stayed still and aimed the rifle. He knew what lynx eyes looked like, bears, wolves, and the beast watching him was none of those. Wyatt fought the urge to turn tail and run, but the gun in his hand evened out his nerves. It was time to put a bullet between the creature's eyes.

"Is someone there?" came a strangled voice from beyond the eyes. "Help me. Pleaa…" The voice ended in a gurgle that sounded like Ned was throwing up.

The eyes disappeared.

Wyatt jumped back, stomach burning. He'd lost sight of the beast, and it could be coming at him through the blackness, working its way behind him, using the forest as cover. He panned the flashlight around wildly, the rifle barrel hissing as it scythed through the air.

Branches cracked and popped, harsh gurgling, then a stifled cry that could have been the beast or Ned. With no options left, he moved through the undergrowth. His fellow officer was alive, and he had to do everything he could to make sure he stayed that way.

The rank scent of rotting fish mixed with garbage filled the woods. A scream of unimaginable fury and the side of Wyatt's face was splattered with saliva as the shrieking beast surged from the shadows, massive jaws extended, pectoral fin arms out like wings as the beast sailed through the air.

Wyatt turned and made himself thin, and the creature sailed by, its hoof-like claws missing him by inches. He swung the rifle around and fired, but his footing was unsteady, and the long gun was difficult to aim with the beast in close. The shot missed and the bullet smacked into a tree as the rifle was knocked from Wyatt's hands.

He hit the ground hard, but he managed to roll and pull his Glock. Mud splattered Wyatt's face as he pressed to his feet and lifted the flashlight, which he'd somehow managed to hold onto.

The gunshot had given the Akhlut pause, and the creature pressed itself to the ground like a massive cat coiling to strike. Dark, white-rimmed eyes glowed with hatred and intelligence, the beast's smooth black and white skin slick with mud. Its jaws fell open and white railroad spike-sized teeth gleamed as the Akhlut growled and sprang.

Wyatt fired three times, fast shots, the Glock bucking in his hand, the scent of cordite filling the air.

The Akhlut twisted like a cat that's been dropped upside-down, streaks of black and white flashing through the night. The beast contorted and shifted in the air, avoiding the first two shots.

The third shot smacked into the Akhlut's right forward leg, and with a *slap* and *pop* the bullet pierced skin, passed through the appendage, and buried itself in a tree trunk.

A primal screech of pain pierced the night and the beast plunged into the woods and was consumed by darkness.

Wyatt pointed the light in the retreating creature's direction and fired. He pulled the trigger four times before he realized a stray bullet cold hit Ned and stopped. Sweat dripped into his eyes, and he spun around, the gun out before him, his nerves stretched to the breaking point.

A hush settled over the forest, and Wyatt knew what that meant.

Splashing, and the pucker and plop of footsteps moving through mud.

Without thought, Wyatt yelled, "Ned! Ned! Are you O.K.?"

Nothing except the low rumble of the wind and the scrape and scratch of the trees.

Wyatt had feared the Akhlut. He could sugarcoat things for his mother, but he couldn't fool himself. He'd been afraid, but he wasn't now. Anger and hatred rose in him, memories of his father, and uncle, Jesse… Ned. The Akhlut had taken so much from him, and now the beast was trying to take all.

He licked his lips and let loose with a battle cry as he drove forward, gun up. The forest was tightly packed with undergrowth, and as the fury drained and reality kicked Wyatt in the ass, he realized how exposed he was.

Wyatt skidded to a stop and put his back to a thick tree trunk as he tried to control his breathing and be silent. His lungs burned, tiny stars blossoming before his eyes, his stomach screaming, his legs like sandbags.

The glare of the flashlight was blinding, and he shut it off.

Moonlight painted the world in silver, and a large shadow moved through the trees to the south. The patch of blackness eased through the evergreens with the fluidity of water, and as Wyatt stared, he wasn't sure if he was seeing the beast or its shadow.

"Help. Please help me," came a faint cry from nearby.

"Ned!" Wyatt almost put a hand over his mouth in response to his stupidity. If he'd been hidden by the darkness, he wasn't any longer.

A low, laugh-like bark massaged its way through the woods, and Wyatt forced himself into motion, slipping around trees and undergrowth like a wraith as he searched for Ned.

Wyatt recalled hearing something about how orca have sensitive eyes, and that bright lights sometimes disorientates them. He needed to see where the hell he was going if he was going to help Ned, and who was he kidding anyway? The beast could probably see him better in the dark than within the glare of the LED light.

He flicked the flashlight back on.

A huge mouth of teeth separated from the darkness, and the air shimmered with energy and fear.

14

Wyatt went slack like he'd fallen while skiing or been buried under a wave while surfing. His muscles failed to tense and fight gravity, and as he dropped to the ground the Akhlut sailed above him, the air between them crackling with static electricity, the huge beast's passage heating Wyatt's face. He rolled as he struggled to aim the Glock, but the monster was a blur, and he was as slow as molasses in January.

A terrible howl thundered through the night as the beast landed and spun around so fast all Wyatt saw were streaks of black and white and the Akhlut's glowing eyes and shining teeth. The beast crouched, its tall dorsal fin swaying like a cat's tail, its right front hoof-like paw raking the mud as if spoiling to run.

He fired and the bullet hit the ground before the beast and splattered its wolf-like face with mud. The Akhlut slithered into the shadows like smoke as Wyatt fired again.

The night symphony went still, the only sound the gentle wind pushing around pine needles and the rumble of the river.

"Ned! Are you out there, Ned?"

"Wyatt?" A beaten voice filtered through the trees. "Oh, thank God."

No, thank the polar plunge kegger. Ned's voice was coming from the southeast and as Wyatt panned the flashlight around, he saw no signs of the beast. The speed and smoothness with which the creature moved was disconcerting, though the Akhlut seemed to fear the gun, or at least the blare of a gunshot.

"I'm coming, Ned. Call out if you see the…" Wyatt paused, his heart dancing on the underside of his rib cage. He'd accepted the existence of the Akhlut, but at the same time, he'd never acknowledged its existence by speaking its name. "Call out if you see the Akhlut."

"O.K.," came Ned's pain-ravaged voice. No hesitation. No question any longer about Trooper Simmons believing in the myth… which, Wyatt corrected, was no longer a myth but his reality.

In the distance, the sharp bleat of an emergency siren echoed over the peninsula.

Driven by the knowledge that help was on the way once again, Wyatt picked up his pace, bracing the Glock on his left arm which held the flashlight. Shadows partied in the undergrowth, tiny eyes darting around like sparks, the smell of rotten fish and garbage filling the woods.

Ned had his back to a tree trunk, the thick evergreen branches shielding him in shadow. When the flashlight beam found him, the trooper raised his arm to shield his eyes and relief flooded Wyatt, pain settling in his lower back. Losing a fellow officer, a man who was basically his partner, would have set things in motion that would have irreparably damaged Wyatt's life. But that hadn't happened. Ned was alive.

The trooper coughed and spat up blood as Wyatt rushed to his side, gun up as he scanned the area for those menacing eyes. When he arrived at Ned's side the elation of finding him alive drained from him along with his energy and resolve.

Ned's chest was gashed open, his orange vest, jacket, and uniform shirt in tatters. Wyatt was no medic, but he had extensive emergency training, and it was obvious he needed to stop the flow of blood. It looked as though the ribs had done their job and protected the inner organs, but the way Ned was breathing and the way his eyes were rolling in his head like pinwheels told Wyatt the trooper's status was critical.

Wyatt cursed himself for not bringing the first aid kit, and he considered backtracking to his ATV to retrieve it. But the siren was getting louder, the Akhlut was stalking the woods, and time was critical.

"Hang in there, Ned," Wyatt said as he knelt beside the man. He put down the flashlight, angled it up, and stripped off his jacket.

Ned's chest heaved, and muscle and fat oozed from tears in the skin like meat from a cracked lobster tail, but his leg wound looked worse. A broken tooth protruded from the appendage, and blood poured from the wound.

A dilemma. Pull the tooth, which would increase the bleeding, or attempt to stanch the bleeding around the tooth? He cycled through all the medical training he'd endured as he holstered the Glock.

Wyatt tore his jacket arms off and used his father's knife to cut the coat into strips.

The gleam of his stainless-steel belt buckle caught Wyatt's eye and he knew what he needed to do. He pulled off his belt and used it as a tourniquet, wrapping it around Ned's left leg above the tooth, feeding its end through the buckle, and pulling it tight.

Ned wailed and blood bubbles spewed from his mouth, but he said, "Thank you."

Then Wyatt went to work using his jacket-bandages to cover the chest wound.

Ned was shaking like a leaf in a gale, and his hands were cold, beads of perspiration rolling down his forehead in rivulets. The trooper reached out and grabbed Wyatt's arm, and a zap of energy ran through him.

"Wyatt, I'm not… Can you go see my family? Settle things with my boy. Keep an eye out for him?" Ned convulsed in pain, his eyes going wide as he stared at something Wyatt couldn't see.

"Don't talk like that." Wyatt stripped the man's claw-like hand from his arm. "The ambulance is almost here. We'll patch you up, get you a change of blood. Maybe it'll help your attitude."

Ned laughed and choked up blood.

"Oh, shit, sorry… I…"

The dying trooper grabbed his arm again. "Don't be. Will you do as I've asked?"

Wyatt nodded. "If it will shut you up. Save your strength."

Ned's eyes slid closed.

Wyatt shook the man awake. "I said save your strength. Not go to sleep. You need to stay awake until they get here with the meds."

The trooper seemed to be fading as he continued to stare at something far away. "Meds?"

"Oh, yeah. You're headed for fantasyland, pal."

"Fantasyland," Ned said. "That sounds nice."

Wildlife Trooper Richard "Ned" Simmons's eyes slid closed, and his chest stopped heaving.

Wyatt fell back, mud soaking his ass. He felt tears building in his eyes, but his mouth twisted in anger, and he bared his teeth as he slowly rotated his head, searching for the Akhlut. He never thought his job was to hunt beasts or any wildlife. But rabid wolves, overly aggressive bears, and troublesome hawks often had to be killed for the benefit of the peninsula's wildlife as well as the human population.

He would hunt the Akhlut. Kill it, and if it had a family and friends, he would kill them as well.

A tree branch snapped and a flash of black and white streaked through the forest to Wyatt's right.

Wyatt drew down, aimed, and with a round already in the firing chamber he squeezed the trigger, peppering the trees and undergrowth, the sharp stench of gunpowder tickling his nose.

The siren was close now and Wyatt pulled his radio and gave dispatch an update, along with general directions to Ned.

"I'm going after this thing," Wyatt shouted into the radio.

"Nega—"

Wyatt turned off his radio, clipped it on his belt, and gave chase.

Terror Lake glared to the north, and the rumble of the nearby river filled the forest, shadows and mist swirling around Wyatt as he picked his way through a dense thicket of hemlocks. Wherever there was free-flowing water there was bound to be plenty of freeloading plants. Pine needles cleaned the mud from his clothes as he muscled his way through the vegetation, all thoughts of the beast lurking beneath the dark boughs of an evergreen lost in a haze of fury.

All Wyatt could think about was Ned's eyes closing for good, and the urge to kill felt so natural angst stirred his stomach. But he didn't slow.

The forest gave way to a gentle slope crowded with boulders and patches of spouting devil grass. Moonlight angled through the thin clouds, the night orchestra wailing, mist creeping down the incline and dancing with the shadows.

Forty yards away, the beast was perched atop a large flat stone. Its white patches glowed in the gray haze, its pectoral fin casting a long shadow over the boulder-encrusted slope. Its eyes glinted under the harsh gaze of the LED light, but the beast didn't flinch. It lifted its wolfish snout, teeth glistening, and threw back its head and howled, letting Wyatt and any other living thing within earshot know who was in charge.

Wyatt screamed as he fired, and when the Glock clicked empty, he let the magazine drop from the gun, then slammed home his spare. As he chambered a round, a cloud of mist swirled around the beast, and when it cleared the creature was gone.

He surged up the incline, weaving around boulders, gun at the ready. He wouldn't let the Akhlut work its way around him again and regain the element of surprise. This was the beast's turf as much as it was Wyatt's and the creature—

That thought stopped Wyatt in his mental tracks, even as he ran toward danger. Whatever the Akhlut was, however it had gotten here, regardless of how it was created, it called the peninsula its home and it had the same right to be here as Wyatt did.

But Wyatt wasn't running around killing and eating people.

Wyatt didn't see the Akhlut as it attacked, but he felt its hot breath on his face, sensed its presence and its insatiable hunger.

A fist of black and white snarling teeth and rippling muscle poured from the darkness. If the beast had possessed claws like a bear Wyatt would've been killed. As it was, the hoof-like talons at the end of the creature's pectoral fin legs were hard, but not sharp, and the Akhlut's main weapon was its mouth, like the biggest killer to ever live, the T. rex.

The beast crashed into Wyatt, and he was knocked from his feet, the Glock and flashlight flying from his hands.

Wyatt landed in a tangle, his teeth rattling in his head, his bones screaming from the impact. But even as pain coursed through him like wine, he knew he had to move, or he was a dead man. He rolled onto his back, the star-filled sky spinning across his field of vision. The flashlight lay ten feet away, its harsh beam cutting across the slope.

The Akhlut powered to a halt and slipped in the mud. It growled and bared its teeth, threw back its narrow head, and bark-howled. The call was answered by a wolf, or…

He thought of the Glock, realized it was gone, got to his feet, and sprang into the forest. Darkness consumed him, and visibility dropped to five feet. The thunder of water crashing over stones filled the forest, and Wyatt felt the gentle touch of mist on his face.

Deep sorrow and shame washed over him. Wyatt thought of Jesse, Ned, and what had he done to help the citizens of Mount Aire? He'd allowed his anger to control his actions and he'd underestimated the beast, despite everything he'd seen.

Two large boulders that looked to have once been one blocked his path and Wyatt nestled into the shadows between them, crouching behind a pricker bush with thick green buds surrounded by two-foot-high devil grass.

Below the flashlight angled across the slope like a marquee spotlight, Wyatt saw the Akhlut. It sniffed the area where the Glock had landed, its chuffing and snarling rising above the rumble of the river.

Then it was gone, and Wyatt's flight or fight debate began hammering his head. No way he could outrun it, and without a gun, he didn't have a chance of fighting it. Being wedged into the crack provided protection on three sides, but he had no means of escape. All that added up to him being screwed.

Wyatt thought he heard voices on the wind, but with the yammering of the river, it was difficult to tell. He wasn't that far from Ned, and if the backup had arrived maybe he could call for help. Lights. People. Guns. It might be enough to scare the thing away before it found him.

But Wyatt couldn't bullshit himself. The Akhlut knew where he was, and hiding was futile. He slipped from between the two boulders and headed east, leaving the sparse incline for the cover of the forest. As darkness wrapped him in its cold embrace, Wyatt feared for his life.

Now he was the hunted.

15

As Wyatt ran blindly through the forest his mind searched for an answer to a critical question. How many times did he have to screw up before the captain relieved him of duty? The lynx incident, and now he'd run off into the wilderness alone chasing a wild animal, and the chief wasn't aware that said animal had already bested him.

Spotlights of pale moonlight knifed through the tree canopy, illuminating sections of the woods, the undergrowth a tangle of pricker vines, scrub pine, and sprouting weeds.

He slowed, lungs sucking for air as tree branches, holes, and stones impeded his path. The moonlight that knifed through the tree canopy angled east, and that suggested the moon was on the western horizon. That meant Terror Lake was to his left and he was running east. Stupid move, Trooper Wyatt.

The Jenki River ran down the stone escarpment he'd just climbed part way up and spilled into a series of shallow waterfalls before dumping into Terror Lake. The river was wide in spots, and he'd have to head south to get to the narrow section, which meant climbing higher.

Or he could change direction entirely.

Before him, a large evergreen had given up the ghost and cleared a path on its fall to the ground. Wyatt climbed through the dead branches and paused, staring back the way he'd come.

The narrow clearing was awash in silvery starlight, the dark line of the forest like the barrier of outer space. The evergreens argued, the wind played the vegetation, and insects bleated and buzzed.

Wyatt's eyes had adjusted to the darkness, but it was still next to impossible to see what was happening beneath the thick tree canopy. He shifted his position and one of the dead tree's branches poked him in the side. Pain stabbed him, but it sparked a thought beyond running for his life. He snapped the branch from the trunk and a loud crack echoed through the forest like a gunshot.

The staff was an inch round and made of flexible but strong pine, and both ends had broken points. He spun the stick in his hand as he scanned the area. Still no beast, despite the gunshot-like crack. Wyatt thought the noise could work for him by either scaring the creature or drawing it out.

He'd decided to backtrack when the Akhlut materialized from the gloom.

An amorphous absence of light marred only by flowing patches of white and glowing eyes slithered from the forest into a patch of moonlight. The creature pushed back onto its hindlegs, its dorsal fin stabilizing the beast like a tail, the animal's snout rising skyward as it sniffed the air.

Wyatt licked his finger like a little kid and stuck it in the air. Wind swirled as it angled into the narrow path of destruction left by the fallen tree, and Wyatt couldn't determine which direction the wind was blowing. He smirked. If he couldn't, neither could the beast, so even if it did catch his scent, it wouldn't know which direction it had come from.

All that assumed the Akhlut had an overdeveloped olfactory nerve. The two slits he'd seen at the end of the beast's snout looked more like gills than nostrils, but maybe they provided superior sensory perception.

Wyatt had a weapon now—not much of one, but something—

He rocked back like he'd been punched, the depth of his stupidity jolting his muscles into motion before his survival-addled mind registered the thought. He reached into his jacket, pulled free his father's utility knife, and flicked it open, the five-inch stainless-steel blade glinting faintly in the gloom.

Wyatt flipped the blade in his hand, catching and gripping the handle tightly, blade out. The knife didn't provide much reach, but there weren't many weapons that could do as much damage in close hand-to-hand… hand-to-fin… combat as a sharp blade.

He still had his wooden staff with its pointed ends, so if the creature had lost his trail Wyatt could wait the beast out. And how long could that be? He'd moved farther away from Ned, but it was only a matter of minutes before flashlight beams pierced the darkness.

Except the Akhlut hadn't lost Wyatt's trail.

The creature dropped back to all fours and snarled, its vicious warning cutting through the rumble of the river. Pressing low to the ground like a lion coiling to spring, the massive beast sniffed as it inched forward and disappeared into shadow.

Wyatt thought his heart paused, but he found he was holding his breath. An overwhelming urge to run engulfed him. He'd seen this movie. Knew how it ended, and his little sharpened twig and his dad's pocketknife weren't enough.

The Akhlut slipped into a cone of light forty yards from where Wyatt hid, its dark eyes aglow, teeth bared, and a gurgling laugh pierced the night.

Make no mistake, there was a threat in that cry. A promise of menace and death to anything that heard it. The tingle of fear put pressure on Wyatt's bladder, cold sweat covering the nape of his neck. Running made him even more vulnerable to attack, so he made the unpopular decision to stand his ground. At least until he had no ground left.

With a primal cry of bloodlust, the beast rushed forward, eyes fixed on Wyatt where he stood within the dead evergreen.

Wyatt moved deeper into the tangle of tree branches, using them as protection. If the Akhlut wanted to pounce on him through the army of natural spears, more power to it.

Thing was, Wyatt was used to bears, wolves, and beasts that let their fury outrace their physical abilities. The Akhlut was no such creature.

The adolescent elephant-sized apex predator crossed the space between itself and Wyatt in a frighteningly short interval of time.

Wyatt blinked and instinctively brought up the knife, despite the natural wooden pikes all around him.

Branches snapped as the beast's rear pectoral fin-like legs churned, its wolfish head rising as its jaws flexed open. When the Akhlut reached the fallen tree the beast used its front hoof-like paws to break the fallen tree's branches.

The sound of splinting wood filled the forest, the Akhlut on its hind legs as it methodically powered forward, its front legs clearing away Wyatt's protection.

"Over here!" The cry was barely audible with the fuzz of river water falling over stones filtering through the woods.

The beast paused for a heartbeat, its head jerking toward the voice.

Wyatt threw his spear, aiming for a white-rimmed eye. There was a grunt of pain, but Wyatt didn't wait around to see if his missile had done any damage. He dropped to his hands and knees and crawled out from within the fallen tree, pressed to his feet, and plunged into the forest.

If his toothpick had hurt the beast the Akhlut was filing away its pain for another time because the sounds of pursuit filled the forest.

Stars sparkled through holes in the thickening cloud cover and the land fell away toward the river as the forest thinned. He dared not look back because there was no need. Wyatt's neck muscles were knotted, and the grunts, growls, and footfalls of the beast were so close he could feel the Akhlut on his heels.

Listening to a sixth sense Wyatt hadn't known he had, he dove left, twisting in the air as he brought around his father's knife in a wide arc, slashing the air where he'd just been.

The sixth sense was bullshit, and Wyatt lost his balance and the knife passed through empty air as he tumbled to the ground, his lungs constricting, starbursts painting his field of vision with tiny white explosions.

A thunderous cacophony of snapping branches and the beast straddled Wyatt, the Akhlut's massive girth above him, pectoral legs on each side of him.

Wyatt attacked. Four fast thrusts of the knife.

Four puncture wounds froze the giant in place, blood dripping from the wounds. The beast stood still, its white-rimmed eyes growing wide like a parent that couldn't believe what its disobedient child had done. There was a gash on the side of the creature's snout from the thumping Wyatt had applied, and a dark stain marred its right leg from where he'd shot the beast.

Wyatt rolled, blood dripping on him as the star-filled sky, the dense green tree canopy, and the brown pine needle-covered ground spun before him. He kept rolling, pushing off with his hands and feet, picking up momentum as the incline that led down to the river's edge grew steeper.

The grumble of water cascading over stones blocked all other sounds, and the undergrowth tore at Wyatt as he put distance between himself and the beast.

He came to a jarring stop against an ancient cedar tree, its trunk twisted and bent because its base was angled toward the river. Wyatt staggered to his feet, his vision coming back into focus, the black shadowy landscape taking form and shape.

A shallow valley twisted through the forest, and the river gleamed under the glare of the moon and stars. Mist floated above the rapids like toxic clouds, and the scent of earthen water wafted into the forest.

Tumbling rocks, the crack of a thick tree branch snapping. White patches eased down the slope through the darkness. The Akhlut was close, but it was moving slowly, as if unsure of its prey's location.

Wyatt didn't want to believe in luck. One of the few things his father had ever said that Wyatt considered truth was "A person makes their own luck." The older he got the more he understood that was overly simplistic, but there was a grain of wisdom there. Yet, the ball did appear to bounce better for some than it did for others, regardless of position or skill. Wyatt considered himself lucky, though there was no specific event he could point to that proved this claim.

Despite his self-proclaimed luck, a million years of natural evolution told every nerve and motion center of Wyatt's brain he needed to run.

The Akhlut burst from the darkness, jaws open in a wicked grin.

Wyatt dove into the undergrowth, the beast just missing him as he bounced off a boulder, pain consuming the entire right side of his body.

He rolled over a flat stone, through a patch of devil grass, and then he was freefalling, the snarling growl of whitewater racing up to meet him.

The river was high with snowmelt, the water frigid, and as Wyatt was sucked under a shock of cold cranked up his adrenaline. He was pulled and tossed as the river sucked him into a channel of smooth stones that jettisoned him forward. He wrapped his arms over his chest, legs straight, and for the second time in recent memory, he let his muscles go slack and let the rushing water take him.

Boulders, trees, and swirling whitewater pushed through the blackness. The Akhlut was perched atop a stone that jutted out into the river, and the beast swiped at him, its massive paw raking the air. It missed and the river drove Wyatt over a ledge, and he was submerged in icy black water.

The rapids tossed him around like trash, the river steadily plunging downward as the rushing water guided him between boulders, through waves, and around pools and eddies in the surging flow.

Above the thunder of the water, Wyatt heard the beast wail, and his last thought before he was tossed over a precipice into the lake was the river might kill him, but at least the Akhlut hadn't gotten him like it had his old man.

Arms crossed, feet pointed down, Wyatt broke the surface of the lake. The water was shallow, a mere six feet, but the fall was less. His feet plunged into a layer of mud and brought him to an abrupt stop with his head just below the surface of the lake.

Wyatt stroked his arms, pushing with everything he had to drive to the surface which was only a foot away. He couldn't free his feet from the mud, and he struggled and thrashed.

Above, the bright glow of stars made Wyatt think of his dad, and his mom, how they'd sit and watch the heavens when he was a boy. He hadn't called Kim, but maybe he would.

A great *womp* reverberated through the water as something massive splashed into the lake, and whitewater rolled across the surface, blocking out the moonlight.

Impenetrable darkness engulfed Wyatt. Something rubbed his leg, and with a last pull of his fleeing strength, Wyatt jerked his feet free and pushed through the surface, gasping for air.

Ribbons of white slithered through the muddy water, a tall dorsal fin slashing through the lake toward him.

16

Somehow Wyatt had managed to hold onto his father's knife, but what good it would do he didn't know. The knot of dirty whitewater rolled toward him as Wyatt struggled to keep his feet out of the mud, but there was barely enough room to tread water. He flopped onto his belly and stroked hard, the shoreline a dark rocky vegetation encrusted line ten feet away.

That was all Wyatt could think about, getting out of the water, but as a sickening dread infected every muscle in his body, he remembered the Akhlut was an apex predator on land as well as in the water. Darkness and despair consumed him as he swam, knowing he wasn't going to make it but unable to give up. Had his father fought until the bitter end? Or was he sucked through his ice hole without a struggle, like a turd swirls down the bowl?

A flashlight beam angled through the evergreens, the screech of someone yelling rising above the rumble of the river and the splash and whistle of the waterfall he'd tumbled over.

Whitewater engulfed him like he'd lost a race with a breaking wave. As he was driven forward Wyatt spun like a fish and brought the blade around in a wide arc.

He slashed the air, the smiling maw of teeth hanging below the Akhlut's fiery eyes coming right at him. Wyatt stood and fought through the mud and shallow water to a flat boulder at the lake's edge. It was covered with green slime and Wyatt jumped for it, but changed his mind in mid-flight, contorted his body, and avoided the slick stone. He crashed into a patch of devil grass that slashed at every area of exposed skin, air rushing from his lungs, his already bruised body shrieking and whining.

A gunshot rang out. Another. Loud concussion bomb-like blasts that sounded like a shotgun.

Wyatt rolled onto his ass and crab-walked away from the lake, the undergrowth tearing at his clothes, thin streams of blood from the tiny cuts caused by the devil grass adding to his list of discomforts.

Something grasped his shoulder and jerked him to his feet. Wyatt's self-defense mechanism kicked into high gear, and he lashed out with his father's blade, swinging away, putting his weight into it.

Another hand gripped his wrist and shook the blade free.

"Shush," came a calming voice from the darkness.

As Wyatt's vision cleared, he saw a dark face painted white in the pale moonlight. "Kal?" Wyatt didn't believe his eyes.

"Yes, Trooper Wyatt. Hush now and be easy."

Out on the lake, the knot of churning whitewater and teeth was moving away, the tall dorsal fin diminishing as it sank like a periscope, white and black skin fading into the depths as the Akhlut dove. The lake settled, bubbles popped, and the night symphony resumed its buzzing, chirping, cooing, and bleating.

Pain consumed Wyatt then, his right side pulsing, his muscles like concrete, but as he wiggled his fingers and toes, he didn't think he'd broken any bones. Nausea washed over him, his stomach going sour as the adrenaline fled and Wyatt sagged to his knees.

"Easy now. Easy," Kal said as he helped Wyatt back up and seated him on a nearby stone.

"How…" Wyatt was having trouble forming words. A debilitating chime rang in Wyatt's head, his heart thumping, his vision cycling back and forth from blurry to clear as tears built in his eyes.

If he'd been a pariah before, what would he be now?

As if reading his mind, Kal said, "Your people are still a few minutes away. Do you want me to get them?"

Wyatt understood the question and knew how to read between the lines so well that sometimes he didn't see what was on the line. He said, "Give me a minute to catch my breath and we'll go find them. I need to be checked out, but light duty is torture." Would Kal pick up on the subtlety of his words?

"As you wish," was all Kal said.

With the immediate issue of what he was going to tell the captain tabled, Wyatt asked again, "How are you here? I can't believe it's a coincidence?"

"No, Mr. Wyatt, it wasn't chance."

Wyatt waited, the low chatter of voices getting louder, the flashlight beams getting brighter. He was getting used to the static of the river and hardly heard it anymore.

Kal waited.

Wyatt sighed. "What were you doing?"

Kal looked at the mud-soaked ground, shame creasing his brown face.

"Out with it."

"Please, sir, understand I was trying to help. Watching over the kids. I wasn't…" He looked away.

Now Wyatt understood. Kal didn't want him to think he was watching the kids swim naked in The Hole. "Come on, Kal. I can see you're no child molester. You were keeping an eye on the kegger, and…?"

"Yes, sir, that is what I was doing," the man said. "I was in the shadows, and I couldn't see well. The kids were doing what the locals do— Inuit or not—drinking and swimming naked in the cold snowmelt as I assume you did."

"You didn't?"

"No, sir."

An owl hooted and the rescuers were getting close. They appeared to be following the river and soon he'd have to call out to them, but he wanted to know what Kal had seen first before he talked to the captain.

"The girl, Sissie London I think it was, she screamed out of nowhere. I really couldn't see her because she was at the end of the lake in the shadows with a boy…" He paused as if he didn't need to explain what they'd been doing.

"You didn't see Darrel get taken?"

Kal shook his head no.

Wyatt asked, "Did you see Trooper Simmons when he was at The Hole earlier?"

Kal shook his head no, again. "He must have come by early before I got there."

"What did you do after Darrel was taken?"

"I waited, watched, and then followed you."

Wyatt wanted to ask why, but he knew why and didn't want to hear the man say "because you seem to be in need of help often."

Now for the big question. "What did you see… back there?" Wyatt motioned toward where he was spit into the lake.

Kal's teeth glowed white as he smiled. "I saw nothing in the darkness, Mr. Wyatt, but when you appeared at the river's edge, I gave you a helping hand."

"And the gunshots?"

He hiked his shoulders. "There are always dangerous beasts lurking in these parts and I needed to ensure we were safe. Plus, I wanted your people to know where you were."

Wyatt nodded and said, "Thank you. For everything."

"You would have done the same."

He would have. "Over here! Over here!" Wyatt called, and Kal joined him.

Wyatt was soaking wet, covered in mud, which was to be expected given his chase through the woods, and he'd lost both his guns.

An EMT and the captain stumbled from the dense undergrowth and Wyatt greeted him with a firm handshake. "I'm so sorry, sir. I know I shouldn't have pursued the creature, but Ned was my friend, and I just couldn't let what happened stand. I shot at the thing, and I think I hit it, but it made its way back to the lake despite my best efforts which almost got me killed." He explained what had happened, leaving out his negligence as he described the beast again.

To Wyatt's relief, he saw the skepticism thaw from his boss's face.

"Kal here," Wyatt paused and pointed as he presented his savior. "He was out and about hiking and assisted me, though the beast—no, the Akhlut—got away. I did everything I could for Ned. I'll speak with his family."

"Wyatt, I don't think—"

"He asked me to, Captain. Please, it's my—"

"Shut it! Now!" screamed Captain Udell.

Water lapped gently against stone, insects tittered and squeaked, and birds cooed from within their nighttime hiding places.

"Ned isn't dead," Captain Udell said.

Wyatt's head jerked back like he'd been punched, his eyes going wide, the sorrow he'd felt for his friend and fellow officer washing away. "But? But…"

"Yeah," the captain said. "There's an EMT with him right now back at the ambulance. We're going to medivac him to Anchorage, but it looks like he's going to make it."

"How can that be? I… He was gone or I never would have left him alone." Despair was starting to leak through him again. Had his fury almost killed Ned?

The captain dismissed him with a wave of his hand. "Who knows? We must have just missed you because when we arrived the paramedics were able to hit him with the defibrillator and his heart snapped back to life. There's nothing you could've done."

"And… He's himself?" Wyatt didn't know how to ask if the trooper's brain had been without air for too long.

The captain nodded vigorously. "He's already spoken to his wife and has tried twice to change the EMT's mind about the trip to the big city. I think he'll be fine."

Wyatt looked at Kal and the two men nodded at each other.

"Let's get you checked out," the captain said, and the four men began picking their way through the forest.

Distant thunder boomed in the west, the thin covering of clouds growing thicker as they streaked west. Storms moved fast across the peninsula, and as the temperature changed and pockets of cold air met the warm fronts that flowed north it wreaked havoc on the peninsula's weather. Isolated thunderstorms were common in spring when the local weather swung wildly as summer asserted itself. Storms appeared as if by magic, and were often gone just as fast, leaving only a coating of moisture.

Wyatt sat on the rear bumper of the ambulance within the shelter of the open doors. He refused a gurney and transport to the Mount Aire Medical Center, a small operation that was always open to people who needed around-the-clock care. The facility was overseen by a small group of professional staff supervised by the local town doctors. The EMTs took Wyatt's temperature, gave him a concussion test, and when the captain told the medic there was no brain in Wyatt's head to get hurt, he knew he was heading home.

"Take these for pain and get some sleep," said the EMT as he handed off pain meds. "Check in with your doctor first thing tomorrow…" The EMT glanced at his watch and amended his statement. "See your doctor later today after you get some rest."

Wyatt nodded and didn't protest. His egg had been a little scrambled, but he'd played high school sports and knew how to beat a concussion test, or the person administering the test to be more accurate. A distant chime still rang in his head, and he was nauseous, but he knew once he had something to eat, he'd feel better, and there was no way he was letting the captain put him on light duty. Not when his new goal in life was to hunt the Akhlut down and kill it and its kin.

The thought made him feel less than human, but at the same time, he knew there was no other path. He heard his father in his head praising him, telling him hunting the creature during the year of the beast was his destiny.

An hour later, as Wyatt was being driven home by the captain, thunder cracked, and the heavens opened up. Large raindrops blurred the windshield, the incessant tapping on the roof filling the vehicle. Captain Udell grunted, slowed, then gave up because he couldn't see. He pulled to the side of the road and put the patrol car in park so the duo could wait out the driving rain.

Under the pressure of silence, and not wanting to answer any questions the captain might pose, Wyatt asked, "How well do you know Kal? I mean, Mr. Kalvak Renne?"

"We've met several times," the captain said. "I know his brother, Adamee, better."

Wyatt felt the captain's gaze drilling into the side of his head, and he turned to face his boss.

"He tell you about the curse?" Captain Udell asked.

Wyatt nodded. "Not tonight, but yeah. I'd heard some of it, but I'd never heard it told by…" He didn't know the right way to say it, so he left his thought unfinished.

"By a native Alaskan?" the captain offered.

"O.K.," Wyatt said. "It's just… it sounded so crazy, but when you lay the story over the facts, especially now, it's hard not to put the pieces together."

The captain harrumphed. "I don't know, coincidence can be a mighty powerful thing."

"Is that what you think all this is?"

"No," the captain said. "But I sure wish it was, and failing that, I wish we had a picture of the thing."

"Me too," Wyatt said. In his fury, he hadn't thought to pull his phone, not that it would have mattered in the dark.

The rain diminished and Captain Udell put the car in gear and pulled onto the road. Neither man spoke as the captain drove, the clouds glowing with moonlight, stars already blinking through gaps in the dying storm.

17

Mount Aire, Alaska, ***11:19 AM AKST, June 18th, 2017***

As Wyatt stared at the moose head above the bar at Buck's, he considered leaving Mount Aire for the first time in his adult life.

It no longer hurt when he walked, and his vision had returned to twenty-twenty, but the right side of his body was still a nasty purple-orange-yellow and hurt to the touch in spots. He'd taken a beating and he was lucky he hadn't been severely injured or killed. He thought about doing the same things but expecting different results. Though the captain hadn't pushed him on the issue because of Ned, Wyatt couldn't deny the fact that he'd pursued the beast twice, and the Akhlut had gotten the better of him both times.

The year of the beast had cooled even as the summer heat and humidity grew. The Akhlut hadn't made an appearance—that he knew of—and there'd been no more murders, at least of the human variety. Wyatt had no way of knowing what wildlife the Akhlut might be eating as it built its strength. Time heals all wounds and lessens all pain, and even the hard stones that called the peninsula home had let the myth of the Akhlut fade into the blur of their daily lives, despite numerous hunts and related attempts to find the creature before the summer tourist season went into full swing.

Soon the peninsula would have a new population of summer adventure seekers, and the local support facilities would be stretched to their maximum. This was great for the town, but also difficult, and though many folks on the peninsula relied on tourist dollars for part, if not all, of their income, most folks looked forward to fall when things went back to normal.

Wyatt took a sip of beer and looked at his watch. 7:04 PM. He was waiting on Ian and his wife Cindy, and Kim. Wyatt had agreed to the double date—was happy about it, in fact. The women could talk, Ian and Wyatt could talk, and it would take some pressure off himself and Kim to carry the whole affair.

The various investigations surrounding the Akhlut had ground to a halt. Jesse was still at the forefront of the town's collective mind, and it was discovered that Harry Toad, the longtime resident who lived on Terror Lake and owned the abandoned skiff, was missing. A canvas of the area had revealed the old man's dogs barking and braying as they tried to escape their kennels because they hadn't been fed in days.

Darrell was still missing and shadows were all the trail camera at The Hole captured, and none of them were large enough to be the beast. Though a coordinated hunt was being organized, there were still many folks in Mount Aire that didn't believe the myth and thought Wyatt and Ned had seen a bear or another freak of nature in their frantic states.

Though open season had been declared on the Akhlut, not many folks were hunting the creature, and he couldn't blame them. He emptied his beer and lifted his mug. He wasn't chasing with whiskey. That would come later when he didn't give a hoot about embarrassing himself.

A fresh brew appeared before him like magic and Wyatt took a long pull, relishing the tang of hops, the refreshing effervesce of wheat. The alcohol warmed his stomach and massaged his shoulders, and the stress drained a little faster than it was building.

"Howdy, stranger," soothed a gentle female voice.

Wyatt looked over his shoulder. It was Jada Harvnor. He hadn't seen her since the day of the race when Jesse disappeared. She looked good; her black hair pulled back, her dark complexion moving toward a summer tan. Jada looked down at him—she was tall, more than six feet. Her eyes ranged toward the empty seat beside him, a question in her eyes.

He said, "I'm expecting someone, but have a seat until they get here."

Her lips formed into a thin red line, she looked at the moose head, and said, "I just wanted to say hello." She took a sip of something green from a martini glass. "Are you doing O.K.? I've heard things haven't gotten much better for you since the incident during the race."

"Things sure have picked up speed, though the beast appears to have taken a holiday."

She chuckled, but it was forced. She said, "You know…" She licked her lips. "Those who have the least information and facts usually talk the loudest."

Wyatt wasn't sure what the woman was trying to say, and his face must have told the story because she continued.

"Nobody I've talked to blames you… No, that's not right. Many folks in town believe you, Wyatt, and those who don't understand, it's not like they think you're…" She hiked her shoulders and took a long pull off her frog drink.

"Crazy?"

She said nothing.

"Me and Trooper Simmons, who's still in a hospital bed in Anchorage fighting for his life?"

"I just want you to know many of us… all of us," she said as she looked around. "We're behind you."

He nodded as he searched for words, but Ian, Cindy, and Kim arrived and saved him. Everybody knew everybody so introductions weren't needed, and after Jada politely declined an invitation to join their party, Wyatt and his crew made their way to a table.

A barrier of heat separated Wyatt and Kim. He'd never felt literal heat between them, and he smiled at her, and Kim smiled back. Maybe his mother had been right, though that was a tough turd to swallow.

"I like her," said Kim as she motioned toward Jada, who was back at the bar.

Wyatt sensed a trap, and he said nothing.

"Do you know her well?" Cindy said. "My brother still hasn't settled down."

Ian chuckled, caught Wyatt's eye, and smiled. Cindy was laying it out there. Direct, to the point. Is this chick a threat to Kim? If not, let's get it off the table and clear away the stink.

"Not really," Wyatt said. "From around town, the race committee. I think she's single, not sure." He guessed that was the right answer because there were smiles all around. Wyatt was so bad at small talk, which was such a large part of human interaction, even out on the peninsula, that he always felt uncomfortable unless he was talking with Ian or someone he knew well.

The foursome ordered drinks and scanned menus and specials.

Wyatt said, "Ian, do you know Kal?"

"Renne Kalvak? Sure," Ian said.

"Very nice man," Cindy said. "He came into the shop recently."

"I met him out on the lake a couple of weeks ago and he told me an interesting story," Wyatt said. "About the curse of Terror Lake?" He searched his companions' faces for any signs of recognition and saw only confusion.

"Which one?" Kim asked.

Cindy nodded vigorously.

Wyatt relayed what Kal had told him. How the Inuit people believed Terror Lake contained an untold number of dead, all victims of the Akhlut, a beast created from stardust and dirt by the ghost of a young Inuit princess named Madeleine.

Their drinks arrived and the waiter, a young kid Wyatt didn't know, was told they needed more time to decide on dinner.

After taking a long draw on her glass of red wine, Cindy said, "I recognize the name Madeleine."

"Isn't she the princess who fell in love with a non-native fisherman? Way back in like the 1800s?"

"1700s, actually," Wyatt said. "The fisherman came to love her as well, and they hid their relationship because the chief forbade his daughter from seeing her lover."

"Right," Cindy said. "Then one day he left her, or something like that."

"In the end, she rowed out to the middle of the lake and stabbed herself in the heart. Her spirit created the Akhlut, and every six years the lady of the lake commands the beast to bring her men to replace her lost love."

That last part sat out there like a fart in church, the four friends sipping their drinks, Wyatt waiting for the inevitable arguments of denial. No one spoke, and the chatter of the bar, the gentle music from the jukebox, the tinkle of silverware on plates, and the push of air through the HVAC system filled the stillness.

"Sounds crazy, I know," Wyatt said.

Kim put a hand on Wyatt's thigh.

An explosion of heat and the tingle of excitement spread through Wyatt like an electrical shock.

"It doesn't sound crazy at all," Kim said.

In that moment, as warmth filled him, Wyatt wanted to take Kim in his arms and kiss her. She smiled at him, and he said, "Thank you." Though he wasn't sure what he was thanking her for.

The foursome ate, drank, laughed, reminisced, and Kim gave the group an update on Coco, Wyatt's mother's new dog. Dessert and coffee came and went, and when the evening came to an end Wyatt surprised himself.

"Would you like to come back to the casa for a nightcap?" Wyatt asked Kim.

Ian and Cindy stood back like proud parents, their matchmaking completed.

Kim accepted Wyatt's invitation, and after a bottle of chardonnay and playing some video games, Wyatt asked Kim to stay the night and she accepted.

Monday dawned bright and warm, and Wyatt woke to find Kim gone. There was a note on the pillow beside him that read simply, "Thanks for a great night. Call me." He would.

Wyatt fumbled for his phone and found a text message from Captain Udell. The boss wanted to have coffee at 9 AM.

His head ached from the prior night's festivities, and the last thing he wanted to do was meet with the boss, but Udell rarely requested meetings, so when he did Wyatt had little choice but to comply. He considered not responding. Wyatt wasn't connected to his phone twenty-four-seven like the kids these days. But... he was being an intolerable ass.

He texted back a thumbs up and let his head fall back into his pillow.

An hour and forty minutes later he pushed through the entrance at the diner and found the captain sitting at the counter. The place was mostly empty, the breakfast crowd having already come through, and he took a seat next to his boss.

Captain Udell had a notebook open in front of him, and there was a mug and coffee urn at his elbow.

"Joe?" the captain asked.

Wyatt nodded and grabbed an upside mug from the place setting before him and poured a cup from the urn.

"How are you feeling?" Captain Udell asked as he read from his notebook.

"Hurts a little when I run."

"You were never very fast."

Crickets. Whatever shit the boss had to shovel Wyatt wasn't lending a hand.

"You heard I'm setting up a meeting with anyone who will come about the hunt?"

"Yes," he said. "I've been working on the section maps to hand out, remember?"

"Of course, I thought that, maybe... No matter. You'll be in charge locally, but I plan to be around more over the next couple of months."

Great, just what he needed. Wyatt said nothing.

"I'll cut to the chase because I don't have much time, and you need to get to work," the captain said.

Wyatt sucked in a deep breath. Here it comes.

"Given that Trooper Simmons won't be healthy enough for active duty until the winter, at the earliest, I've made some reassignments."

Wyatt's stomach sank. Help was always welcome, but if he drew some yahoo, some cowboy...

"I'll be assigning five officers to you until the end of summer. Two pairs and a partner."

Wyatt licked his lips. He and Simmons were kind of partners, but they did their own thing and always patrolled alone. But what could it hurt to have help? “I do—”

The captain put up a hand. “I know you like riding alone, but this is for the best, and it's only temporary.”

“Fine.”

The captain’s eyes grew wide.

“Who?”

“I’m not sure about the pairs yet, but I’m pulling in someone from Anchorage to accompany you. A Susannah McFarely. She goes by the name of Suzie.”

Wyatt had never heard the name before, so he stayed silent.

“Don’t get prissy. This is to protect you from yourself and help put folks’s minds at ease. It’s not an indictment of you or anything you’ve done.”

Wyatt said nothing as he sipped his coffee. The more he ran things through his filter the more he liked the idea of backup.

“Questions?” The boss didn’t give Wyatt time to respond. “Good. Let’s get on with it then.” The captain went back to reading his book.

Wyatt had been dismissed, and he was fine with that. It was time for the year of the beast to end.

18

A rainbow arced over the Zodiac's rooster tail, a cloud of mist hanging above the churned water, the outboard screaming as Wyatt piloted the boat across Terror Lake. The bow was steady as it sliced through the calm water, the wind nothing more than a soft puff from the south. It was the calm before the storm, the convergence of warm and cool air, which caused atmospheric pressure to drop, leading to stillness before the chaos.

He'd chosen the lake as his patrol zone because he knew the area best, and it provided fast and easy access to the surrounding areas. Not to mention the Akhlut called the lake home.

His new partner, Wildlife Trooper Susannah McFarely, sat on the bench seat before the command console, her short black hair twisting in the wind. The orange Rabbit Ranger vest she wore was brand-new, and its reflective markings glowed faintly in the midafternoon gloom.

Suzie was quiet and reserved, but Wyatt liked her. She was fresh out of training and had zero experience, but that wasn't necessarily a bad thing. He recalled the saying, "If you don't want a rotten apple, don't go to the barrel, go to the tree." Suzie was clay, and Wyatt found he enjoyed teaching and passing on his knowledge and experience.

Then there were the feelings he was doing his best to control. He couldn't get Suzie's hazel-brown eyes out of his head, the way they sparkled with life. Her lips were always twisted in a smile, and she smelled like a sea breeze scented with wildflowers. Wyatt was attracted to her, but it was more than her physical appearance. She was smart, a great listener, and he would be hard-pressed to find someone as easy to spend a day with, including Ian. Wyatt's stomach curdled as he thought of Kim. They'd been seeing each other a lot recently, and though he couldn't say he loved her—not yet—the attraction to Suzie made him feel guilty and uncomfortable.

Wyatt rolled his shoulders and cracked his neck. She was his partner, and he had a girlfriend, so Wyatt would bury any feelings he had. Not a problem, that was standard procedure.

The surface of Terror Lake glistened, rays of sunlight cutting through the thickening clouds. Suzie's eyes were pressed to binoculars as she scanned the lake's western shoreline. Several boats dotted the lake, folks fishing and enjoying the early season peace and quiet. The tourists would start rolling in any day now, and along with them would come radios, children playing handheld video games, and a cacophony of noise. The thought of what it must be like to live packed together with other people all the time reminded Wyatt why he lived in Mount Aire, his crazy thoughts of leaving town filed away under he'd had too much beer.

Suzie raised her hand and made a fist, but never took her eyes from the field glasses.

Wyatt eased back the control lever and the growl of the outboard diminished as the boat slowed and the bow dipped. "Got something?" he said.

She pointed.

Wyatt lifted the binoculars that hung around his neck and adjusted their magnification as he peered through the eyepieces.

The glare on the water made it difficult to see, even with the dark clouds rolling in.

"See that movement? In that thick patch of Hemlocks?" Suzie asked.

Wyatt saw something, but what he didn't know. He let the binoculars drop to his chest and said, "Hold on."

He punched the throttle and the engine screamed as the Zodiac surged from the lake, the engine's propellor clawing at the still water, the bow rising. Mist settled on Wyatt's face, and he felt at ease, which told him the Akhlut wasn't near.

The depth finder chimed, the dark line marking the lake bottom filling the screen, the reading cycling back and forth between a depth of one and two feet.

Wyatt eased back the throttle. The following sea crashed into the transom and bubbled over, the hum of hydraulics carrying over the lake as Wyatt angled up the outboard and killed the engine.

A soothing wind tugged the boat east, away from the lake's edge.

The shoreline was packed with evergreens, and trees towered over the lake, their branches reaching for the clouds. A spidery network of limbs covered in needles filled the dense canopy and filtered the sun, casting a soft green light over the landscape. The air was heavy with the scent of pine, and the sound of the lake gently lapping against the shore played second fiddle to the squawking and braying wildlife.

Wyatt was awe-struck at the sheer size of the trees and vastness of the woods. The massive pines went on forever, their trunks growing thicker and taller as the forest marched away from the lake. Underbrush encroached around the base of each tree, and wildflowers in shades of purple, yellow, and pink bloomed among the ferns and water reeds.

Tiny ripples rolled over the lake, the water reflecting the evergreens and a cloud-darkened sky. Fish darted about just below the waterline, and insects alighted on the rippling surface. A small waterfall cascaded through the woods, tumbling down a series of rocks and reminding Wyatt of his fall the night Ned had been injured.

A family of ducks swam in the shallows, and a doe drank along the water's edge. The wildlife was unafraid, and the creatures went about their business as if Wyatt and Suzie weren't there, and that confirmed in Wyatt's mind that the Akhlut wasn't in the area.

"I can't tell what all the commotion is about," Suzie said. She was still staring through her binoculars. "Can you get us in closer?"

The outboard was angled as high as it could go and still have the propeller and cooling intakes in the water, and the bow floated in a foot of water. He could push in further, and if the Zodiac bottomed out, they could don their waders and walk the rest of the way in. Or…

"Give me a minute," Wyatt said. He lifted the radio handset and opened a channel. "Rogue One, do you copy? This is Wyatt, over."

"We copy, Wyatt," came the voice of Wildlife Trooper Denis Freed. He was teamed up with Rolly Langdon.

"What's your current position?"

"Up on the glacier checking for tracks."

"Anything?"

"Not yet. Do you need us? Over."

It would take Rogue One at least twenty minutes by ATV to get to the location. "Negative," Wyatt said. "Report in if you find anything."

"Copy that."

"Rogue Two, do you copy?" Wyatt said.

The other pair of wildlife troopers were up on the western ridge and couldn't provide any immediate help. Wyatt dropped the handset back in its cradle and said, "O.K., let's move in closer."

Wyatt cranked the engine and gently eased down the throttle control as he spun the ship's wheel and turned the bow toward shore. The boat glided slowly through the shallow water, the lake's depth increasing and decreasing with the uneven lake bottom.

Three minutes later the Zodiac slid into mud and Wyatt killed the engine before the water intakes got fouled.

"False alarm. It's not the Akhlut, but check it out," Suzie said.

Wyatt harrumphed and lifted his binoculars.

A huge hawk had a mouse in its powerful talons, and the predator fought to control its prey. The bird's wings flapped wildly, brown and white feathers fluttering, bronze pine needles flying as the two animals crashed through the green vegetation.

The gray field mouse struggled, but the hawk held the tiny creature tightly, its grip unyielding.

With a muffled shriek, the giant bird of prey tilted its head back before pistoning forward and driving its beak into the mouse's tiny body.

A final, pitiful squeak carried over Terror Lake as the hawk began to feed. The bird ate methodically, carefully tearing off pieces of the mouse's flesh and swallowing them whole. Wyatt watched with strange fascination as the mouse's body was quickly stripped of all meat, leaving only bones, skin, and entrails behind.

When the hawk finished its meal, it lifted its head and looked out over the lake and noticed the Zodiac for the first time. Then it squawked, its shrill call like a great pterosaur's cry, or at least what Wyatt believed the legendary flying reptiles might have sounded like.

The bird of prey flapped its massive wings and pushed into the sky, soaring over the lake, and angling away from the Zodiac as the wildlife troopers watched.

"I've seen that happen like five times already, and I still find the circle of life amazing," she said.

Wyatt hated that phrase—the circle of life—but he couldn't deny that the saying had merit. He said, "You'll see things out here that most Americans wouldn't believe."

"Like the Akhlut?"

He said nothing. Since Suzie had been out on the lake with him there'd been no signs of the beast.

A chill breeze pushed off the glacier and Wyatt felt cold despite the heat pressing on the lake. Thick clouds rolled in from the west, and soon the rain would come. The Zodiac was an open eighteen-foot center console, and there was no cabin, no head, no shelter at all, but it was too early to call it a day.

With the spectacle of the hawk done, Wyatt fired up the engine and slowly backed out into deeper water as he lowered the motor. When the depth finder read six feet, Wyatt cranked the throttle and pointed the bow south.

"We'll take a couple of laps around the lake's edge before we head in," Wyatt said.

Suzie nodded. She hadn't moved from her position on the bench seat before the command console and suddenly Wyatt felt guilt surge through him. Was he treating her like an ornament and not taking advantage of her skills? She needed to learn, and to do that he needed to let her take the lead sometimes.

"Do you want to pilot the boat?" he said.

Suzie turned to look at him, her eyes wide, her mouth hanging open.

"What?" Wyatt said, but he was gaslighting her, and his stomach burned. "I mean… Do you want to or not?"

"Sure." Suzie got up, stretched, and worked her way behind the command console and Wyatt relinquished the ship's wheel for the first time in his career. That realization made him uneasy, but at the same time, he knew he was doing his job. Piloting the small Zodiac wasn't a major task, yet he needed to see how she handled the craft.

Wyatt took a seat before the command console, happy for the break. He took his turn scanning the shoreline, but soon grew bored and gave up.

The rain came in sheets, beating against the surface of the lake, turning the once calm water into a chaotic mess of swells and splashes, as if the lake was alive and fighting the storm.

Wyatt sat before the command console watching nature vent. The rain slid off his raincoat, but the wind picked up, and water splashed his face, and he was mesmerized by the power of the storm, the way it transformed nature into a wild and untamed adversary.

The outboard whined as Suzie arced the ship's wheel and headed for the marina, the western shoreline a gray outline dulled by the driving rain. Lightning illuminated the sky, casting an eerie glow over the lake, and Wyatt counted the seconds between the flashes of light and the claps of thunder, waiting for the storm to reach its peak.

The rain was cleansing, and it washed away some of his worries and brought back an odd sense of peace.

"Let's head in," Wyatt hollered over the wind.

Suzie gave him a thumbs up, and as she piloted the Zodiac back to the dock the storm slowly died down.

They'd failed to catch even a whiff of the beast, but tomorrow was another day.

The remainder of the week passed slowly, each day blending into the next like colors on a painter's palette. Time stretched out, endless and uninterrupted, like a river flowing towards an unknown destination. Wyatt and Suzie patrolled the lake and watched the sun rise and set and waited.

Wyatt tried to hold onto his calm, telling himself the Akhlut could be done for the year, but he couldn't shake the feeling that time was his enemy, and sooner or later the beast would return.

"You in there?" asked Suzie.

"Sorry," he said. "What is it?"

"You don't hear the radio?"

Wyatt had been so lost in thought he hadn't, but he did now. He pushed to his feet, moved around the command console, and grabbed the comm handset. "It's Wyatt. Go ahead."

"We've got Kim Farret here, Wyatt, and she needs to speak to you. Says it's an emergency."

Suzie and Wyatt exchanged a glance through the drizzle as Kim's voice burst from the radio. "Wyatt?"

"What is it? Kim, are you alright?" Wyatt felt responsible for Kim and cared about her well-being. This was exactly why he didn't get close to people.

Kim's voice was frantic. "I'm fine. It's your mother, Wyatt."

19

The medical center was a quaint, two-story building with a white exterior and blue metal roof. The front entrance was surrounded by lush green juniper bushes, and as Wyatt pushed through the front doors the cacophony of street noise died away and the smell of evergreens faded and was replaced with the stink of disinfectant.

A knot grew in Wyatt's stomach as he thought about his mother, who was in critical condition and fighting for her life in the closest thing the center had to an ICU. Though their relationship was strained, the thought of losing her was unbearable.

The interior of the medical center was simple but functional. The lobby was brightly lit and clean, with a reception desk on one side and a seating area on the other. Wyatt headed to the desk, where a security guard Wyatt didn't know asked him to sign in, though he didn't bother with a visitor's pass because in Mount Aire, Wyatt was the law.

"Through those doors there, down the hall, and the day nurse will assist you," said the guard.

Wyatt nodded his thanks and took a deep breath.

The first floor of the Mount Arie Medical Center had exam rooms, a laboratory, and a small pharmacy. Though tests often had to be sent to Anchorage, the center's lab handled routine blood tests, X-rays, and other diagnostic tests. There had been a fundraiser the prior year for an MRI machine, but it fell way short, which didn't matter because the center couldn't afford a full-time technician. The pharmacy was well-stocked with all the necessary medications and supplements to support patients' health and wellness, and other than some basics that Ian carried, it served as the area's RX supplier.

An additional wing housed the emergency room and the two ICU-like rooms for patients who required around-the-clock care. There was a basic surgical center, though any operation requiring a specialty or new equipment was transferred to Anchorage if the patient's condition permitted it.

The second floor housed the offices of the healthcare providers and specialists where routine business was handled. Thanks to the failed MRI fundraiser, the raised money was used for the center's newest feature; telemedicine services so patients could visit healthcare providers from the comfort of their own homes, making it easier for the elderly and injured to receive care.

As he walked down the sterile, white-walled corridor, hopelessness leaked through Wyatt again, and the beeping of machines and the hushed whispers of the staff only added to his unease.

Wyatt reached a desk manned by a nurse in purple scrubs and wearing a name tag that read Dot.

"Officer Wyatt, we've been expecting you," Dot said. The knot of blonde hair atop her head swayed when she talked. Before Wyatt could start firing off questions Dot continued, "Your mother is stable and doing O.K. The doctor is in with her right now and she'll be out to see you in a minute. Have a seat."

"Who's on tonight?"

"Dr. Riole."

Relief washed through Wyatt. He'd just seen Janet and she was good.

He took a seat, and as Wyatt waited, the preciousness of life filled him with worry and love for a woman he dreaded seeing. Nothing was guaranteed, and guilt consumed him. He should have been there to help her. Visited more. Been a better son.

Kim pulled him from his pity party. She came down the hall with a cup of coffee, her face gray with weariness, black bags hanging beneath bloodshot eyes. They hugged and Wyatt thanked her for getting her mom to the medical center.

"I just went out back with Coco, and your mom was fiddling in the kitchen, you know how she is."

Wyatt nodded.

"When I came back into the house with Coco, she was on the kitchen floor," Kim said. "I almost panicked."

He took her in his arms and hugged her. "But you didn't."

She nodded and wiped her eyes.

The door next to the reception desk opened and Dr. Riole appeared. The regal physician nodded to Dot and waved at Wyatt and Kim. "Sorry to see you again so soon."

He nodded, but said nothing as he vaulted to his feet.

"Easy, sit down. Hi, Kim."

Wyatt's nerves danced, his stomach turning sour, but Janet didn't look upset. He sat, his heart pounding with anticipation.

Dr. Riole seated herself next to him. There were no other patrons in the area. "Wyatt… is it O.K. if I speak freely in front of Kim?"

Wyatt nodded without thought. Their relationship aside, Kim had just as much right to be there as he did. She had taken better care of his mother than he had recently.

"I'm pleased to tell you Helen is making great progress," the doctor said. "Her vital signs are stabilizing, and she's responding well to the treatment."

A wave of relief washed over Wyatt, and he couldn't help but smile. "That's great news. Thank you, Janet."

Kim took his hand in hers.

"Good news, yes, it is. However, I do have some concerns," the doctor said, her smile slipping away. "Your mother's condition is still critical. She's had a heart attack."

Wyatt gasped then put his hand over his mouth like a southern bell.

Dr. Riole put up a hand. "She scored a three on the Penn Scale, and that's middle of the road, and I think it would be best if she were transferred to Anchorage General due to her age and the advanced care provided there."

Wyatt's heart sank. He knew that his mother was in no condition to be moved that far, and he was afraid that the transfer would do more harm than good. "Is it necessary?" he asked, trying to keep the tremor out of his voice.

"In my opinion, I'm afraid it is," the doctor replied. "The medical center here is equipped to handle most emergencies, but your mother's condition is complex. A larger hospital will be better equipped to handle her needs and provide her with the care she needs."

"Is she awake? Can she talk?" Wyatt asked.

The doctor shook her head no. "She's intubated and sedated."

"Can I see her?"

"Sure, but don't take too much time deciding," the doctor said. "The bird is on the pad, ventilator onboard, and she can be in City General in an hour. This kind of thing is done all the time. Don't let the actual transfer and distance affect your decision."

As Wyatt and Kim were led into his mother's room, Wyatt couldn't help but think of himself, how the timing of all this couldn't have been worse, not that there was ever a good time to die.

When Wyatt saw his mother lying in bed, hooked up to multiple machines and tubes, pain stung his chest, and a block of ice formed in his stomach. He couldn't believe that this was his mother, the strongest person he had ever known. She looked like she'd lost half her body weight and the tube sticking from her mouth and the puff and sigh of the respiratory machine brought tears to his eyes.

He approached her, took his mother's hand in his, and she squeezed it back.

"She's still there," the doctor said, and as if on cue Wyatt's mom opened her eyes.

"How long... how long before the breathing tube can come out?" Wyatt asked.

Dr. Riole hiked her shoulders. "Don't know. She's on a high percentage of oxygen and until we're sure she can breathe on her own, I don't want to take the tube out, because putting it back in could do significant damage. Those decisions will be in the hands of the specialists at City General."

"Any estimate?"

She threw up her hands.

Wyatt knew that his mother's health was the top priority, and he couldn't deny the importance of getting her the best possible care. "Okay, let's do it," he said, his voice firm, though he felt anything but sure.

The doctor nodded and the next forty-five minutes were spent filling out forms and signing documents. Wyatt wrote what was happening on a pad and showed it to his mother, but she became agitated and had to be sedated further.

Wyatt joined his mother on the copter to Anchorage, and as the sun set on what felt like the longest day of his life, Wyatt found himself on the return flight coming back to the peninsula. Going back and forth to Anchorage would be difficult, but he wasn't helping anyone sitting by his mother's bedside. The doctors had promised to keep him up to date, and Wyatt planned to be back at the hospital two or three days hence when it was hoped an attempt could be made to remove her breathing tube.

Before he left, Wyatt managed to sneak in a visit with Ned, who was two floors up from his mother and a couple of weeks away from being transferred home to the peninsula. He said he would keep half an eye on Wyatt's mother when he could and that eased Wyatt's guilt some.

His shoulders ached, and he felt older than he had in his entire life, but still, the day wasn't done. He pulled his phone and called Kim, who had agreed to take Coco until alternate plans could be arranged.

"Hello?" she sounded frantic.

"It's me."

"Everything go O.K.?"

"As best as can be expected. I'll be going back in a couple of days if she continues to improve, and there's talk of her coming back this way in a week or two."

Kim sighed. "What a relief. Any long-term ramifications?"

"Still unknown, but everyone is hopeful. That's the only reason I'm coming home," Wyatt said. "They'll be running a battery of tests over the next day or so and that will tell us more, but Dr. Riole said not to worry. Mom's tough and she should come out of this one."

"This one?"

Wyatt didn't want to sound like an asshole, but he was under no illusions. "This is how it starts, right?"

Kim said nothing. Her mom had died several years ago of pancreatic cancer, and she'd never known her father.

Realizing what an insensitive ass he'd been, Wyatt said, "Sorry."

"Don't be," she said. "You're right, so since you know that, there's something you can do about it."

He thought he understood. "Yeah, I need to be around more, even if it's…"

"Torture? She could have died, and then you'd never be able to speak to her again."

That thought brought an odd mixture of pain and guilt. He changed the subject. "How's Coco?"

"Fine," Kim said. "But she knows something is up."

"Can I come by tomorrow and pick the girl up?"

"No rush, and…"

"What is it?"

"Those stairs to get up to your place," Kim said. "Her hips aren't what they once were."

"I'll come by in the morning to visit her and we'll talk. I've got a teleconference with Mom's docs at eleven." Wyatt declined an offer to come by now, he was exhausted, and the pair closed with pleasantries and said goodnight. Wyatt went straight home, downed two fingers of whiskey, and went to bed.

Sleep wouldn't come, thoughts of his mother hundreds of miles away, lying in the dark by herself filled him with guilt, and when the sun came up, he got up, showered, dressed, and headed out to the woods. He patrolled until 9 AM and then headed to Kim's, where he found Coco loving life.

The dog was a proud and majestic beast, and her patchy coat of white and gray fur glimmered in the sun. Her once bright eyes had faded to a soft, gentle gray, but despite her age, Coco still had a lively spirit.

She loved to play, though she was also content with spending her days napping and receiving belly rubs.

Life dragged on and Wyatt's life consisted of patrolling and sleeping, and trips to Anchorage. Kim agreed to keep Coco at her place until things settled down for Wyatt, and this made things much easier, and since he and Kim saw each other most days he also got to see Coco and help out with food and such.

The days slipped away with no sign of the Akhlut, no reports of dead farm animals or missing persons. Terror Lake was packed with fishermen and recreational boaters, and with the Fourth of July coming, Wyatt's stomach got tighter with each passing hour.

Six days after his mother's heart attack, Wyatt took a ferry to Anchorage and arrived at his mother's bedside an hour before the doctors yanked the breathing tube from her throat. To say his mother had choice words for the doctors and him was an understatement, but after she got some water and a sleeping aid, she was able to rest comfortably. Her throat would be sore for weeks, and her voice sounded more smoke-torn than ever. She hadn't taken the news that she could never have another cigarette well.

"When do you think she can be transported back to the peninsula?" Wyatt asked the attending physician.

"Two more days, maybe three," said the tall doctor whose eyes were so blue Wyatt couldn't believe they weren't contacts. "We need to run some more tests and make sure your local doctors can handle her treatment plan. She got lucky this time, but she needs to make some changes. Right, Helen?"

Mrs. Wyatt harrumphed, then promptly fell into a drug-induced sleep.

He spent the rest of the day sitting with his mother, and when she woke, he endured a tongue-lashing about him being single when there were perfectly good women around. Kim for example.

Wyatt decided to toss his sick mother a bone. "Actually, Kim and I have been seeing each other. She didn't mention it to you?"

The first genuine smile he'd seen on his mother's face in years made his stomach grow hot.

His mother was happy, and she was done with him and told Wyatt to go home. "The people of Mount Aire need you. Coco and Kim need you."

Coco and Kim didn't need him, but he smiled, kissed his mother's forehead, and left her to rest.

The trip back to the peninsula was uneventful, and when his mother arrived home four days later there had still been no sign of the Akhlut.

20

As the last days of June gave way to July the peninsula became crowded—at least what Alaskans considered crowded. July was usually the warmest month of the year, and the beauty of nature was on full display. The forest was alive, and the soft light of dawn filtered through the trees, casting pale light on the forest floor. Wyatt sucked in the crisp air and took a pull off his canteen as he scanned his phone. He had marked locations that appeared to be good access points for the Akhlut on a chart of Terror Lake, and now he was checking them out on foot, searching for any sign of the beast along the shoreline.

Wyatt was anxious beyond anything he'd ever experienced, and he almost wished he'd get a call about a mutilated horse or a destroyed henhouse. That would tell him the beast hadn't changed its habits.

But surely it had. The Akhlut's entire world had transformed since the year of the beast began.

The thick forest blocked the view of the western horizon, and sunlight danced across the treetops, creating a pattern of light and shadow beneath the tree canopy that slithered and shifted with the breeze. Birds sang, insects buzzed, and animals rustled in the underbrush.

The lake was a glassy silver field of tiny whitecaps and swirls of eddying dead leaves and twigs. A four-point buck dipped its narrow head into the cool water, a doe, and several fawns filing in behind the alpha.

Despite all the prey, he hadn't found any of the odd slash-like hoof prints of the Akhlut.

Wyatt reported in and checked with his crews. Suzie was hiking the opposite side of the lake, and she'd had no more luck than Wyatt. Rogue Two was taking a turn patrolling the lake and Rogue One was testing out the backup boat because it would be needed on the Fourth of July when the locals that lived around the lake provided the residents of Mount Aire with a private fireworks show, and the best seat in the house was on Terror Lake.

He would be working, but if all went well the plan was for Kim to bring Mom and Coco to Lakehead Beach to watch the festivities, but that depended on how she felt and her mood. His mother's recovery had slowed, and she was frustrated and fought bouts of constant depression while lashing out at those who were trying to help her.

What must it be like to know that your time was coming to an end? To be able to look back on life and know that time was running short? Would his mother feel at peace, knowing that she had lived a full life? Or would she be filled with regret, wishing she'd done more, seen more, experienced more? Wyatt thought the latter.

He mused about his own life and all the things he had yet to do and accomplish. There were so many places Wyatt wanted to travel to, so many forests, bays, and lakes, so many things he wanted to learn, and so many people he wanted to meet. The thought that he might not have enough time—like his father—to do it all, was sobering. At the same time, there was something freeing about the idea of death. It was the ultimate reminder that his time on Earth was limited and that every moment counted.

Wyatt reached a thick tangle of scrub pine and pricker bushes that ran to the water's edge and marked the end of his hike. Rather than backtrack, he planned to cut through the woods to Circle Road, then grab a ride, or walk, back to where he'd left the ATV.

He felt insignificant as he made his way through a dense stand of firs, and he marveled at the towering trees. The giant fir trunks were straight and tall and packed tight like an army guarding their queen. The tree needles rustled in the wind, a soothing whisper that filled the woods. A soft blanket of bronze needles covered the forest floor and muffled the sound of Wyatt's footsteps. The air was fresh and crisp, and the scent of fresh water and evergreens filled his nostrils and tickled his senses.

Ahead, in a knot of brambles, two golden eyes floated in the shadowy darkness like glowing orbs, their yellow-green hue piercing the gloom beneath the dense tree canopy. The eyes watched Wyatt, unblinking and intense.

Wyatt's heart galloped and invisible spiders ran down his spine as a primal fear consumed him, the terror that comes from knowing he was being watched by a predator in the shadows.

The eyes belonged to a lynx, he knew that much, but Wyatt couldn't see the rest of the animal. It was as if the eyes were suspended in mid-air, disembodied and haunting.

Wyatt stood still as stone and stared down the cat, and the lynx revealed itself. It was a sleek and powerful creature, its fur blending seamlessly into the shadows of the forest. The cat eased into a ray of light that knifed through a gap in the trees and pressed its stomach to the ground, a low growl carrying on the breeze.

The lynx was medium-sized with a stubby tail, large ears with black tufts at the tips, and a ruffed tangle of dark hair around its face. Its fur was reddish-brown with black spots and stripes, providing excellent camouflage. The animal's large paws had sharp, retractable claws for climbing trees and catching prey. As carnivores, the cats regularly hunted rodents, hares, and birds, and it wasn't unheard of for lynx to prey on larger animals such as deer when the opportunity presented itself. Wyatt knew of documented attacks on people, but in almost all those cases it had been the human that had instigated the confrontation. He recalled his tangle with the lynx earlier in the season, and he didn't think he'd provoked the beast.

A sour-sweet wind pushed through the trees. The lynx regarded Wyatt for a moment longer, and then, with a flick of its tail, it disappeared back into the darkness, leaving only the memory of its piercing eyes behind.

Wyatt licked his lips as his heart slowed, sweat running down his back. He had his guns back, but the last thing he wanted to do was kill an innocent lynx and deal with all the associated reports and disposal procedures. And what would the boss say? He was already watching him like a hawk.

He continued his trek and when he reached Circle Road Wyatt's radio squawked. It was the captain.

"Wyatt, can you come in? I've got Billy-joe Tolliver here. He was out on the lake and took a picture I think you might find of interest."

"I'm on Circle Road and I've got a half-hour walk back to my ATV if nobody drives by… unless you want to send someone out to pick me up?" A brief pause and Wyatt assumed the captain was doing the same math as he had. Rogue One and Rogue Two were patrolling on the opposite side of the lake, and it would take someone coming from town almost half an hour to get to him.

"Negative," came the captain's voice over the radio. "Doesn't make sense. Get to your unit and double-time it to my office. Copy?"

"That's a 10-4."

Wyatt didn't catch a ride, and fifty minutes later he pulled up outside town hall and killed the ATV's engine.

The stink of the dental offices assailed him as he made his way to the captain's closet of an office where he found the boss and Billy-joe engaged in a debate about who was going to win the Stanley Cup.

"Let me tell you something, Billy-Joe," said Captain Udell. "The Jets are going to crush the Flames this year. Mark my words."

“Oh, I highly doubt that," retorted Billy-Joe, a mischievous grin spreading over his round face. “The Flames are going to take the cup, and there's nothing you can do about it.”

Captain Udell scoffed. "You’re dreaming, my friend. The Jets can take down any team.”

Billy-Joe leaned back in his chair, his sly grin running away from his face. “You know what? I think we need to settle this once and for all.”

The captain raised an eyebrow. “How do you propose we do that?”

“A good old-fashioned game of pond hockey," said Billy-Joe.

“The winter classic!” said the captain.

The two men laughed and turned their attention to Wyatt.

Captain Udell said, “Wyatt, you know Billy-joe, right?”

“We’ve met.” Wyatt saw the man in Buck’s from time to time.

Billy-joe was a rugged, rough-around-the-edges guy, with a wild beard and calloused hands that told the story of a life spent outdoors. He had climbed the peninsula’s highest peaks, crossed its most treacherous rivers, and hiked through some of the wildest terrain in the country. Despite his rugged exterior, Wyatt knew Billy-joe had a big heart and a soft spot for animals, and he was quick to help anyone who needed it.

Wyatt held out his hand and the big man took it.

“Check this out.” The captain tossed a photo across his desk and Wyatt picked it up.

He felt the captain and Billy-joe staring at him, both men willing him to see what they wanted him to see.

The photo was grainy, clearly shot with a cell phone, and blown up. Moonlight painted the lake glimmering white, and in the foreground, a tall shadow fell across the water.

Wyatt pulled the photo closer to his face as if that would improve its quality.

“What do you think? That your Akhlut?” Billy-joe rasped.

A clock ticked, air moved through the vent above the captain’s desk, and somewhere a child cried, most likely a youngster getting a tooth drilled.

Wyatt turned the photo in his hand and willed his eyes to see something that wasn’t there. He thought it was the beast’s dorsal fin in the foreground, its tall shadow falling over a patch of moonlit lake. It was the Akhlut alright, but the photo wasn’t enough to convince someone who hadn’t seen the creature. “Is this the only shot you got?”

Billy-joe nodded.

“I think it is the beast, but there’s not enough here to go to the media. The picture could be anything. Did you see it, Billy-joe?”

The big man shook his head no. "I felt it, though, you know? You're a hunter, right? I got that feeling when you know there's a buck there, right in front of you, but you can't see it."

"Did you smell anything?"

The captain and Billy-joe nodded in unison.

"Garbage and rotting fish," Billy-joe said.

Wyatt licked his lips as he handed the photo back to the captain, who dropped it into the open file.

"I agree about the photo," the captain said. "Not media worthy, and all releasing it would do is stir everyone up before the Fourth." The captain stood. "But thanks, Billy-joe. Please continue to keep an eye out and holler if you see anything else."

Handshakes, goodbyes, and when the captain and Wyatt were alone, Captain Udell said, "The picture isn't the only reason I asked you to come in."

Wyatt lifted his eyebrows.

"What's the plan for the Fourth of July?"

"I'm closing the lake." If it was up to Wyatt, that's what would be happening, but it wasn't.

The captain laughed, a full-throated obnoxious braying that made Wyatt feel small. Captain Udell slapped his leg, wiped a tear from his eye, and said, "Like that would ever fly on a holiday. Do I need to issue a warning? Terror Lake is going to be packed."

There were no simple answers. Wyatt said, "A notice couldn't hurt, but anyone who hasn't heard about the Akhlut has been living under a rock, and even the folks who believed the myth before things went to shit this year aren't going to hole up in their house on the Fourth."

The captain waited.

"The plan for the fireworks show is simple: both boats will patrol the lake, and I'll have one crew patrolling the shoreline. Suzie will be with me and I'm going to deputize Kal and his brother, maybe Billy-joe since he's already involved, Jada, and a few others. The more sets of eyes we have the better, and of course, you're welcome to stand a post if you're up for it."

The captain smiled, but said nothing.

"As far as state support—" Wyatt threw up his hands.

The captain sat in silence for several minutes, lost in thought. Finally, he said, "Tell me what you're thinking. Are you concerned?"

Wyatt laughed, and it was genuine, but he reigned it in fast and transitioned to a cough. "Excuse me, sorry."

The captain showed Wyatt his teeth, his eyes narrowing like his mother's did when she was aggravated.

“Would you take your family out on the lake and make a lot of noise and set off explosions when you knew there was a huge apex predator sleeping below the lake’s surface?” Wyatt said.

“A little dramatic, no?”

Wyatt said nothing, which meant no.

“O.K.,” the captain said. “Let me know if you need anything, and I’ll be on Lakehead Beach, so no need to put an officer there.”

Wyatt nodded. “If all goes well, Mom will be there to watch the show.”

“Good.” The captain closed the case file and got to his feet.

Wyatt took the hint and said goodbye. He still had to stop at Kim’s and see Coco before he called it quits.

He had a milk bone for the huskie and Coco sniffed it out as soon as Wyatt entered Kim’s house, a ranch three streets over from his mother’s place.

Kim talked Wyatt into staying for dinner, then T.V., then for the night. Coco watched the couple as they made love, and when they were done Kim fell off to sleep immediately. Wyatt lay awake, his mind churning through all the things he had to do over the next couple of days, his thoughts drifting to Suzie and how he’d had no thoughts of her while he was making love to Kim. That was a good thing. A very good thing.

He closed his eyes, listening to Kim’s steady breathing and the faint buzz of the night symphony leaking through an open window. Wyatt smiled, content. He might be falling in love, and he dared to dream that the Akhlut might have taken a holiday.

21

Terimore Lake, Alaska, ***9:19 AM AKST, July 4th, 2017***

The first sign of trouble came long before the first rocket rang clear.

Wyatt and Suzie were sitting on the dock eating breakfast sandwiches when Kal called.

Yelling and laughter came from the line waiting to use the boat ramp, and people of all ages fished off the pier that jutted into Terror Lake. The village of Mount Aire loomed to the south, its buildings scattered about the hillside as the town climbed out of the thin lake valley.

"Kal, you're on speaker," Wyatt said. "Everything O.K.?"

"Was just getting an early start on the day, taking a look around, and I found something a little… disturbing."

Wyatt met Suzie's eye and she stopped chewing.

"Where are you?" Wyatt said.

"Just north of The Hole along Mud Cove."

"On our way."

Wyatt pressed to his feet and jumped onto the Zodiac as Suzie untied the aft and bow mooring lines. The engine fired up, and Wyatt piloted the boat out of the harbor, going as slow as his nerves would allow, but still leaving a considerable wake.

Unease, anxiety, and concern fought for control of his body, and his armpits bled moisture and he could barely focus. Wyatt considered handing the wheel off to Suzie, but his partner didn't look much better. She was pulling at her hair, her eyes locked on the lake. Wyatt rolled his shoulders, trying to ease his concern, but his mind kept building horrible scenarios that ended with him being unable to prevent the Akhlut from killing. He knew that was crazy, but he couldn't ignore that the worry had motivated him to be extra careful and consider all outcomes. If the beast showed, he'd be ready.

Except, Wyatt knew that was bullshit. If he'd learned anything, he knew the beast wasn't of this world, and he couldn't make the mistake of underestimating the creature's abilities or overestimating what he thought he knew about the Akhlut.

The sky was a clear blue, the breeze light and fresh with the scents of evergreen and wildflowers, and there was scarcely a cloud in the sky.

The weather forecast called for a perfect day, and though the people of the peninsula deserved a peaceful, relaxing, sunny day off, Wyatt had been secretly hoping for rain. Then folks would've stayed home, and the fireworks show would be postponed, and each resident would ultimately do their own thing. Without any coordination, the crowds on the lake over the following week would be less.

Ducks squawked, flies buzzed, and a gentle wind massaged the lake's surface as the Zodiac sliced neatly through the calm water, the bright sunlight painting the lake silvery-white. The outboard hummed, but the boat threw little spray. There were already more boats out on the lake than Wyatt could count, and by nightfall, anything that could float would be out on the lake for the festivities.

A deep shadow loomed on the western shoreline, and Wyatt slowed the boat as he approached Kal. The bow of the man's kayak was wedged onto a mud flat that stretched out from Mud Cove, thusly named because it slowly drained as the lake level dropped and was nothing more than mud for half the year.

Soft, black sediment that looked like dark chocolate mousse stretched to the west where it met a line of pine trees. The flat was vast, and there was a network of channels and pools. A rank aroma of decaying organic matter mixed with water reminded Wyatt of the smell of diarrhea, and he avoided Mud Cove when he could. To the north and south the clear waters of Terror Lake lapped gently against the mud, slowly pulling it apart as if teasing out cotton, the dirty strands of dirt, twigs, and gobs of green vegetative matter polluting the clear lake water.

"Hello!" called Kal as the wildlife troopers approached.

Wyatt waved, the sound of servos echoing over the water as he tilted up the vessel's outboard and shut the engine down. The Zodiac stopped alongside Kal with a gravelly gasp as the hull ran aground on mud.

"Happy Fourth, Kal," Wyatt said.

The man's wool hat had been replaced with a baseball cap displaying the American flag. His face was creased with worry lines, and his eyes were sharp as ever. "To you as well, Trooper Wyatt."

"Just Wyatt is fine."

Kal licked his lips and cast a gaze at Suzie, who sat on the bench seat staring through binoculars.

"You haven't met my new partner yet, right? This is Suzie."

Hearing her name, Suzie dropped her field glasses, and introductions were exchanged.

"So, you're not going to start my day off bad, are you Kal?" Wyatt asked.

"Were it that I controlled such things."

Wyatt waited and smiled at Suzie, and his partner nodded. Their communication was almost at marriage level, and they'd gotten adept at reading each other's minds in a very short time.

"Over there." Kal pointed south.

Twenty yards off the port bow a reddish-brown substance clouded the water. The large plume was several feet in diameter and thin around the edges as it dispersed. Tiny fish darted in and out of the cloud, their silver scales catching the sun's light and sparkling like diamonds.

Wyatt had seen whales defecate, and he knew the beasts expelled their waste with such force the explosion of crap spread through the sea like a toxic chemical. But this was no whale feces.

His breath caught, and for a horrific heartbeat Wyatt thought he'd found one of the missing Mount Aire residents, but his panic soon passed.

A mutilated deer floated at the center of the waste cloud. Its body was limp and lifeless, the animal's eyes glassy, its fur matted with blood and water. Pieces of its flesh were missing, exposing its bones and organs. The animal's legs were splayed out awkwardly, and its antlers were tangled in a ball of lake debris held together by a jumble of fishing line. The water around the animal was tinted a rusty red, as if the deer's life force was still draining away, and flies swarmed the decaying flesh.

The sun reflected off the lake ripples, casting a warm glow over the macabre scene, mud leaking into the plume of waste.

"Holy shit," Wyatt said.

"Can't see what makes it holy, but it's certainly shit," Kal said.

"We should get a sample," Suzie said.

Wyatt was struggling to hold down his egg sandwich, so he simply nodded.

"Thanks for calling, Kal," Wyatt said. "Are you going to be out here tonight?"

"Wouldn't miss it. My brother and I are going to drop his sailboat and bring his family out."

"Where's your family?" Wyatt asked.

"The wife passed, and the kids live in the real world down in the forty-eight."

Kal said this with no emotion, which told Wyatt he'd hit a nerve. He said, "Sorry, I didn't mean…"

The wind gusted and Kal looked away. "Not your fault."

Suzie wrapped a towel around her face to dull the smell as she leaned over the Zodiac's gunnel and filled her empty water bottle with the reddish-brown feces. Red lines of blood ran through the waste like fudge through vanilla ice cream, and shards of bone and sinew glistened as she held the bottle up.

Sample taken and scene documented, Wyatt said, “I need you to be on the watch tonight. I’m sorry to impose, but we need all the help we can get.” He knew he was asking a lot—folks like to let it all hang loose on the Fourth and have a few cocktails.

The native Inuit waved a withered hand. “I’ll have my phone and we’ll move around. Find us. I’m sure my brother’s wife will have an extensive selection of food.”

Wyatt waved, lowered the engine, and fired it up. As he backed off the mud flat, he said, “Let’s head back to the dock and finish getting ready and update the boss.”

Suzie nodded in agreement.

The marina was like a beehive that’s been smacked with a stick. To nobody’s surprise, the line at the boat ramp had grown longer, and a crowd was already forming on Lakehead Beach, the scent of charcoal wafting over the water. That reminded Wyatt that he needed to check in with Kim and his mom.

Captain Udell didn’t have much to say about the pictures of the deer corpse floating in feces and he told Wyatt to hold onto his bottle of shit.

As the day wore on, Wyatt and his team made sure both boats were ready to roll, the ATVs, and he gave out assignments. Rogue One, Troopers Freed and Langdon, would patrol the northern section of the lake because they were much more experienced on the water than Rogue Two. Troopers Sanford and Kai Ai were top woodsmen, so they would patrol Terror Lake’s shoreline. The captain was on the beach, and Wyatt and Suzie would roam.

Everything was set, yet unease continued to poke at his insides, and it was more than the dead deer and the beast’s waste. Wyatt felt like he was standing on the train tracks with a blinding light and blaring horn bearing down on him, but he was unable to move.

He called his mother, hoping she’d decide to stay home, but of course, she was having one of her good days and said she wouldn’t miss the show for anything. Kim would pick her up at eight and bring Mom and Coco to the lakeside.

By 7 PM Terror Lake was packed with boats. The gray half-light of dusk pressed in on the lake, and chatter, laughter, and pungent white smoke carried over the water, interrupted occasionally by the random pop and crack of fireworks, the scent of rotten eggs filling the air. It was the period of calm and anticipation before a show.

As dusk settled into shadowy darkness tension crept through Wyatt, his muscles tightening, his mouth going dry as his stomach rumbled and whined. Dusk was a dangerous time in the wilderness, a transition period between daylight and darkness, which makes it an ideal time for predators to hunt. Many of the peninsula's predators had heightened senses and moved stealthily, which made them more effective hunters in low-light conditions. Dusk is also a time when many animals that are active during the day are settling down for the night, which makes them vulnerable.

Wyatt wondered about the beast's circadian rhythms, its biological clock that regulated its daily activity and behavior. Another puzzle piece he didn't have.

The outboard screamed at full throttle and Suzie was piloting the Zodiac, when the first call came in. Rogue One was up by the glacier and they thought they had eyes on the beast.

Suzie didn't wait to be told, and she arced the ship's wheel and changed course.

The duo arrived on the scene two minutes later to find Troopers Freed and Langdon staring through their binoculars.

Darkness pressed in on the lake, the setting sun nothing more than a purple-orange glow filtering through the mountain peaks on the western horizon.

A knot of whitewater rolled through the smooth water, a tall dorsal fin casting a long shadow over the darkening water. Misty spray and whitewater trailed after the fist of water, patches of white sliding through the blackness, and a loud exhale chanted over the lake's surface as something massive expelled air from its lungs. A sliver of white arced from the lake, the Akhlut lifting its girth from the water, pectoral arms and legs fighting gravity, the creature's tail churning the lake as it rose like a leviathan from the depths.

The rank scent of rotting fish and garbage wafted over the lake.

Wyatt covered his mouth with the back of his hand, but he couldn't dull the putrid overpowering mixture of rotting fish and decomposing organic matter. He drew his Glock, but it was more out of habit than an intention to use the weapon. The beast was moving away and there were no civilian vessels in the immediate area.

Yet, there were currently a couple of hundred people out on the lake, and he knew from experience that the beast moved fast, and if it went—

A loud boom, followed by a shriek as the first Mount Aire resident fired the first rocket, and the lake was illuminated by the shimmering reflection of the white starburst, pushing away the thickening gloom.

Then all the residents around the lake went to work and the sky filled with bursts of brilliant red, blue, and white. Color danced and shimmered against the black canvas of the night, creating a loud spectacle.

As the display continued, the fireworks grew larger and more elaborate as neighbors competed for best in show.

When Wyatt turned his attention back to the Akhlut the glow of the fireworks illuminated a shrinking surfboard-sized dorsal fin as the beast slipped beneath the water.

22

Undoubtedly it was the earsplitting shriek of the rockets and the thunderous booms and related cracks and pops that provoked the monster.

As Wyatt and Suzie patrolled, wailing rockets, concussion bombs, and gunshot-like thunder reverberated off the mountains as the sky filled with sparkling explosions, the myriad of colors reflecting off the lake, white clouds of pungent smoke licking the water. A rumble of cheering carried over the festivities, the smell of sulfur thick in the wet summer air. The woods surrounding the lake were dark save for the occasional bonfire, dock light, or flashlight beam that revealed parties and amateur pyrotechnic engineers.

He smiled as he took it all in. This was his home, and he'd spent many Fourths enjoying the summer's biggest gathering. A huge rocket burst overhead, spewing smaller rockets that fizzled and wiggled their way higher into the sky before popping. This big boy spurred on others, and soon the constant flurry of sparks, the rat-a-tat of a one-thousand-cracker bundle, and the thumping of a Roman candle spewing colored fireballs competed for the crowd's attention.

Three M-80s detonated in fast succession, the deep thuds vibrating the lake. Illegal in Alaska, M-80s are known for producing a deafening explosion and a large burst of sparks and flames roughly equal to an eighth of a stick of dynamite.

There was a brief lull in the action as the pyros restocked and took pulls of beer as their guests debated who had won that round of a contest that nobody officially won and for which no prize was given, other than bragging rights, which were often disputed.

In the stillness, Wyatt heard Trooper Sanford's voice blaring from the radio.

"Go ahead, Rogue Two."

"Wyatt we're up in the northeast quadrant east of the glacier and we're tracking…"

Static crackled over the line. Wyatt knew how Sanford felt. Believing in something that wasn't supposed to be possible was one thing, articulating that belief out loud for the world to hear was something else altogether. Most of the folks out on the lake were monitoring the emergency channel, so Wyatt appreciated the trooper's discretion.

"I'm not sure what we're tracking, Wyatt," said Sanford. "But whatever it is, it's big and we found prints that match the description you gave us for the… For the Akhlut."

So there it was. The beast had escaped Wyatt by leaving the lake and traveling on land.

"What direction is the contact moving in?" asked Wyatt, but he knew in his gut the beast had been roused by the noise and crowd and would head toward it.

"It appears to be heading south, back toward the lake."

A sharp pain settled at the base of Wyatt's spine as he pondered what to do. He should clear the lake, but that would cause chaos. A suffocating heat radiated out from his chest to his extremities.

"Wyatt?" Suzie said. She'd come around the command console and was standing next to him. "Orders?"

Snapped from his reverie Wyatt spoke into the radio's handset, "Pursue the beast but keep your distance. Do not engage unless human life is threatened. Keep me up to date as needed."

"Copy that, Wyatt."

"Rogue One, did you get all that?"

"We did," came the voice of Trooper Langdon.

"Head to the northeast quadrant toot sweet. We'll meet you there."

Suzie took the wheel and spun up the engine. The Zodiac surged from the lake, propeller churning the glowing water, the bow angling up. As the boat came up on plane, Suzie buried the throttle and the outboard yelled, the boat's wake spreading over the lake like a tsunami and rocking boats as their passengers stared upward at the show.

A series of massive explosions rocked the sky, sending cascades of color and light raining down on the lake. The sound was deafening, and the audience was mesmerized.

The emergency channel erupted with offers of help and questions. Before Wyatt could shout them down, the captain came on the line and took control.

Wind pushed around the clouds of smoke, and white tornadoes danced over the surface of Terror Lake. Wyatt saw many boats under the glow of the fireworks, and when he zipped past a red boat with its sails down, he saw Kal waving at him through the gloom.

The fireworks show slowed as word spread and flashlight beams bounced through the night as folks along the lakeshore headed for the cover of their houses. Outboards screamed through the night, and boats began to move south toward the marina. What a free-for-all that would be. Wyatt didn't even want to think about it, but at least the captain was on the beach and could take control of the chaos.

Wyatt turned on the Zodiac's light array, and the boat raced forward within a cloud of light, everyone watching. Despite the fleeing crowd, he was aware of those watchers and knew that everything he did from this moment forward would be analyzed and judged, not only through the lens of his job, but his family history.

A chill rankled his neck and sent shards of pain jolting through his arms and legs. Mom was on the beach. He breathed deeply. She'd be fine. Kim was with her, and the captain was there along with many other people. But still, he felt he should be with her.

The Zodiac reached the center of the lake and Rogue One arced in behind Wyatt and Suzie, the old vessel settling into the Zodiac's wake.

Wyatt called Kim.

"Wyatt, what's happening? Talk here is the Akhlut attacked a boat."

Not yet. If good news traveled as fast as bullshit the world would be a much better place. Wyatt sighed, then spoke into his cell. "Not true. My people are tracking something up by the glacier, and nobody has been attacked."

"People are saying the Akhlut was spotted."

"Possible. I'm on my way to investigate," he said. "Not that it needs to be said, but get Mom and Coco out of there at the first sign of trouble."

"She's ready to leave now, so given the situation I think I'll take her home."

Relief flooded through Wyatt, and not only because his mother was going to safety. He was happy Kim was leaving the lake also, and he wondered how much he cared for her. He'd ruminated on whether he loved her… or could love her, and with each passing day he thought he could… might… perhaps already did.

He said, "Thanks, Kim. I…" He wanted to tell her he loved her, that he couldn't wait to see her again, and that he looked forward to every second they spent together. But all he could muster was, "I appreciate everything you've done… do. I don't know what I'd do without you."

She said nothing, the disappointment leaking over the invisible cell wave connecting them palpable.

"I'll see you later," he said, lamely.

"Your mom says be careful."

Coco yelped as if to emphasize the point.

"Will do." As he tapped end call, he decided he needed to move things along with Kim. They had to have the dreaded "talk." Yet, for the first time in his life dread wasn't the right word. It was more excitement for what the unknown would bring. He needed to put himself out there more, spend more time with people instead of the creatures of the peninsula.

The glacier licked the lake, its dirty white surface shining faintly. The dark tree line loomed like a wall, tall shadows reaching out over the water. The roar of ATVs grumbled beneath the booms and pops of the fireworks.

In the glare of the fireworks painting the world in a garish rainbow of color, the Akhlut emerged from the vegetation as large waves from the Zodiac's wake slapped the stone shore.

Suzie spun the ship's wheel and brought the forward light array to bear on the beast.

Rogue One inched up and did the same.

The monster was unearthly, unlike anything ever to walk the peninsula. Its baby elephant-sized frame moved with the grace of a cat, its dark, white-rimmed eyes blinking spasmodically under the brightness of the harsh LEDs. Wyatt recalled that orcas had sensitive eyes, and the Akhlut looked to be just as much orca as wolf.

Wyatt stood in awe for several heartbeats before he drew his Glock.

The Akhlut's slick black and white skin shimmered as the beast made its way forward on all fours, using its muscular pectoral legs ending in flat black talons to propel itself with perfect coordination. Its tall dorsal fin swayed, casting a wobbling shadow over the underbrush, and the creature's thick, muscular tail ended in two flukes. Its wolfish head had a narrow snout that housed a mouth full of three-inch teeth, and its long ears were pressed against its head, the beast's eyes endless black pools perched above a gill-like nose.

Suzie followed Wyatt's lead and drew her weapon, though the trooper looked odd with one hand on the ship's wheel and the other holding a gun.

Trooper Freed yelled, "Shouldn't we move in closer and try to drive it back toward land?"

Wyatt said nothing, his mind churning.

ATV headlights approached the lake's edge—Rogue Two, and the Akhlut appeared to be running from them. Given the situation out on the lake, Wyatt preferred to have the beast on land if it could be managed.

Every move the creature made was calculated and purposeful, like a well-trained predator stalking its prey, and as the beast reached the water's edge and climbed atop a large boulder, Wyatt knew what needed to be done.

"Yes! Drive it back in the woods," he yelled to Trooper Freed. Wyatt lifted the radio handset. "Rogue Two, do you copy?"

The roar of the ATVs lessened, and headlights stopped bobbing through the forest.

"Go ahead, Wyatt."

"Back off," he said. "Stop, shut down your machines, and wait. We're going to try and drive it away from the lake."

Static. The pops and cracks of the dying fireworks show.

"Rogue Two, did you get that?"

"10-4," came Trooper Denny's worried voice. "What are our orders? Do we have authorization to engage?"

Before Wyatt could speak, the captain, who was monitoring the emergency channel, said, "You are authorized to use all force necessary to take down the ani—the Akhlut. Understood?"

"Copy that," Wyatt said.

With open season declared, Wyatt holstered his Glock and fished out his rifle. He could almost feel half the residents doing the same thing and worry nudged the side of his mind that would always be one hundred percent cop. People were afraid and panicked, and it was more likely that an innocent would be shot than the beast, but there was nothing he could do about it.

Suzie and Denny piloted the boats slowly toward shore, the beast framed between them.

The creature was watching the boats like a diver surveying its audience before taking the plunge.

Wyatt chambered a round, put the rifle's stock to his shoulder, and peered through the night scope.

As if sensing the weapon, the creature sprang, black and white patches sliding through the darkness, teeth bared, eyes aglow.

Gunshots rang out, and bullets peppered the lake as the Akhlut's pectoral fin arms stroked the water, its dorsal fin disappearing into the inky lake.

Wyatt's heart pounded and his body tensed. He felt an immense sense of unease as his worst nightmare became reality. Thoughts of death and destruction consumed him as a surge of adrenaline jolted him with pain, and fear and worry made it difficult to think or act. Despite this, he knew he had to stay calm, so he breathed deeply and told himself it was time to end this. For good.

"There!" yelled Suzie.

A patch of white streaked through the water on the starboard side of the Zodiac.

Wyatt swung the rifle around, but Rogue One's vessel was too close and was partly in the line of fire. He let the tip of the rifle barrel dip as the beast darted between the police boats and headed toward the heart of the lake.

"Stay with us!" Wyatt yelled at Rogue One.

Suzie needed no orders. With a deftness that surprised Wyatt, the trooper holstered her weapon and dropped the hammer as she spun the ship's wheel.

The Zodiac twisted in the water and the bow lifted and the outboard howled, water splashing over the sides as the bilge pump kicked on.

Suzie let the wheel slip through her fingers and the vessel straightened.

Wyatt scanned the SONAR.

The screen showed a series of dots and lines that represented sound waves bouncing back to the device after hitting an object in the water. A dark amorphous shape could be seen moving fast through the lake about twenty feet below the surface. The beast's body appeared as a large, elongated black smudge.

A few cracks and pops still rang out, but the show was over. Those with inventory left would have to hide away their inner child for another day. Tendrils of white smoke spiraled into the star-filled sky, the scent of evergreens and gasoline driving out the stink of rotten eggs.

Wyatt's ears rang, the hum and gurgle of outboards like background static. His skin itched, and the conversation with the captain came rushing back. Wyatt had wanted to close the lake and the boss had laughed. He should have fought harder and argued his point more stringently. But he didn't, and his father's voice poked him from beyond, making sure Wyatt knew any blood spilled this night would be on his hands.

A line of boats trailed south toward the marina, their lights bobbing in the darkness.

The radio crackled. "Wyatt, status?" It was the captain.

"We are southwest in pursuit of the creature. Over."

Static popped, the ring in Wyatt's head reaching a fever pitch.

"This is Kal… Renne Kalvak. Wyatt, are you there?"

"Go ahead, Kal," Wyatt said.

"My brother and I have a visual on the beast. Orders?"

"Blow it back to hell!" yelled Captain Udell.

There was a brief pause, then, "Copy that, Captain."

Wyatt glanced at the SONAR and it was clear, the pixelated image rolling steadily across the screen as the minutes slipped away and the Zodiac closed in on Kal's position.

Half a mile off the starboard bow muzzle flashes lit the darkness, and a volley of gunshots pierced the night. Shrieks and screams carried over the water, followed by a howl that teased Wyatt's neck muscles. He'd heard only one creature make that sound.

The Zodiac bounced and listed as Suzie pushed the craft as hard as she could. The scents of evergreen, sulfur, and gasoline were driven away by the stink of garbage and decaying fish.

A blast of static made Wyatt jump. "Wyatt? How close are you? Our little motor barely moves this thing and putting up the sails—" A scream of human agony echoed over the lake, and the radio fell still.

"Kal! Kal!" Wyatt screamed into the radio, but there was no response.

A thin haze of firework smoke hung in the air, eddying and swirling in the calm breeze. As the Zodiac raced toward Kal's location a debilitating sense of failure and remorse engulfed Wyatt. Terror Lake was his jurisdiction, his responsibility, his home, and he'd failed to do his job, and tonight the residents of Mount Aire would pay for his negligence. But as gunshots tore through the blackness, hope surged in him. This wasn't over. Not by a long shot.

23

Captain Udell's voice blared from the radio. "Blow it to hell!"

Kal looked at his brother, Adamee, who nodded.

"Copy that, Captain," Kal said, and closed the connection.

Adamee's eighteen-foot fiberglass sailboat had a single mast, and the mainsail was down, the jib tied off on a port side cleat. The cockpit area behind the cabin was filled with Adamee's family; his youngest boy, Trip, working the tiller and the small electric outboard.

Kal ushered his brother's wife and two daughters below deck and fetched the guns as Adamee secured loose items above deck and passed out life preservers.

"Take this, son," said Adamee as he held a shotgun out to his boy. The Browning had been in the family for years and carried five shells of buckshot.

Trip flipped a switch and the buzz of the electric motor died as he accepted the gun. The kid looked like he weighed a hundred pounds wet, all skin, bones, and lanky uncoordinated limbs. But he was tough, and he was a decent shot and showed remarkable judgment for a boy of fifteen. Kal had gone skeet shooting with the teenager, and the kid hit more clay pigeons than he had.

Adamee handed a pistol to Kal. It was a Colt revolver six-shooter that looked like it had seen better days, but Kal knew his brother was meticulous about cleaning his weapons. The walnut handle was covered with black duct tape, and the blue steel finish on the barrel was scratched. "It's loaded with three regular .45s and three hollow points. Aim for the eyes."

Kal aimed the pistol at the dark water and cocked the hammer.

Adamee lifted his weapon and pumped a shell into the firing chamber of the Beretta Xtrema his wife had bought him for his birthday a few years back.

The two generations of Inuit Kalvaks stood with their weapons trained on the lake, the scent of garbage and rotting fish assailing them.

A bright column of light from the sailboat's deck lamp illuminated the lake, revealing a dorsal fin as it emerged from the murky water. The fin grew in length and width, creating a knot of whitewater underneath it. White and black stripes slid through the lake, and a mouth filled with teeth hanging below two dark eyes materialized amid the rising water.

Kal fired first, holding the pistol in a doublehanded grip as he squeezed the trigger, the gun's sight moving in small circles as he struggled to aim the weapon as the boat listed and dipped.

Adamee and Trip opened fire with their shotguns, the booms echoing over the lake, the tiny pellets from the shells peppering the water like so many thrown pebbles.

Gunsmoke filled the air, cordite stinging Kal's eyes, his forearm muscles aching. The revolver clicked empty, he dropped to a knee, flicked open the cylinder, and let the spent cartridges fall to the deck.

The Akhlut dove and left behind a thin undulating blood slick on the surface.

As Kal thumbed bullets into the Colt, Adamee and Trip emptied their shotguns into the swirling water.

Kal snapped the Colt's reloaded cylinder closed and cocked the gun's hammer.

"Did we hit it?" Trip asked. The kid's voice was steady as he stared into the turbulent lake, gun still aimed at the water, though the weapon was empty.

Adamee stuffed shells into his Beretta, laughing, and said, "You bet your ass we hit it. Get on the horn to the captain and let him know we—"

The Akhlut breached, the creature's sleek, muscular body surging effortlessly from the water. Its wolf-like head was aimed at the boat, jaws open in a rictus tooth-filled grin. The beast gurgled, slim and water flying as the Akhlut defied gravity and hung in the air for a moment before crashing down onto the sailboat.

Screams of panic from the cabin knifed through Kal, and heat burned his chest as he questioned the decision to bring the kids for the thousandth time. It hadn't been his decision, and Adamee had said some animal wasn't keeping him and his family from enjoying what he considered his country's most important holiday.

The Akhlut landed on the boom arm and tiller, and the bow of the boat rose from the water as the boat's deck tilted at a thirty-degree angle. Water surged over the sides, and Kal was smacked in the face by a wave of cold water that knocked him from his feet. The Colt went flying and landed in the lake.

With a cry of rending metal, cracking fiberglass, and splintering wood, the bow came down, the entire front end dipping beneath the surface and sending a wave of lake water washing over the boat. The Akhlut howled, then growled in anger as it rolled off the sailboat.

Kal grabbed a side rail and worked his way to his knees just in time to grab Trip as he was swept down the deck. The boy had managed to hold onto his gun, but he was dazed and spitting up blood.

Adamee held onto the jib arm while trying to aim his shotgun, but he wasn't having much luck. The gun barrel dipped and shifted as he wrestled with the weapon, the shotgun too heavy to fire with one hand.

Screams of concern and worry rose above the cacophony of rushing water and the grunts and howls of the beast. The cabin was filling with water.

The Akhlut surfaced, its dark eyes fixed on the swamped sailboat, its dorsal fin swaying, pectoral arms and legs clawing at the water.

Kal stumbled forward and managed to get hold of the tiller. He jerked it left, and the wind nudged the sailboat right as the vessel turned away from the beast.

With a cry of anger and fury the Akhlut dove and rammed the bottom of the boat, and again water coursed over the gunnel. The boat's bilge pump was on, and water jetted from the side of the boat, but it wasn't keeping up with the inflow and the vessel was going down.

Spinning in the current, the sailboat's lights rotated like a lighthouse, casting wavering light over the inky surface of the lake. Bubbles popped and snapped, and tiny whitecaps rippled over the surface. The wind cried, and the hum of outboards and the chatter and screams of the fleeing spectators filled the night.

Trip and Adamee reloaded.

"Daddy?" came a scared voice from the cabin.

"It's O.K.," Adamee said. "Stay down there unless I tell you to come out."

Water drained from the boat's cockpit, but Kal could tell by the sound of the straining bilge pump that the boat's battery would die before all the water drained. The lights of the approaching Zodiac were getting close, and Kal breathed a sigh of relief.

A hollow *womp* carried over the lake.

The Akhlut drove its massive girth into the underside of the sailboat again, and the adjustable centerboard missiled from its slot and disappeared into darkness. Whitewater roiled around the boat and a loud pucker carried over the water as the eighteen-foot sailboat was driven from the lake.

Time is funny. A second can be the blink of an eye, or it can last half a lifetime, and as the sailboat hung in the air, the beast using its strength to thrust the boat from the water, Kal felt all his cares slide away. He saw his mother's face, his wife and children, the stern face of a father he'd barely known. "Adamee!" he screamed as he was tossed from the boat.

Trip yelped as he too was thrown from the safety of the sailboat and landed face-first in the churning lake.

Kal's stomach dropped as he sailed through the air, the dark star-filled sky, black water, and the flash of approaching LEDs spinning across his field of vision. With a bone jarring splat he hit the water, and starbursts danced before his eyes.

The sailboat crashed back into the lake, and a mountain of whitewater washed over Kal, lake water forcing its way into his mouth, nose, and ears. Funny thing was, Kal felt no pain as teeth stabbed his torso and blood gurgled up his throat.

Trip screamed in terror, this time his voice cracking and fading as Kal called out his brother's name again and again as he slipped into oblivion.

Suzie yanked back the throttle lever and the Zodiac bobbed to an awkward stop, the following sea smashing into the transom. A knot of whitewater churned around the capsizing sailboat and Wyatt saw Kal and a young boy in the water.

Rogue One screamed onto the scene, rubber squeaking on rubber as it pulled in alongside.

Wyatt aimed his rifle at the erupting lake but didn't dare fire for fear of hitting Kal or the boy.

The lake flattened, and Kal called out to Wyatt.

A circle of twisting water formed around Kal, and he was sucked under.

"Shit!" Wyatt shouted.

The Akhlut propelled itself out of the water, jaws open, teeth glinting under the LEDs. Glistening white patches caught the light, white-rimmed eyes blinking as the beast used its muscular, pectoral legs to sweep away the water. The tall dorsal fin that jutted from its back swayed and bent, and the creature's thick, powerful tail twisted like a sea serpent.

Wyatt fired, and the shot plunked into the creature as it dove and slipped into darkness.

He dropped the rifle, drew his Glock, chambered a round, and opened up as fury consumed him, bullets peppering the lake.

Rogue One opened fire and even Suzie joined in, both hands on her weapon, the ship's wheel spinning free.

Kal was thrust from the lake, the Akhlut's wolf-like head silhouetted in the pale light. Its jaws crunched down on flesh as the beast surged from the water, the sounds of cracking bones and tearing meat rattling Wyatt's spine.

Suzie screamed, and Adamee fired, but soon stopped when he realized he was most likely hitting his brother as well as the beast.

Not that it mattered.

Kal's corpse was bitten in two with a sickening snap, everything from his waist down falling from the creature's jaws into the water. Spinal cord, muscle, and skin hung from the severed torso, the dead man's head and shoulders within a cage of sharp teeth. The Akhlut slid back into the lake with a bear-like snicker, whitewater bubbling around the creature as it slipped into the depths.

The ensuing splash and shockwave of water crashed into the Zodiac, and the craft listed and bounced as it was knocked around. Bailing gaps allowed the water to drain quickly, and before Wyatt could give the order, Suzie spun the ship's engine and put the bow on the sinking sailboat.

Blood bubbles popped on the lake, tiny pieces of skin and fat floating thereon, the greasy slick dissipating in the turbulent water.

Wyatt screamed in rage so loud his throat hurt, and when he finally stopped his ears were ringing.

Suzie stared at him.

To the south, a fist of whitewater broke the surface, and for a horrifying instant, Wyatt saw Kal's arm hanging from the creature's mouth as it snaked from the water like a dolphin, moving at an incredible speed.

"Are you alright?" Wyatt yelled to Adamee.

Kal's brother looked down, eyeing the water that flooded the cockpit. "How are things down there, Renna?" Adamee called to his wife.

"Wet, but we're O.K."

Adamee's gaze shifted between the sailboat's cockpit, Rogue One, the fleeing beast, and the remains of his brother floating like dead leaves on the surface of Terror Lake. Then he yelled, "Go get it!"

Wyatt considered leaving Rogue One behind to help, but he needed the backup and others could help Adamee and his family. He grabbed a life ring and tossed it to Trip, who deftly caught it and placed it over his head. With the beast moving away, Adamee could deal with his son.

"We'll send help your way."

Adamee gave a thumbs up.

"Get on its ass!" Wyatt yelled. Then to Rogue One, "Follow us!"

"Yes, sir," Suzie said as she spun the wheel and pressed the throttle down as far as it would go. The outboard hollered and coughed as the boat leaped from the water, the wake rocking the swamped sailboat as Suzie adjusted course and headed south, the Akhlut nothing more than a mound of churning white in the gloom.

24

Wyatt switched to a private channel and hailed Billy-joe.

"Go ahead, Wyatt," the big man said.

"Can you head north and help out Adamee? His sailboat has been attacked and is sinking, and Kal…" It hit Wyatt for the first time, a full-blown smack to the face. Kal was dead, taken to his watery grave by a creature conceived by an Inuit princess named Madeleine.

Static crackled over the open comm line.

"I've got one fatality, and the creature is heading for the marina. Can you help Adamee?" Wyatt relayed the sailboat's position.

"On my way," Billy-joe said.

Wyatt fiddled with the radio and switched back to the emergency channel. The radio handset was still in his hand, but he didn't depress the talk button.

Should he put out a general warning?

He could announce who he was and inform the people of Mount Aire of the current situation. But that would cause more panic than there already was, and as Wyatt gazed at the navigation lights clogging the southern horizon, he didn't know what folks in boats could do anyway. Head to the nearest shore? What kind of protection was that?

Or he could continue on his current path and chase the beast down and do his best to kill it before it reached the knot of boats.

Wyatt held up the handset to Suzie. "What do you think? Would telling folks what's happening help or hurt?"

She hiked her shoulders and said, "I think the secret's out, boss. But if it was up to me, I'd say we go get the thing before it gets there. But…"

He raised an eyebrow, a light sheen of mist settling on his face as the Zodiac pounded over the churned-up lake.

"But it never hurts to cover your ass," she said.

At first, he didn't know what she meant, but as understanding blossomed within him, shame and pride washed through him in equal measures. Wyatt nodded and pointed at his partner. "Now that is brass thinking."

Wyatt pulled his cell phone, called the captain, and updated him.

"For Christ's sake… Can't we get five minutes of peace? Do you and Rogue One have a visual on the creature?"

Wyatt lifted his binoculars, which had night vision capabilities, but all he saw was the powerful glare of the boat's LED lights. He shut them down and with blackness forcing itself on the boat he scanned the shimmering surface of the lake, green-tinted moonlight splashing over the troubled water.

About two hundred yards ahead of the Zodiac the black dorsal fin of the Akhlut scythed through the lake, leaving a thick line in its wake.

"I have a visual," Wyatt said into the handset.

"You're a good shot, take it out!" the captain said.

Wyatt wanted to say they'd tried that but didn't. He was sure he, his fellow troopers, and the Kalvak family had hit the beast, but if it was working off its final supply of adrenaline the beast had a deep well. "I'll try," he said as he reached out and gripped the stainless-steel handhold on the side of the command console, the Zodiac bouncing and throwing spray.

"The beach is already clearing out and I can move people along, it's the line for the boat ramp that I'm worried about," the captain said.

White, green, and red lights dotted the horizon as vessels crowded toward the marina and fought for position in line for the ramps. There were still boats out on the lake, their solitary white pilot lights bobbing in the gentle breeze.

Wyatt fetched the rifle and put it to his shoulder, but he didn't have a shot. The creature was sixty yards distant, and with the Zodiac bouncing and listing the best marksman on the peninsula wouldn't have been able to make the shot. He paused, finger wrapped around the trigger, scope pressed to his eye. A little closer…

An unsettling and haunting sight appeared in the green glow of the water off the Zodiac's port bow.

A hand bobbed on the surface of the water, surrounded by ripples that distorted its reflection in the moonlight. A dark, murky green cloud surrounded the hand, and it appeared delicate, almost fragile like a flower petal floating on a storm-swept sea.

Wyatt's skin crawled and when he looked at his partner, he saw Suzie had covered her mouth with the back of her hand.

He thought of Kal, the man's kind face, and an anger built in Wyatt that superheated his chest and set the bells to chiming in his head. Wyatt squeezed the rifle's trigger and fired at the mound of whitewater, knowing he had little chance of hitting the creature, but the shot made him feel like he was doing something.

Wyatt, Suzie, and Rogue One were a hundred yards out from the marina when the first emergency call burst from the radio.

That first call reporting a dorsal fin sighting was quickly stepped on by others, and soon the emergency channel was a cacophony of partial sentences, bursts of static, and the captain yelling and trying to get control.

In the distance, the dark mound of whitewater moved towards a group of boats huddled together. Bow lights shifted and swayed as the knot of boats broke up, each captain hoping the beast would choose another vessel to play with.

Boat lights and flashlight beams cut across the water as Wyatt and Suzie entered the fray.

The first boat to get tousled was a dinghy. With a cry of anger, the Akhlut passed within feet of the small vessel, rocking it awkwardly as the boat's occupants screamed in terror as they were hurled into the chilly water.

Suzie didn't slow, and neither did the Akhlut. The Zodiac's outboard was roaring at full throttle, and as the duo passed the folks in the drink Wyatt saw they were O.K. and didn't need rescue. Their small craft hadn't capsized, and one of the two people in the water was climbing back into the boat.

The second boat, a tiny motorboat with a two-person cockpit, was flipped over by the Akhlut's massive tail, its two passengers scrambling for purchase on the overturned hull as they struggled to stay out of the water.

With a suddenness that made Suzie jerk on the Zodiac's wheel, the Akhlut made a sharp left as it breached from the lake, twisting in the air.

Relief flooded through Wyatt, but it fled quickly when he saw why the creature had changed course.

The beast was heading right at an old wooden skiff with a five-horsepower beater. The passengers of this vessel were more adept, and they managed to avoid the Akhlut's initial onslaught by gunning the outboard and moving sporadically and fast. But the beast circled, churning the water with its pectoral legs, its wolfish jaws flexing. With a deafening roar, the creature drove its head into the vessel, pounding the boat like a battering ram. The vessel listed dangerously to starboard, its passengers clinging to the boat's gunnel to avoid getting tossed into the drink.

A pontoon boat eased slowly over the lake beyond the rocking skiff, and Wyatt thought the boat was too big for the beast to mess with, but the Akhlut wasn't deterred. With a massive leap, it launched itself at the pontoon boat, a mountain of whitewater smashing against the craft, the weight of the water causing the boat to tilt dangerously. The passengers on board screamed and scattered as the Akhlut began to thrash about, its massive jaws snapping at anything that moved.

Wyatt considered stopping and helping, but he had to stay on the Akhlut. If he did that, everyone in his wake would be fine.

"Rogue One, do you copy?" He realized he was using the emergency channel, but it didn't matter anymore. Everyone on the lake had eyes and could deduce what was happening.

"Go ahead, Wyatt," said Trooper Freed.

"Hang back and get these people out of the drink and to safety."

"Copy that." The second boat peeled off, its engine dying away as the boat bobbed to a halt.

Boats capsized and passengers were thrown into the water as the Akhlut continued its rampage and unleashed its fury on the hapless boats that waited in line for the boat ramp.

And then, as suddenly as the assault had begun, it was over. The Akhlut abandoned its attack and dove as it swam for the marina, its tall dorsal fin slipping beneath the inky water like the mast of a sinking sailboat.

That made Wyatt think of Adamee, and he checked in with Billy-joe. Everything was fine, and Adamee and his family were on Billy-joe's boat.

Suzie piloted the Zodiac through the maze of overturned vessels, passengers scattered across the water, the sound of screams and shouts echoing over the lake.

A line of armed civilizations stood at the end of the pier that extended out into Terror Lake. Abandoned bonfires lit the beach in an eerie orange glow, but Wyatt saw no people. A long line of red taillights ran away from the marina parking lot.

Wyatt smiled and he allowed himself a brief moment to collect himself, his pride at the resolve and strength of his fellow Mound Aire residents reminding him yet again why he called the peninsula home.

As if sensing the danger that awaited it on the pier, the Akhlut arced away from the dock and the battery of guns that awaited it there.

"Fall back!" The captain's voice came from the radio, and Wyatt didn't understand that the order was for him until stray bullets started slapping into the water around the Zodiac.

"Cut off its angle," Wyatt said.

Suzie matched the beast's speed, but instead of following the creature, she charted a course due west which would put the Zodiac in front of the creature if it didn't change direction.

With a screech and another jumping twist, the creature turned around, the knot of whitewater and black dorsal fin powering over the lake and locking Suzie and Wyatt in a deadly game of chicken.

The Zodiac's blinding LED lights illuminated the rhino-sized beast as it rose gracefully from the depths, its dark, white-rimmed eyes blinking under the unforgiving glare. Its white spots blazed against its glistening black skin, its arms and legs stroking the water as its wolf-like head pushed from the fist of water embroiling it.

Water splashed as the Zodiac bounced and jumped, the beast fifty yards away. In the darkness, with the boat rising and falling, Wyatt couldn't get a bead on the creature, and unease lit his stomach on fire, his muscles aching as adrenaline filled him with a false strength.

Two black vacant eyes, perched above a slim, slit-like nose appeared in the knot of whitewater, the beast's jaws flexing open at the end of its narrow snout, long ears pressed to its head, its dorsal fin rigid, the slap of its thick powerful tail pounding the water driving away the rumble and shriek of the surrounding chaos.

The boat rocked and heaved, the knot of water and teeth and fury twenty yards away. He aimed the gun again, but it was impossible, despite his best efforts, to brace his legs and hold the weapon still.

The Zodiac hit a small wave, jumped, settled, and Wyatt fired.

25

Suzie jerked the ship's wheel two heartbeats before impact, and the boat listed sharply to port as the Akhlut slammed into the bottom of the Zodiac's hard composite hull.

Wyatt launched from the deck upon impact, but he grabbed hold of the safety bar on the command console, his feet flying behind him, dark water racing by beneath him as the Zodiac slewed on its side, the engine screaming bloody murder as the propeller lifted from the water. The rifle fell and splashed into the lake, and pain numbed Wyatt's arms as he held on for his life.

The beast screeched, a ragged, broken sound that sounded like an elephant dying, and blood splattered the water as the propeller tore into the creature, carving up flesh and bone.

Suzie worked the wheel, and with a crash and a tumult of water, the Zodiac was once again upright and zipping over the turbulent lake.

Wyatt landed on his feet, but would have gone down had it not been for his fingers wrapped tightly around the handrail.

For a heartbeat, the water settled.

He steadied himself, knees weak, heart galloping, a knot of pain forming in his lower back as the adrenaline fled. A wicked grin spread over Wyatt's face. Even if most of the gunshots hadn't had an impact, the stainless-steel propeller sure had.

But the Akhlut was stronger than Wyatt could have ever anticipated. Its huge lungs and orca-like body allowed the beast to take a tremendous beating and keep going, at least in the short term. The beast was grievously wounded and when it floated to the surface off the starboard bow hope surged through Wyatt. A dark cloud spread around the creature and its dorsal fin had been chopped in half, white bone, cartilage, and skin hanging from the broken fin like bloody hair.

Wind gusted over the lake and stars blinked down from the night sky like the eyes of spectators.

Suzie slowed the boat and circled back toward the beast.

Wyatt sat on the gunnel, his muscles bitching, his joints trying to keep up. He was exhausted, and the bells still chimed in his head, but he was relieved. With the beast dead he could go back to his life. That thought sent a wave of depression crashing over him. Without the creature, he'd be just another wildlife trooper again.

When he focused on the beast again it was gone.

He frantically searched the lake's surface and saw the Akhlut's wolf snout pushing from the water twenty yards from the Zodiac, its one remaining eye staring at Wyatt. An unnatural silence settled over the lake, the stink of trash and rotten fish filling the air. The creature was missing its right forward appendage and its left rear leg. With the horror balanced out, the beast lurched through the water like a zombie, its eye rolling as the creature came at the Zodiac one last time.

Suzie cycled up the motors and headed toward the monster.

"Where is it?" said Suzie. Without the tall dorsal fin marking the creature's passage it was difficult to track the beast.

Wyatt scanned the SONAR and yelled, "Hold on!" On the screen, a giant black smudge was rising next to the boat.

With a mighty roar the beast launched from the water, a snarling wave of whitewater, rage, and teeth. Its vise-like jaws clamped down on a rear section of the Zodiac, and a hollow *pop*, like an old musket firing, echoed over the ring in Wyatt's head and the hiss of air pissing into the water.

But the Zodiac had sixteen separate air compartments, and it would take more than deflating one to take the vessel down. Despite this, Suzie was forced to muscle the wheel because the maneuverability of the vessel was affected by the deflating compartment. Water cascaded over the breach, though the water drained quickly.

The Akhlut thrashed, its jaws tearing at rubber, its damaged body flexing and jerking, blood splattering the deck and turning the flood waters a ghostly pink.

An outboard screamed in the night, and a cloud of white LED light cruised across the lake, heading toward the fight. Rogue One.

The beast's tail slapped the water, driving the creature's bloody torso onto the Zodiac. With a squeal of metal on metal, the bow was submerged as the transom lifted from the lake, the motor screaming from lack of cooling water.

A howl of crying metal, then the pop of an explosion as the Zodiac's outboard ground to a stop, black smoke wafting over the boat.

Wyatt held onto the handrail with one hand and drew his reloaded and ready to fire Glock with the other, the deck tilting beneath his feet. He aimed at the creature's head and squeezed the trigger as fast as he could. He hardly noticed Rogue One screaming onto the scene, lights helping to drive away the shadowy darkness, guns blazing.

The Akhlut slipped into the lake and the Zodiac came crashing down, water spilling through the gap in the boat's side.

A stifled gurgle carried over the chaos and the beast slipped down into blackness.

The Glock clicked empty, and Wyatt let the weapon fall to his side as he stared at the swirl of water where the beast had been, pieces of white bone, red muscle, and dark fat heaving on the churning blood slick.

"Are you O.K.?" It was Trooper Sandford, but Wyatt hardly heard him.

Wyatt dropped onto the bench seat before the command console, holstered his empty weapon, and let his head fall into his hands. It had almost taken everything he had, but in the end, he had gotten the Akhlut. His head snapped up and he focused on the swirling knot of water, but no corpse had yet to float to the surface. He rolled his shoulders. No matter. There was no way the beast could've survived the pummeling it had taken, and it had probably used the last of its life to go to a certain place to die.

"Wyatt?" called Trooper Sandford again.

Suzie put a hand on Wyatt's shoulder and he looked up at her and smiled.

Most of the floodwater had drained from the Zodiac, but the engine was slag, so Wyatt threw a tow line to Rogue One.

Cheering erupted from the end of the pier, and in the hazy light, Wyatt saw a line of people high-fiving each other and sharing congratulations.

Wyatt met Suzie's eye. "You O.K.?"

She nodded. "You?"

He hiked his shoulders. Wyatt wasn't sure how he felt yet.

The snap of an outboard dropping into gear rang over the lake, the tow line went taut, and the disabled Zodiac lurched into motion, water lapping through the gap in the boat's side.

Though relieved, pain still cycled through Wyatt like an irregular heartbeat, his skin crawling with tension as his nerves calmed and the bells tolling in his head died away. Wyatt was in no mood to celebrate. The people on shore might not know that Kal was dead—and who knew who else—but the damage was done, and he didn't know if he'd ever be able to wash the blood from his hands.

When the small armada arrived at the dock Wyatt and crew were surrounded by residents, many holding weapons they hadn't gotten the opportunity to fire. Wyatt was thankful for that, and as far as he knew, there had been no incidents involving friendly fire.

Captain Udell pushed through the crowd and held out his hand to Suzie and helped her off the Zodiac. Someone threw a blanket around Wyatt, but he was in a daze and hardly recognized the faces swarming around him and he ignored the many questions.

Wyatt was seated on a storage crate, and the laughter and celebration died away as Suzie recounted what had happened. His gaze fell on Lakehead Beach and the dilapidated KYES news van in the barren parking lot, the station's roving reporter that covered the peninsula, Glenda Dainy, standing before a ring light, Terror Lake in the background.

By morning everyone would know what happened, and his world would be turned upside-down. He chuckled to himself. That happened a long time ago on a cold day in February when Jesse Ombridge had been killed.

It was midnight, and the lake was free of boats when the captain insisted that everyone involved in the night's activities get checked out at the Mount Aire Medical Center.

Wyatt was exhausted, but he felt fine, aside from his bumps, bruises, and hunger, but he complied. The EMTs and medical professionals, many of whom were volunteers drafted during their holiday celebrations, were stretched to the breaking point, and most of them used personal vehicles to transport the injured to the medical center.

The hospital was organized chaos. The lobby had been converted to a triage center, and every room was full with the twenty-seven people who were injured in the attack on Terror Lake.

Wyatt and Suzie were separated and handed off to nurses, and leaving his partner rattled Wyatt's nerves and an overwhelming sense of loss filled him. He had put the woman in harm's way, and the ease with which he'd done it made him feel small and dirty. His rage had taken control, a hatred that he'd never felt before, and it had almost gotten him and his partner killed.

A nurse probed Wyatt, took his vitals, and gave him some Xanax and pain meds, neither of which he would take. After getting an O.K. to go home Wyatt found himself aimlessly wandering through the wounded. Most of the injuries had been caused when folks got tossed around in their boats. Heads smacking decks, hands and limbs getting sliced, or puncture wounds and deep bruises caused by flying objects were the common culprits.

Only Kal had paid the ultimate price this time, and Wyatt supposed he should be thankful for that. The year of the beast was over, hopefully for good.

When he left the hospital most of the lobby had been cleared, and only eighteen people were being held overnight for observation. Captain Udell stood watching a TV mounted in the corner of the waiting area. Glenda Dainy's report was on.

"Are you going to live?" the captain asked, but he was smiling. "With the state budget being what it is I don't know how long it would take to replace you."

"Always good to know you care."

The captain sucked on his lips.

"I'll get out there at first light and see if I can… retrieve Kal's corpse."

Captain Udell nodded and said, "Look at this." He pointed at the TV. "What the hell are we going to do?"

The image on the TV shifted to shaky cell phone footage, the reporter's voice continuing over it. "This footage was taken just hours ago as the creature wreaked havoc on this small community's Independence Day celebration."

Dark, choppy water filled the TV screen, moonlight dancing on the surface of Terror Lake. Small boats floated in the distance, their NAV lights shining through the darkness. The person working the phone turned on its light, and the area around the boat was illuminated.

The reporter paused, letting the gasp of the photographer fill the silence. Two white-rimmed eyes appeared in the lake, the tall shadow of a dorsal fin falling over the silvery water. Teeth glinted in the blackness, and someone screamed, a shrill cry that made the photographer jerk the cell phone downward, where it caught an image of red sneakers before angling back up.

Black and white skin oozed from the water, the creature's wolf snout lifting from the lake, muscles rippling beneath slick skin. More screaming and yelling and the glow of approaching lights.

The Akhlut rammed the boat, and the cell phone fell to the deck, the TV screen filling with the side of a blue cooler. Glenda Dainy appeared on the screen again, the dark pool of Terror Lake behind her as she droned on about what would happen in the days to come, and she ended with a lengthy soliloquy about the single fatality, and how the body count was expected to go up.

"Will you listen to this shit," Captain Udell said.

It angered Wyatt also, but it wasn't a total lie. Who knew what the morning would bring? He said, "Kal might not be the only victim."

Captain Udell sighed, and said, "Go home and get some rest."

Wyatt nodded, but his hands were still shaking, and he didn't think any amount of whiskey would soothe his pain and worry.

26

Wyatt was forced from the twilight world of half-sleep by the sound of his cell phone blaring. It was under his pillow and the volume was set to maximum. It was the captain.

The Akhlut's corpse had washed up on Lakehead Beach.

Usually, the day after the Fourth was meant for nursing hangovers, eating leftovers, and reliving the prior day's festivities, but Wyatt's day was a shitstorm that started as soon as he hung up with the captain.

An elderly woman had died overnight. Cardiac arrest brought on by the stress of the accident and her internal injuries. The Akhlut hadn't munched on the woman, but it had killed her all the same.

He dressed, grabbed coffee, and drove his ATV to the beach where he found the pier cordoned off by deputized civilians wearing loaner orange vests. The boat ramps were closed, and Rogue One and Rogue Two were patrolling Terror Lake and its shoreline. Suzie was still at home sleeping. He'd seen no reason to wake her, and she'd earned some downtime.

Captain Udell stood with a knot of officers, two of whom were wearing suits. When the brass showed up that was the final sign things had fully gone off the rails. What better way to exacerbate a situation than to bring in opportunistic law enforcement officers from Anchorage that didn't know shit about the peninsula?

Wyatt's boss waved at him, but didn't break off from his conversation. He figured the captain was doing him a favor. Wyatt was already tired of telling the story of what had happened, and the idea that he would have to repeat the tale many times over the course of his life turned his stomach.

The black and white skin that covered the Akhlut's carcass was shriveled and bloody, the massive animal's thick layer of blubber already decomposing. Birds divebombed the corpse, and crabs scuttled across the hardpacked sand like ants, tearing off a piece of the dead monster and slipping back into the lake. Gulls screeched and cawed, the smell becoming more pungent as Wyatt got closer to the dead beast. To Wyatt, it smelled like generations of vindication.

Wind gusted and sang, the sound of sand scraping over sand like the rustle of dead leaves. The once mighty Akhlut looked like a deflated balloon, and it was now nothing more than a tangled mass of bones and ligaments. Patches of brown rot and strands of gnawed gristle hung from where the beast's two limbs had been severed, its dorsal fin was half gone, and gunshot and stab wounds pocked the beast's sagging skin. Entrails leaked from several holes, the creature's remaining eye clouded over with death, the decaying orb staring toward the western shore of Lake Terror as if expecting one of its kind to come and take it away.

A fart-like push of air blasted over the beach, and Wyatt jumped. The dead beast's body sagged further. Wyatt held in a snicker as he watched one of the suits throw up his eggs. As the Akhlut's internal organs broke down the corpse released gases that caused the corpse to bloat. As nasty as the carcass was, the wildlife trooper in Wyatt knew that despite the unpleasantness of the rotting creature, its decomposing corpse would provide valuable nutrients for the ecosystem. That idea made him pause. The Akhlut would certainly go under the knife, and he had a feeling it might be a long time before this dead soul got to rest.

The faint *womp womp* of airfoils pounding the air carried softly on the breeze.

Sadness washed over Wyatt as he stared at the beast. He didn't feel so powerful and strong anymore. Yes, the creature had killed, but there was still something horrific about destroying something so terribly unique. Even though Wyatt and his family history had been forever cleansed, he would have rather not been a part of it, and he wondered how many rounds he'd punched into the monster.

Something struck Wyatt as odd. He knew that in death, with muscles decomposing and flesh decaying, the beast would be smaller than in life, but this beast… It looked much smaller than the creature he'd seen prior.

But was he sure? Sure enough to open his mouth with the brass fifty feet away?

Wyatt was able to push off the decision because as the thunder of the approaching helicopter increased Wyatt understood that Captain Udell and everyone who worked for him was about to be usurped.

A black SH-60 Seahawk arced over the trees, cutting sharply south and heading for Lakehead Beach.

The suits all paused and looked north like sheep who had heard the call of their shepherd. Wyatt sighed. Everything that happened in the next few days depended on who was in charge of the approaching team, whether he got a cowboy or a player. A cowboy wanted to get the job done no matter the cost, and a player wanted to be in control no matter the cost, even if it meant losing.

The helicopter was loud, and it left a rooster tail as it came in low, something dangling beneath the fuselage.

A black rectangle hung beneath the bird, and it swung in a wide arc from a tether. The gale caused by the SH-60 Seahawk flattened water reeds, tore leaves from trees, and stirred the water.

Wyatt turned up the volume on his hip radio and checked its handset, which was clipped to his vest.

A voice unknown to Wyatt blared over the radio, "It's an NSW."

"What?" the captain responded, but it was difficult to hear him over the pounding of the rotors and churning winds stirred by the chopper.

"Naval special warfare insertion," said the unknown voice.

Wyatt was familiar with the acronym, and as he watched the SH-60 Seahawk descend from the blue cloud-streaked sky, he couldn't help but feel a bit jealous. The feds always had the coolest shit. The SH-60 was a solid craft. A heavy lifter. It had a top speed of a hundred and sixty-eight miles per hour with a load capacity of five thousand pounds.

The copter pulled up and settled, treading air and holding steady a hundred yards off the tip of the pier. A black Zodiac special ops boat hung from cables beneath the chopper, and slowly the SH-60 began to drop toward the lake.

When the hanging boat was ten feet from the surface of the water, a soldier dressed in black and wearing full body armor stood up and pulled a quick release. The black Zodiac dropped the last ten feet, landed with a loud *smack*, and started toward the beach straightaway.

The whirlybird's engine cycled up as it lifted away and rolled west, and before the new arrivals were within fifty yards of the beach, the Sikorsky was nothing but running lights and background noise.

Collective silence stretched over the lake. The black Zodiac was under power, but Wyatt couldn't tell what was driving the vessel. As the newcomers got closer, Wyatt saw two guns, barrels down, mounted on the boat's bow, though he couldn't tell what type they were. Soldiers in full body armor and helmets with tinted face shields sat at attention on each gunnel, their dark silhouettes casting long shadows across the swaying water reeds. A man in green fatigues stood in the bow, one foot on the gunnel.

A faint buzzing sound rolled across the lake and as the black Zodiac slowed the sound diminished. The boat crunched onto the beach and the man in green jumped to shore and started walking toward the cluster of staties.

As the man approached, the volunteers moved in closer like a flock of geese protecting injured members of their flock.

The newcomer said, “Who’s in command here?” No handshake was offered.

“That would be me, sir,” said the oldest-looking suit. Wyatt didn’t know the man’s name, but learned it a second later. “Deputy Commander Justin Greger. Who am I talking to? I mean, I called you sir because anyone that can drop out of the sky like that is of higher rank than me, but forgive me if I’m suspicious. It’s been one of those days.”

“I heard,” the man said. “Harry Silva. I work for the federal government and specialize in anomalies, and I think your creature qualifies.”

“You Navy?”

“I’m everything,” Agent Silva said.

“Aren’t we confident,” DC Greger said.

The agent’s gaze ranged over the assembled crowd. He said, “I know you all think this is the end, but in my experience, that’s when the biggest turds fly.”

A cough, wind pushing sand over sand.

“And what is it you think you can do in our backyard that we can’t?” DC Greger said.

Agent Silva shifted his weight and looked up as if asking for divine patience. “You see those five guys? They’ve got missiles,” he said. He held out his hand and one of the soldiers stood and displayed a sleek shoulder-fired rocket launcher. “They’ve got grenade launchers, drones, and armor-piercing bullets. See those two guns on the bow of the Interceptor? One fires three shells per second, and the other is a laser. Any more concerns?”

Water lapped on the shore and the wind argued.

“Didn’t think so,” Agent Silva said. “Where is Wildlife Officer Terry Wyatt?”

Wyatt’s bowels loosened, and the coffee he’d had for breakfast threatened to make a curtain call. Suddenly Wyatt wanted to be small, to slink away, but all eyes had turned in his direction.

When Wyatt didn’t step forward, everyone else stepped back, leaving an open path between Agent Silva and Wyatt.

As the agent strode forward, he reached into a pocket of his fatigue pants. “I believe this is yours,” Silva said as he handed Wyatt the tooth the captain had sent off to the lab in Quantico. It was in a clear plastic bag and there was a card next to it.

Wyatt blinked as he stared at the man. His mouth dropped open as he thought to ask if the analysis had revealed anything, but he decided to be a clam.

"In case you're wondering, the analysis showed mostly what one would expect from a marine animal's tooth," he said. "It has a series of concentric layers that grew over time, and new layers of dentin were added, which caused the tooth to grow longer and thicker. Based on this, the bigheads said the tooth is at least forty years old."

Wyatt felt the sweet sting of vindication again.

"The texture of the tooth has a slight serration, which suggests the Akhlut evolved to grip and tear prey. The inner layer of the broken tooth is composed of a soft, porous material called pulp, and there are many blood vessels and nerves, which provide the nutrients needed for the tooth to grow and repair itself." The agent paused and turned to the bag of bones on the beach. "Does that have a broken tooth?"

There was a flurry of activity, and someone yelled, "Not that we can see, sir."

A low murmur leaked through the crowd and a suffocating heat spread through Wyatt.

His attention back on Wyatt, Agent Silva said, "I'm going to need your help in the coming days."

"I'm not sure what I can do that your team can't," Wyatt said, and he wasn't just being polite. Silva and his team looked like they could take over a small country.

"You know the area, all the ins and outs." The agent turned to DC Greger. "Is it a problem if Officer Wyatt and his team are assigned to my detail?"

DC Greger gave Wyatt the dirty eyeball, then said, "We want to help in any way we can." The suit smiled tightly.

"Good," Agent Silva said.

"Still, even with my knowledge…" Wyatt shook his head. "Our track record isn't great."

"We shall see," said Agent Silva, and for the first time the fed smiled.

27

In the days that followed Wyatt was a permanent fixture at Agent Silva's elbow. Though there was no official report yet, word of the tooth and everything it meant had leaked through Mount Aire like floodwaters infected with raw sewage. More news vans arrived, helicopters, the governor, and even the nutty one herself, Sarah Palin, made an appearance, standing on Lakehead Beach yelling about how socialist policies lead to all kinds of mutant creatures, most of them human.

Silva brought in drones, dive gear and frogmen, underwater ground penetrating radar, and the search for the Akhlut… the search for Akhlut, as in more than one, was ongoing. Wyatt had always known on some level that there was more than one beast. Procreation notwithstanding, he just couldn't believe there was a single creature that had managed to live over four hundred years.

Kal's memorial was a solemn affair. There was no burial, and his children, with help from Adamee and his family, had the pieces of Kal that were recovered cremated. Kal's children planned to get him a headstone down in the forty-eight where they lived, and thus another of the Akhlut's victims fell into memory.

Wyatt told Silva all the tales he'd heard about tunnels at the bottom of Lake Terror, and the agent was convinced one of those caves, maybe even a grotto free of water, was where the Akhluts called home.

"I'm bringing in a submersible, but it's going to take a few days for it and its crew to get here," Silva said. "In the meantime, my guys will be out on the lake with the underwear drones, and we'll see what there is to be seen."

"In many spots, the bottom is made up of thick mud," Wyatt said.

"That might help us. Mud underwater can eddy and drift like snow in the wind, and if there's a flow of water in and out of the cave system the patterns in the mud could help us find it."

Wyatt and Silva sat on the dock that circled the marina. There was no line at the boat ramp because the lake was closed indefinitely, despite it being the dog days of summer. Silva was surprised the chief had to issue the ban. Lakehead Beach was empty except for camera equipment and ring lights, though there were no reporters. Out on the lake, he saw Suzie patrolling and the Interceptor bobbing at the lake's center as agents controlled the robots beneath the clear water. Wyatt said, "You sure know a lot about geology for a guy who investigates freaks."

Silva laughed and sipped his coffee. "Anomalies. But, yeah, sometimes that means freak. This though…" He pointed at the lake with his coffee cup. "This could be something else."

"Seems to meet every definition of a mutant," Wyatt said. "Extremely limited habitat, rarely seen, its body comprised of seemingly two different animals of two different species. If not a mutant, what?"

Silva hiked his shoulders. "A disease, maybe?"

It sounded more like a statement than a question to Wyatt.

"I've seen things, Wyatt. Stuff that shouldn't be that I shouldn't be talking about. Stuff that goes way beyond cells mutating. On Long Island, there was a giant sea scorpion, in Florida a beast straight out of the past that I can only call an aquatic dinosaur. Those were freaks of nature that had no business living. One of a kind. But this…" He shook his head again. "Did you hear about what happened out on that research station in the Atlantic a few years back?" Silva asked.

Wyatt searched his memory and seemed to recall there had been a fire and all aboard were killed. "Some kind of explosion?" he guessed.

"Fire was the official line, but the truth is the place was overrun by sea spiders, and not the gentle spindly type you've seen. The creatures were infected with a mutation of chronic wasting disease. You know what that is, right?"

"It originated in deer, though we haven't seen cases out this way," Wyatt said.

"You might have now."

Wyatt said nothing.

"We found the disease in orca down Washington's way last year," Silva said.

"I remember. The beasts attacked Friday Harbor. The orcas were trapped, right?"

"Some got away, but yeah, the bigheads have been studying the creatures and they have a strain of this mutant disease."

"And you think that's what caused… made the Akhlut?"

"Don't know, but that's why I'm here. This is bigger than Mount Aire."

"What if…" Wyatt felt a chill of terror seize him. "What if it spreads to all the creatures in the ocean?"

To that, Silva had no response, because the answer was that would bring about the end of a huge chunk of humanity.

"The Akhlut carcass can tell you that, right?" Wyatt asked. The Akhlut corpse had been moved to a fish packing plant, where it was on ice and being documented and dissected by Silva's team. Wyatt glanced at the nasty stain on the beach where the carcass had washed up, and he could still smell the lingering scent of garbage and rotting fish on the breeze.

"Hopefully," the agent said. "Scientists live by a different clock, but I know some of the biological experiments need time. A test could take five minutes to prepare, but five days to complete and obtain results."

Wyatt nodded.

"Oh, and I forgot." Silva reached into his bag which sat on the dock beside him and pulled out a bottle filled with a viscus fluid. "You can keep your shit."

It was the water bottle Suzie had used to collect waste out on the lake. "No use?" Wyatt asked.

"Not anymore," he said. "I think we know the creature was full of shit. Let's go." Silva pushed to his feet, dumped his empty coffee cup in a trash can, and grabbed his bag.

Suzie had the new Zodiac, and Silva's crew had his fancy ride, so Wyatt and Silva took the backup boat out. The lake was calm, the air thick with humidity, the heat of midsummer like a suffocating winter blanket. He fired up the engine and wiped perspiration from his brow with the back of his hand.

Silva untied the mooring lines and jumped aboard.

There was no rush, so Wyatt took it slow, the outboard gurgling gently, bubbles snapping as the propeller churned the water and drove the boat across the lake. "So, you really think it's a disease? I mean, everything you mentioned was recent. The legend of the Akhlut goes back way further."

"Who knows?" Silva said. "We search for answers… it's my life… but rarely do we get the ones we want. If the Akhlut was the product of a disease, it would take the mysticism out of it, and we could deal with the problem rather than spend half our time trying to convince people the threat exists." Wyatt felt the agent's stare like the glare of the hot sun, but didn't turn to face him. "Yeah, I know you understand that more than most."

Wyatt looked at Silva.

"What? Did you think I didn't have you checked out? I know your family history, but…"

"But what?" Wyatt felt his hackles rising with anger.

"But what proof do we have of the cycle, really? We have proof of the creature now, but there are some gaps in the evidence going back through the years, and as you know legends grow in the telling."

"Understood," Wyatt said. It burned him, but he had to agree. The evidence was what it was. "But let's assume the cycle is real, what does that mean? Have you seen anything like this before?"

"A fellow agent told me about a creature under Niagara Falls. Big thing, that appeared every sixty years or so like clockwork. Cicadas of all types keep the same life cycles, regardless of the particular generation, so there is evidence to support hibernation or extended life cycle theories."

Wyatt harrumphed. "For a fed with top clearance you don't *know* very much."

"The more you learn the less you know," Silva said. "But what I do know is we need to kill the fucking things."

"Why no trap and study like the orcas?"

Silva shook his head. "The brass aren't skeptics. They've seen the evidence and know the disease is real and mutating regularly. So, no, the Akhlut… Akhluts are to be put down."

Wyatt knew that's what he should want. The beast had killed people he called friends and terrorized the town's Fourth of July celebration and all but destroyed tourist season, and yet… He was a wildlife officer for a reason. He felt the creatures of Earth had just as much right to live as humans did—shoot, in many cases more so. At some core level he had an issue with killing a beast living in its natural habitat just because it posed an inconvenience for people. Regardless of where the Akhlut had come from, it had just as much right to the lake as the folks of Mount Aire. Wyatt reached into a pocket and felt his father's knife, memories of how the beast had killed his kin wiping away the feelings of fairness and symbiosis.

Sensing his unease, Silva said, "This is personal for you, I get it, and it goes against your wiring. Trust me, I understand. Nobody likes… well, not nobody, but most people don't enjoy killing. Shit, I go out of my way not to step on ants, but…" He threw up his hands.

The Interceptor bobbed off the port bow. Two of Silva's men were working drone remotes and a third sat at the pilot station. In the silvery haze, the black boat stood out as it drifted with the breeze because the water was too deep to drop an anchor.

"Anything?" Silva hollered to his men.

"Mud. Mud, some mud, and a few fish, plants. Oh, and did I mention mud?" said one of the agents. It was all hands on deck, and everyone was working around the clock. Wyatt hadn't spoken much with Silva's crew, and he didn't know the man's name.

"Holler if there's anything to see," Silva said. Then to Wyatt, "Excuse me while I check in."

Wyatt raised an eyebrow.

"Everybody serves somebody," the agent said as he went aft for privacy.

Who did Wyatt serve? He pulled his phone and called his mother, and she picked up on the second ring. Coco had fallen back into her routine thanks to Kim, and Mom was doing well, feeling better, though "the goddamn heat is like getting roasted in an oven. You'd think my bigshot son would invest in a better air conditioner for his mother."

"You leave the windows open, Mom," Wyatt said. But the funny thing was, he wasn't angry, or even aggravated at her jabs. When she'd almost died, Wyatt had come to terms with the fact that though he loved his mother very much, and would do anything for her, she was a miserable person who constantly felt the need to spread her displeasure around. Kim said to just let her talk, but it bothered Wyatt that his mother didn't razz Kim at all, but never stopped busting his peanuts.

"How's Kim?" his mother asked.

"She's next on the call list."

"Then get on with it."

Happy to. "Bye, Mom. Love you." He killed the connection and immediately felt guilty, all the thoughts of never talking to her again rushing back like a bad hangover.

Kim didn't answer her cell, which wasn't unusual. She was probably busy at work. Not everyone got to float around Terror Lake all day.

Silva rejoined him just as one of the drone pilots yelled, "I've got something here."

A line was tossed, and the two Zodiacs were lashed together, and Wyatt and Silva stepped on the gunnel of their boat and jumped over the Interceptor.

Two agents were huddled next to the drone pilot who had proclaimed eureka, the screen showing the drone's feed awash with white light, specks of sediment, and encroaching blackness. Mud swirled along the lake bottom, and there was no vegetation.

"What am I looking at?" Silva asked.

"Give me a second to bring it around again." The agent worked a joystick, the drone's umbilical slowly unspooling and snaking over the gunnel into the water.

The image sent back by the drone was clouded with mud, the unit's harsh light blinding as it refracted in the water. The screen showed a clear patch of seafloor, and what looked to be the dark maw of a cave mouth. But that's not why Wyatt's jaw dropped open a crack and made a swarm of invisible mice nip at his skin.

Before the cave entrance, in a hollow of thick mud created by the push and flow of the lake water, there was a pile of bones. All sizes, shapes, and species appeared to be represented. There were bear skulls, ribcages large and small, femurs, hip bones, and an assortment of cracked and broken bones that stuck from the lake bottom like protective spikes.

The water around the drone undulated, its light went out, and the screen went dark.

"What happened? Why did we lose the—" Silva croaked.

The remaining umbilical line unspooled and flew off the boat's deck as if it were being yanked on by Godzilla. The line went taut, sang as it stretched, and the boat listed. Then the line snapped and snaked into the lake.

"Good thing we've got another drone," Silva said.

28

Mount Aire, Alaska, ***9:47 AM AKST, September 19th, 2017***

The drone search of that first underwater cave, like the many others found after, yielded nothing. The submersible arrived, more divers, drones. More piles of bones were found, and the areas were marked for further investigation in the future. Wyatt and Silva felt there were human bones in the piles, and they might bring closure to the families of the missing, like Jesse Ombridge. The smashed drone was also recovered, and there were signs of the Akhlut everywhere, but over the two and a half months since the Fourth of July attack, there hadn't been an Akhlut sighting.

To Wyatt's surprise, Silva stayed and handled what he deemed cases of lesser importance from his base in Mount Aire. The government man was paying big money at Gigi's Inn, one of the best hotels on the peninsula, for accommodations for himself and his crew, visitors, and a meeting room that also served as a command center.

Wyatt had settled in as the buffer between the fed and the captain, who was happy to step back and let the big boys run the show. After the Fourth, there had been much second-guessing, and the chief's balls were in a vise for not closing the lake. But the heat blew over, as storms do, and Wyatt found himself liking Silva, becoming almost jealous of him.

The agent appeared to have no personal ties, though he occasionally mentioned a sister and nephew, but other than that he was a blank slate. When Wyatt tried to pull information from the man, Silva would always tell him a war story, and Wyatt was beginning to believe those were the only stories the guy had. That was kind of sad, yet he knew this wasn't uncommon. Certain jobs were an all-in proposition, and there was no time for family, fun, or love.

The command center was abuzz. Two agents manned computers, and they were going through the hours of footage recorded by the robotic drones that crawled across the lake bottom and through its thick mud, watching, recording, and waiting. Two agents were out on the Interceptor, and one was patrolling with Suzie. Because of the increased fed presence, Rogue Two, Troopers Sanford and Kai Ai, were sent back to their regular posts. Rogue One, Troopers Denis Freed and Rolly Langdon, were still assigned to the Mount Aire region because though

Ned Simmons had been transferred home from Anchorage, he wouldn't be back on full active duty until the new year, and he was still weeks away from working light duty taking calls and making reports.

Silva was waiting on a call from the lab boys back in Washington, and when his phone played the Imperial March, he rubbed his hands together and let Darth Vadar's theme song play through before he answered. "Silva," he said, and his face immediately went sour.

"Yeah," Silva rolled his eyes and mouthed "the boss." "Yeah. O.K., but we're still going to patrol, no reason we can't do that, right?" The agent looked exasperated. "I know a watched pot doesn't boil, sir, but I… Yes, sir." Silva stabbed his phone and said, "The submersible is shut down for the next couple days. Captain Howier says it's not safe."

"Because of that?" Ellis pointed at a TV mounted on a wall that was tuned to the local weather station.

Silva nodded.

A blonde weatherwoman stood before an old-school map, waving her arms, and Wyatt grabbed the remote and unmuted the T.V.

"There's a high-pressure bubble of arctic air coming in from the north and the pocket of warm air sitting over the lower forty-eight is pressing our way. This sets up the perfect conditions for an early winter storm."

Wyatt hit mute and said, "Great."

Silva said, "How do you do it? That summer was pretty short. I figure you like the cold."

He thought it over for a few seconds before responding. Did he like the cold? Or did he dislike people? Wyatt loved the summer weather, but when mid-September rolled around and the last of the fair weather adventurers left to go home and the peninsula settled from a churning hive to dormancy, he felt the knot in his stomach loosen. He said, "I don't love the cold, but I've lived here all my life so it's part of me, I think. But it's the solitude, the ability to be in nature and truly hear and see it. I guess you can't understand what I mean."

"No, I can't," Silva said. "Nobody truly knows what another is going through, but I have seen nature do some amazing, and terrible, things. I've had moments like you mention when the woods are so quiet you can hear the rub of the pine needles, the fluttering of flies' wings, and the crackle of ants as they march over dried leaves."

"Yeah, it's hypnotic and soothing," Wyatt said. "When I go to Anchorage, I'm never really comfortable."

Silva laughed. "Ever been to Seattle or a big city?"

He nodded. "A few times. Training, vacations, and such. I've never seen anything, or been anywhere, where I didn't want to come home."

"I guess that makes you lucky," Silva said.

And with that, the conversation ran out of gas. Wyatt thought he detected regret in Silva's tone, but when the agent's phone rang again normal thoughts fled and in an instant the year of the beast reasserted itself.

"Silva. Yes." He put a hand over the phone, and said, "The lab."

So this was it. The moment of truth when they found out just how screwed they were.

Silva nodded, licked his lips, and then his eyes went wide. He said, "O.K. You'll send the report up the chain? Thanks. I appreciate you guys getting to this so fast." He tapped his phone, ended the call, and said, "Now we do have a mystery."

"Do tell," Wyatt said.

The other agents had stopped working and were looking at their boss. "Get the captain on the horn," he said. Then to Wyatt, "The Akhlut didn't have the disease."

That nugget sat out there in the stillness as Wyatt pondered what the news meant. The results were good in that it meant the disease Silva had told him about hadn't spread to the area and created the Akhlut. But it was bad because that meant they had an impossible mystery on their hands.

Silva said, "I guess you were right, Wyatt. They must be mutants. The bastard children of some unholy union that has further mutated over the years as the beasts breed with other species."

Wyatt didn't see any other explanation, but he was no scientist and he and Silva had talked many times about things that shouldn't be.

"What does that mean?" Wyatt asked.

"We exterminate them and that's the end of it," Silva said.

Wyatt didn't like the word exterminate, it just didn't sit well on his tongue, or jive with his ethics and sensibilities, but still… Akhluts were a danger to public safety. There was no way around that. Had the beasts stayed in the woods and killed a few bears, some deer, maybe an elk, nobody would have paid any attention to the ranting of a wildlife officer talking about mythical beasts on a six-year cycle.

But the creatures had killed people and that couldn't stand.

Over the next twenty-four hours, Mount Aire was pummeled by a massive ice storm that spit a mix of hail, snow, and freezing rain. As predicted, the pocket of frigid air pushing down from the north met the encroaching wall of hot summer air coming up from the south, and the two fronts met in a calamitous collision that blackened the sky and caused the temperature to plummet.

Cold specks of ice bit Wyatt's face as the boat sliced over Lake Terror. Suzie was out with two of the feds on the Interceptor, and Wyatt, Silva, and another agent named Quinton patrolled in a twenty-one-foot center console Zodiac. There had been no arguments from the captain, or anyone else about patrolling in the storm. On the contrary. It was believed that the early storm could drive the beast from wherever it was holed up.

Terror Lake was scalloped with tiny waves, the frozen rain spattering the surface, the crackle of lightning and the rumble of thunder echoing over the wilderness.

Static blared from the radio. "Si… might not… cop.." Static.

Wyatt checked his cell phone. One signal bar, and when he tried to call the command center the call didn't go through.

Silva grabbed the handset and opened a channel. "This is Silva. Repeat. You broke up. Please repeat."

Static, broken words, a shriek of feedback.

Silva's phone chimed and he answered. He wasn't on long, and when the call was through, he said, "The repeater is covered in ice, the antenna, so until they can correct the problem, we need to go direct radio to radio."

"Like when we were kids," said Quinton, who was piloting the Interceptor.

"I'll never forget my first set," Silva said, as he pulled the drawstring around the hood of his rain slicker tighter to cover more of his face and seal off his neckline from the driving hail. "They were the G.I. Joe model. Remember those?"

Wyatt did, but he hadn't had anything so fancy. "Probably worked better than my cell phone," Wyatt said. "You better keep your phone on low power because I don't—"

The radio clipped to Wyatt's life preserver squawked.

It was Suzie. "Silva, do you copy? Over."

Wyatt handed Silva his radio, and the fed said, "Silva here. What is it, Suzie?"

"We've got something big on the SONAR."

"What is your current position?"

"We're a quarter mile southwest of the glacier head."

Silva lowered the phone and said, "Isn't that where you first saw the Akhlut on the night of the Fourth?"

Wyatt nodded. The sleeping maggots in his stomach were suddenly awake and looking to party.

Turning his attention back to the phone, Silva said, "We're inbound."

"Copy that," said Suzie.

Quinton dropped the hammer and the Zodiac sprang from the water, the propeller spitting a fifteen-foot rooster tail as the boat cut effortlessly over the lake.

Sheets of rain cut visibility to fifty yards, gray nothingness surrounding the lake. Even the steep mountain peaks that surrounded Terror Lake were obscured, and it made the lake seem very small.

Ahead, the Interceptor materialized out of the gloom.

Quinton backed off the throttle and the Zodiac slowed to a crawl. SONAR showed a large black blotch of nothingness rising beneath the boats.

"What do we do?" Suzie yelled across the gap between the vessels.

Silva hooted, and said, "Get on those guns."

Suzie piloted the Interceptor, and the other two agents went to the bow and positioned themselves behind the big guns, one of which fired three shells per second, the other a laser that could slice through steel.

Silva clicked a safety line onto his life vest, and yelled, "We'll move back." Wyatt and Silva had basic munitions aboard, but the Interceptor was far better equipped.

The black patch rising from the depths had almost reached the surface, and its shapeless form filled half the SONAR screen.

"Brace yourselves!" Silva screamed, but the man didn't appear scared. Instead, he sounded like a surfer getting ready to ride a big one.

The hail died away and cold rain pounded the lake and everything on it.

Through the haze Wyatt saw the tip of a black dorsal fin break the surface, its knife-like shape rising and growing as the beast came on. Wyatt tried to feel his father's knife, which was in his chest pocket covered by his raincoat and life jacket. All he felt was a hard lump, but it was enough. It was his job to protect and serve, both people and animals, but everything he did from this moment on was for his father and uncle.

All eyes were on the Akhlut as it surfaced, tiny waves running away from the beast, a thick line of gurgling whitewater trailing behind.

So it was that nobody saw the second Akhlut until it launched from the water and nudged the Interceptor. The boat listed severely to port. Suzie kept her seat, but the agents manning the guns were tossed from the deck, and had it not been for their safety lines, both men would have ended up in the drink. The agents arced through the air, their safety lines jerking them back toward the boat.

The new arrival roared as it breached, jaws open and reaching for one of the agents as he swung through the rain. Snapping jaws clamped down on the agent's foot, and for a horrifying instant the man was stretched, the safety line singing, before the leg broke off at the knee joint. The agent wailed as he crashed to the deck, blood, tendons, splintered bone, and torn muscle leaking from what was left of his right leg.

"Get me to those guns!" Silva yelled.

29

Quinton spun the ship's wheel, eased the throttle arm down, and the motor grumbled as the Zodiac pushed toward the Interceptor.

Wyatt and Silva drew down but didn't fire because the attacking Akhlut was still too close to the fed boat. The agent piloting the Interceptor was doing his best to get the craft under control as an agent tended to the man with the severed leg, who was screaming in agony.

The Akhlut wedged itself under the Interceptor, and the beast dove as rubber screeched and whitewater churned over the boat's gunnel. A howl pierced the day, and thunder cracked as rain fell in buckets. The first Akhlut on the scene, who Wyatt labeled Thing One, had been forgotten and it moved in to help its mate, Thing Two.

With an earsplitting cry, Thing One, which was smaller than Thing Two, drove from the lake, a mound of whitewater propelling it from the water. The beast came down on the bow of the Interceptor, and the agent tending his fallen mate and the injured guy were tossed in the air again and jerked around by their safety ropes.

This time Suzie didn't manage to stay on her feet, and she too was thrown from the boat only to be reeled back in by her safety line.

Quinton eased the Zodiac into reverse and backed off, giving Wyatt and Silva better angles. Both men fired, and the shots thumped into the creatures, who screamed like pigs as they thrashed and twisted, throwing around their pectoral fin-like arms.

This time the man with the severed leg wasn't so lucky. He landed in the water, and though his mate started reeling him in as soon as he hit the Interceptor's deck, it wasn't enough.

Wyatt and Silva fired and Thing One and Thing Two squirmed and bucked as they struggled to escape from between the boats.

The agent in the drink screamed for help as he struggled to stay afloat, a cloud of crimson spreading around him in the rain-dappled water.

Thing Two had taken most of the shots, and the larger creature submerged and eased back into the depths as Thing One pushed the police Zodiac aside like a leaf. With a wail of anger, Thing One flexed its wolf-like jaws, revealing sharp teeth behind receding gums, the stink of mud-rot filling the air.

The man in the water screamed in panic. Thing One took hold of the guy and began thrashing its head side-to-side in an attempt to rip its prey free of its safety line.

Wyatt placed his shots carefully and when the Glock clicked empty, he reloaded, chambered a round, and began firing again. He aimed at Thing One's head without coming near the agent in the water, or at least what was left of him.

A crunch reverberated over the lake as Thing One bit down on the struggling agent. Crimson rain lashed the lake's surface as Thing One tossed back its head, biting, and crunching on the agent until his corpse broke in two, his legs and the safety line falling to the lake's surface as his entire upper body was chewed. Chunks of muscle, fat, bone, and boat dropped onto the surface.

The sound of cracking bones sent an electrical-like pulse racing to Wyatt's extremities.

Silva screamed as his gun clicked empty, and he dropped the weapon as he darted aft. Before Wyatt could ask what the agent was doing, Silva vaulted onto the Zodiac's gunnel and launched himself across an eight-foot gap onto the Interceptor. He landed on the heaving deck and almost fell but managed to keep his feet. He jumped into the chair behind the laser cannon.

Wyatt hooted. Playtime was over. But nothing happened. The rain roared, Thing One continued dining on the agent, Thing Two disappeared beneath the tossing surface, and Silva sat behind the laser cannon, waiting. Then Wyatt remembered Silva telling him that it took a few seconds for the weapon to charge before it could be used. Something to do with the power that—

Three sharp staccato womps pounded the air, the rain sizzled, and Thing One shrieked as the upper third of its torso was sliced away. There was no blue energy line, no dramatic hiss or Star Trek-like buzz. A black and white chunk of flesh fell into the water, blood spilling from the dying creature as its eyes widened, and it stopped chewing.

The laser cannon fired again, and Thing One's head exploded, a hail of blood, brain, and bone splattering the lake's surface as well as the Zodiac and the Interceptor. With a final cry Thing One heaved itself from the water and crashed back to the lake with a final exhalation of air and blood that sprayed the Interceptor crimson. Suzie and the remaining agent ducked as the boat bobbed and listed, but they were still overrun by the bloody water filled with pieces of the agent's corpse.

Silva recovered first, and yelled, "What's on the SONAR?"

Suzie looked at him stunned, her face splattered with Akhlut blood, her eyes the size of quarters.

"SONAR!" he screamed. "I want it! Tell me where it is! Now!"

Suzie yelled through the driving rain, "Off the port bow and still diving. It's at about fifty feet."

Thing One sank beneath the surface, leaving a swirling mess of blood and whitewater behind. The corpse would float, and they'd retrieve it. And if it didn't, the frog men or the submersible could go get it, but judging by Silva's bloodlust he wasn't too concerned about future research.

The patter of rain, howling wind, and cold bit Wyatt's face. The boats settled, and Wyatt fished spare clips for the Glock from the dry storage compartment beneath the command console.

"It's at eighty feet, and headed for the glacier," Quinton said.

"Pursue," Wyatt yelled.

Quinton spun up the motor and twisted the ship's wheel and pointed the vessel north.

Suzie still sat behind the command console of the Interceptor, not moving, her gaze fixed on a finger floating on the lake's surface.

Wyatt looked over his shoulder and saw the surviving agent take the helm, Silva falling in beside Suzie to hold her up.

Shame and sorrow washed over Wyatt. His partner had just been embarrassed, but the woman didn't seem to care. She appeared to be in shock, which Wyatt figured was to be expected. She was new to the job, and certainly had never seen anything like this, not that he had.

Suzie sat on the bench seat before the command console and snapped into a safety line. She looked done. Used hard and put away wet. Through the driving rain, Wyatt saw her lower her head, and he wished he could comfort her. But there wasn't time for feelings, not now.

The Zodiac and the Interceptor came up on plane, both vessels throwing long rooster tails, the Zodiac's engine wailing, the Interceptor as silent as an electric car. Both vessels' bilge pumps were going full tilt, and streams of water jettisoned from the boats as the units barely kept up with the deluge of rain.

Static, and the radio came to life. They'd thawed out the repeater, and Wyatt listened as Silva reported back to the command center. Silva had arranged for his chopper to be standing by, and he called it in, but with the weather, it was several minutes out and would probably be too late for the party.

Three feet separated the boats as they raced north.

To Wyatt's surprise, Suzie pushed up from her seat and charged to the bow of the boat. She had a brief exchange with Silva, who showed her the basics of how to fire the laser, and then took up position behind the gun as Suzie manned the laser.

Silva jacked back the gun's bolt and chambered a shell. The weapon fired three rounds per second and had a hard recoil, but the laser cannon was smooth as silk which explained why Silva had taken the gun and given the laser to the one hundred and ten pound wildlife officer.

Thunder cracked, and lightning spidered over Terror Lake, the dark clouds glowing for an instant. The rain let up, but round BBs of hail pelted the boats, the wind shrieking and pushing around the boats' spray.

Wyatt focused on Suzie and Silva. "Quinton, slow up and drop into the Interceptor's wake," he said. Wyatt would've preferred to be manning the gun next to Silva, but that was just macho bullshit. Suzie could handle herself, but still he felt the coward as he gave the order to fall back. He and Quinton had Glocks, a grenade launcher, but by all accounts, the Interceptor's bow guns were infinitely more powerful, and with only one beast left—that they knew of—Wyatt was content to let the literal big guns take the prize.

Ahead, the glacier appeared like a giant dirty white tongue through the mix of rain and hail, and the vegetation at the lake's edge swayed and shifted as something large moved through it. Everything was covered in a layer of ice, and the sound of crackling ice and breaking branches echoed over the wind.

Rogue One, Troopers Denis Freed and Rolly Langdon, had taken up position atop the glacier at Silva's command, but Wyatt could barely see them through the driving storm. Gunshots rang out, the laser cannon sang, and Silva opened up with the gun, the thunderous booms pounding over the lake.

The Akhlut crawled from the water, covered in mud, its tall dorsal fin swaying back and forth as it struggled through the thick vegetation to the east of the glacier.

Rogue One moved across the glacier, staying ahead of the beast as it tried to scramble into the woods. More gunfire and the Akhlut changed direction yet again, giving up the landward track and driving back into the shallow lake water, where it half walked, half swam through a thick stew of mud and lake water.

Suzie and Silva fired again, but the beast was fast, the boats were heaving in the turbulent water, and the wind and rain were pushing the vessels around like toys in a bathtub. The northern tip of Terror Lake was deep, the glacier having eaten away at the shoreline over millennia. Soon the beast's dorsal fin was gone, and all that remained was swirling whitewater which dissipated in the relentless rain.

"Orders?" yelled Quinton. He spun the ship's wheel, fighting the wind and the two-foot chop that had consumed the lake's surface.

The SONAR was a mess, and Wyatt didn't see the smudge of the beast on the screen.

Silva stood on the bow of the Interceptor, his head stuck into the gloom as he gazed east, searching for the Akhlut, but the creature was nowhere to be seen. "Shit!" he yelled. "I'm gonna be stuck here until Christmas!"

"I've got a bead on it!" yelled the agent piloting the Interceptor. The SONAR on the Navy craft was light years more advanced than the Zodiac's unit. "It's heading southeast."

"Put us on it!" Silva yelled.

Suzie made Wyatt proud. The wildlife officer, who was unfamiliar with piloting electric-powered vessels, played the boat like a finely tuned violin. With one hand she pushed the throttle arm down as far as it would go, and with the other spun the ship's wheel until the outboard had reached its maximum turn radius. The vessel rose on its own wake as it spun around and jumped from the rain-pocked lake, the electric motor whining as its propeller clawed at the water.

Quinton fell in behind the Interceptor and brought the Zodiac up on plane as he stayed in the fed boat's wake.

The radio blared and Wyatt answered the hail.

"What's happening out there, Wyatt?" It was the captain.

"One Akhlut ready for the canning factory, and we're in pursuit of another," Wyatt said.

"What do you want Rogue One to do?"

Wyatt had forgotten about Troopers Freed and Langdon. The Interceptor was still powering southeast, and he mentally drew a line off the boat's port bow and figured if the creature didn't change course, it would reach the eastern shoreline in minutes. He didn't see how Rogue One could be there in time, but they weren't doing any good where they were.

"Wyatt, did you copy?" the captain asked, static filling the background.

Wyatt chuckled to himself. Guess they didn't get all the ice off the antenna. He said, "Yeah, I copy. Freed? Langdon? You out there?"

"Copy that, sir."

"Follow the eastern shoreline the best you can. Be ready to move in if I call you," Wyatt said.

"10-4. Rogue One out." The Troopers had ATVs, but few trails ran along the lake's edge.

"Wyatt, can I do anything to help?" the captain said.

"Tell that whirlybird to hurry up," he said.

30

The distant *womp womp* of the approaching chopper pounded through the storm, which had taken a break. Thick mist covered Terror Lake and the wind died away as the Zodiac zipped across the water, the Interceptor running beside it.

Suzie's hair blew in the wind as she sat behind the laser cannon, Silva in the gunner's chair next to her. Quinton piloted the Zodiac, but the man's face had slipped from excitement to worry over the last twenty seconds.

Wyatt's thoughts wandered as the boat raced through the rain. Here he was again, chasing the beast. Putting his life on the line for… what? Mom? Did she really need him? She had Kim, Coco, and she'd do just fine. Ian, well, his buddy would miss him, but within a few months the pain would fade, and after a year or two he would be nothing but a distant memory. And what of Kim? They'd been dancing, playing the game, but she would find someone else, and if he didn't commit to her soon someone else would. Shoot, it didn't matter if Wyatt lived or died. The animals. They would miss him, but was that enough?

Gunshots rang out, and Wyatt saw two men standing on the shoreline firing at the creature. Wyatt couldn't tell who the men were, but they stood on the end of a dock that jutted out into the lake twenty yards. The guys had shotguns, and the weapons' thunderous booms drew the attention of the Akhlut, who made a hard turn toward the dock.

The depth finder showed the bottom of the lake rising to meet the boats at a precipitous rate.

Wind hollered and sang as the Akhlut churned toward the dock.

The two men turned tail and ran, but it soon became clear the guys weren't going to make it to land.

Silva's shriek of anger carried over the gale. With the creature between him and the dock, he and Suzie couldn't open fire because the fleeing men could be hit.

Like a battering ram on steroids, the Akhlut crashed into the dock, and wood splintered and cracked. Nails popped and boards sprang up as both fleeing men were tossed into the nasty syrup of mud and water.

The Akhlut was on the men in seconds, and their shrill cries cut Wyatt to the bone.

With the Akhlut working on its new prey, both men in the water were doomed and Silva and Suzie fired. The gun barked as it spit shells, the shots peppering the water and the creature.

Screaming. Wails of agony. Pleas for help.

The Zodiac's motor coughed as the propellor dug into mud.

Quinton killed the engine and the Zodiac slid to a stop in a foot of water, thick black mud splashing the boat.

Wyatt considered telling Quinton to continue. The outboard would eventually get clogged with mud and stall, but if they didn't get on the scene soon it wouldn't matter. But if he needed the boat again and the engine was clogged up…

The scream of ATVs moving along the shoreline knocked Wyatt from his reverie. Rogue One had arrived.

A final scream as the Akhlut chewed. Wyatt couldn't see the carnage from where he was, but he'd seen enough blood on this day that his mind had no problem painting the picture.

The Interceptor pressed into the shallows, its bow throwing mud and water like a snowplow. The fed boat's electric outboard was built to withstand all types of adverse conditions. It didn't rely solely on water as a coolant, and with its reverse propeller, it could drive through the mud as though it were water.

Rogue One dismounted their ATVs and took up positions behind thick trees where the half-destroyed dock met land. The duo fired on the beast, and for an instant, Wyatt thought the Akhlut was going to pursue the wildlife officers, but the beast threw Wyatt yet another surprise.

Through the thickening fog, Wyatt watched with a sense of growing dread as the Akhlut climbed from the lake, its pectoral fin arms and legs churning through the mud.

The Interceptor was bearing down on the creature, and Suzie and Silva both fired their weapons, loosing a barrage of shots that knocked the Akhlut back, the giant creature disappearing beneath a fountain of whitewater mixed with mud.

Rain lashed the lake again and the sound of the approaching helicopter was close now, and the pilot's chatter blared from the radio. The bird was three minutes out.

That was two minutes too long.

With a roar, the Akhlut breached, driving toward the fed boat as Silva and Suzie pounded the creature. Blood spouted from the beast, the top of its dorsal fin was severed by the laser, and its dying shrieks were almost sad.

But the beast wasn't done.

The Interceptor and the Akhlut met in a momentous crash, and the front of the boat lifted. Silva held on, but Suzie was tossed from her seat. Her safety line went taut, and she was tugged toward the rear of the Interceptor.

Wyatt's nerves fought to break through his skin.

Suzie disappeared behind the Interceptor's transom and the electric motor coughed, sputtered, and stalled as it churned part of Suzie into chop meat.

Wyatt's scream hurt his throat and made his vision go red. Rage took command. An anger he didn't think he could control.

The Akhlut headed for the shore, but it kept its distance from Rogue One who were firing at the creature again. The beast was moving slowly, leaving a trail of bloody sludge, and when it crawled from the mud onto the shoreline, Wyatt could see the beast wasn't long for this world.

"Quinton, get me in there!" Wyatt yelled.

The agent's eyes went wide, and he looked toward the Interceptor for Silva, but the agent was preoccupied, his head hanging over the boat's transom. Wyatt figured he was tossing his cookies.

Quinton said, "Do you think that's a good idea? It looks cooked. Why not wait for—"

"I'm not waiting for shit. Get me in there or get out of the way!"

Quinton nodded, angled up the outboard as high as it would go but still function, and cranked up the motor. The outboard wailed and spit mud, but the Zodiac slowly churned toward shore.

The wounded Akhlut was crawling, and Wyatt saw that the beast had lost a front pectoral fin and a rear pectoral fin, its entire dorsal fin was now gone, and several huge gashes marred the creature's flanks. It was missing an eye, and the right side of its wolfish face was crushed, its jawbone visible.

As the beast slipped into the dense vegetation along the shoreline, the storm decided to rear its ugly head. The rain came in hard, sheets of cold water that made Wyatt shiver, but then he realized it wasn't the cold that was rattling him.

He was making the same mistake again. Bad decisions made with emotion. Anger. He'd done this so many times before he wondered if he was losing it. Isn't that what the bigheads said? Doing the same thing over and over and expecting different results was the definition of insanity? But he wasn't crazy. Just angry beyond measure. The beast had gotten his uncle, his father, Jesse, Kal, and countless others, had almost killed his partner, and now Wyatt had Suzie's blood on his hands. The thought of it soured his stomach and he bent over the gunnel and puked.

The Zodiac churned to a stop and Quinton killed the outboard.

Wyatt gathered himself, jumped onto the gunnel, and leaped down into the mud. He sank to his knees, but using the Akhlut's tracks, he and Quinton were able to make it to the shoreline. There they paused and let the rain cleanse them before pulling their Glocks and checking their weapons. The Glock 19s were military grade, and could not only handle rain, but they could be fired underwater, though Wyatt had never tested the assertion.

The land climbed steadily up toward the road, and red lights flashed through the trees. The chopper had arrived and was hovering over the lake, but with the beast on its last legs and Silva still dealing with the mess on the Interceptor, Wyatt didn't see how the bird could help.

Evergreens packed the forest, their needle-like leaves covered in ice, the underbrush a slippery mess of hail and mud. It was tough going, and Quinton and Wyatt struggled to keep their footing, holding onto tree trunks while keeping their guns at the ready. Wyatt didn't think the Akhlut had anything left, but he'd learned to never underestimate the beast.

The forest echoed with a loud squeal, like the largest pig on earth had just been shot. That was followed by a whimpering roar that Wyatt interpreted as the beast's final sounds.

A house appeared to the duo's right, the rain easing, mist snaking around the structure, which looked to be unoccupied. It wasn't uncommon for those who owned cabins in Mount Aire to be long gone when school started up in Anchorage, and this year the exodus had been early thanks to the year of the beast.

The Akhlut's tracks continued through the forest, bypassing the house, and cutting through a thicket of trampled pricker vines.

"Looks like it's come this way before," Wyatt said. The ground was churned up real good, the vegetation flattened, and there were scuff marks on the trees on both sides of the trail.

The stench of rotting garbage filled the wood. Wyatt and Quinton slowed, covering each other as they moved around trees, boulders, and patches of frozen undergrowth.

Wyatt and Quinton found the Akhlut beneath a deadfall of debris at the base of a sheer cliff face that climbed up to Circle Road. A nest of a kind had been built from large branches and other detritus, and a foul reek emanated from the dark maw of a cave mouth.

There wasn't much left of the beast and a deep sorrow washed over Wyatt. That feeling after achieving something you wanted so very badly, only to realize what that success meant, and it wasn't what he thought. The Akhlut was dead, and the species might be gone from the world, but he was fine with that. Some things were just in the wrong place at the wrong time.

The majestic beast, which had been so full of fire and hate just moments before, was nothing but a deflated white and black balloon doused with blood, fat, and bones. Wyatt didn't see how the creature had managed to make it this far from the lake. He couldn't count all the bullet holes, and the fins were mostly gone, and large chunks of flesh were missing from the corpse's torso, but much of the gore had been washed away by the rain.

Wyatt dropped onto his ass, exhaustion overwhelming him.

"Only goes in a few feet," Quinton said as he exited the cave. "There's some bones that look recent."

Snap! Crack!

Wyatt threw himself to the ground, mud splashing his face as he aimed the Glock.

Silva and Suzie emerged from the forest, guns at the ready.

Everyone stood frozen for a moment, mouths agape, rain cleansing them.

Wyatt blinked and rubbed his eyes with the back of his hand. Was he dead? But…

Quinton said, "I'm going to need a bit of extra leave, boss."

Silva laughed. "You O.K., partner?" The agent came forward and helped Wyatt to his feet.

All Wyatt could do was nod, his gaze fixed on Suzie.

"What?" she said. "I'm fine."

"But…" Wyatt stammered. "You were sucked into the propeller."

She nodded. "Almost. I got lucky. It's about time at that."

"What did the propeller slice and dice? I heard it. The engine stalled."

Silva said, "The safety line foiled the propeller, the motor overheated, and the propeller shaft sheared off before it got her."

"There was ten feet of rope left when the engine stalled," she said.

Quinton whistled.

"Yup," she said.

Then Wyatt was a volcano of emotions, and he surged forward and wrapped Suzie in his arms and lifted her from the ground. He knew it was inappropriate, but he didn't care, and he hoped she didn't either.

"Easy, Wyatt. Easy." She was laughing, and when Wyatt put her down, she pecked him on the cheek. "I'm good, boss. Did you think I was going to let you off so easily? Simmons isn't back for months."

"What about you, Silva? You done here?" Wyatt asked. Part of him wanted the man out of his hair, but another part, the part that fantasized about doing a job like Silva's, the part that wondered what it would be like to move off the peninsula and see the world, those parts wouldn't mind if the fed hung around. Kim's face filled his mind's eye, the critters of his woods, and the fish in his lake.

"I think things are in good hands," Silva said. "Maybe I'll come by for Christmas and we can toast to the end of the year of the beast. But if not, I'll be back in six years if the winds of fate allow it and I'm needed. Hopefully, the years will be uneventful, and if you get bored, look me up. I'm always looking for guys like you."

Wyatt laughed. He didn't know about uneventful. Could he be a federal agent? Wyatt didn't see it. But happily ever after? Hell, maybe he'd give that a try.

CODA

The Akhlut had survived so long in the darkness it was fearful of light.

But it was hungry.

Its purpose was to hunt and feed. It didn't know joy or happiness. It didn't feel fear, or pity. It couldn't be bargained with or cajoled. It had no family and didn't know love.

The Akhlut knew only pursuing and killing prey.

As the beast tried to move its pectoral fins it found two were gone, and a numb pain spread through the Akhlut, its body failing, organs shutting down as its last surge of life propelled it through the forest. Its vision was blurry, and the beast only saw blurred gray and black wavering images in the driving rain.

It had seen the deaths of the others, heard the terrible wails as the Akhlut became the last of its kind. The beast didn't know remorse, or loss, yet… there had always been others, even in the early years when few came to the watering spot, the great sea that brought life and allowed it to survive.

Sensing it had now become prey, it fled through the evergreens, ice cracking, the Akhlut leaving a trail of viscus fluid in its wake. It heard faint cries. Angry cries. The beast shifted its massive weight, losing its ability to move as it dragged itself through the forest.

Its remaining eye was ultrasensitive, even in the gray half-light of the storm. There was a den where killers lived, a white orb of light on its side cutting through grayness.

The rain eased its pain for water was its lifeblood. For time uncounted its kind had lived in the cracks of the world, long periods of restful blackness ending in bountiful hunting and fulfillment. Still, the creature doesn't remember the way humans do, in a linear fashion with benchmarks to help place the memories in the proper context and period. Its past is a series of dark episodes of survival and hunting wrapped around long periods of dreamless sleep.

A steep rock wall loomed above. Somehow it had made it. Rarely did it use the den behind the pile of sticks, but the blackness at the edges of its vision was spreading and becoming darker, and the beast knew it didn't have much time left.

It had no time at all.

The Akhlut collapsed, its final reserve of energy expended, its world going black. But… Still… There was something…

It convulsed, the pain becoming everything the Akhlut knew as it overwhelmed what little perception of its surroundings the beast had left. The calf within moved and struggled. There had been no sign from the calf since the killers had attacked and the Akhlut had feared it was dead.

The Akhlut squealed, its final breaths like the coming of a mighty wind.

An eerie buzz, then an answering shriek from within the beast's stomach.

What was left of the dying Akhlut undulated and stretched, the calf within fighting to break free through one of the many gashes that marred the creature's torso.

Skin tore, and blood mixed with a dark greasy fluid leaked from the gash.

A dark talon, like a hoof, broke through the skin, twisting, and widening the hole as blood spilled.

With a grotesque rending of flesh, the Akhlut calf clawed its way from its mother's body. The sounds of ripping skin, cracking bone, and tearing muscles reverberated off the cliff face as two dark talons burst from the dying Akhlut. Then a tiny wolf-like head appeared, and jaws opened, white specks of incoming teeth standing out against black gums.

The dying Akhlut screamed one last time before falling still, its body sagging and losing its shape.

Fighting to get free, the calf tore and bit. Blood spilled onto the hardpan, but it was washed away by the driving rain. The newborn flopped from its dead mother but didn't hit the ground because it was held aloft by its umbilical cord.

Yelling and screaming as the killers got closer.

The baby Akhlut clawed and chewed at its cord as it dangled from its dead mother.

Red lights appeared above in the trees. The sounds of more killers.

The calf doubled its efforts, digging its tiny teeth into the flesh that provided it with life over the last six years as it grew within its mother.

With a twang and slap of meat, the cord snapped, and the calf fell to the ground.

The Akhlut crouched, scanned the area, and scampered away east, away from the killers. Rain pounded the forest, and as the calf slipped away for its long sleep, the rain washed away all signs of its passage.

When it awoke in six years, it would be hungry.

The End

Other Severed Press novels by Edward J. McFadden III: TRAGIC, Predators & Prey, Wolves of the Sea, Fortune's Cypher, Crimson Falls (#1 Amazon Bestseller Tag), Hell Creek, Barracuda Swarm, The Cryptid Club, Dinosaur Red, Drop Off, Jurassic Ark, Keepers of the Flame, Throwback, Sea Tremors, Primeval Valley, Shadow of the Abyss (#1 Amazon Bestseller Tag), Awake, and The Breach (#1 Amazon Bestseller Tag, Amazon #1 Hot New Audio Release Tag). His other novels include: Terror Peak (#1 Amazon Bestseller Tag), the Ellis Parker Adventure Thriller series: The Modern Pharoh, The Doomsday Deception, and The Sigils of Solomon, the Theo Ramage Thriller series: Quick Sands, Sandbagged, and Too Much Grit, and Dogs Get Ten Lives, The Black Death of Babylon, and HOAXERS. Ed lives on Long Island with his wife Dawn, and their daughter Samantha.

CHECK OUT OTHER GREAT DEEP SEA THRILLERS

LAMPREYS
by Alan Spencer

A secret government tactical team is sent to perform a clean sweep of a private research installation. Horrible atrocities lurk within the abandoned corridors. Mutated sea creatures with insane killing abilities are waiting to suck the blood and meat from their prey.
Unemployed college professor Conrad Garfield is forced to assist and is soon separated from the team. Alone and afraid, Conrad must use his wits to battle mutated lampreys, infected scientists and go head-to-head with the biggest monstrosity of all.
Can Conrad survive, or will the deadly monsters suck the very life from his body?

DEEP DEVOTION
by M.C. Norris

Rising from the depths, a mind-bending monster unleashes a wave of terror across the American heartland. Kate Browning, a Kansas City EMT confronts her paralyzing fear of water when she traces the source of a deadly parasitic affliction to the Gulf of Mexico. Cooperating with a marine biologist, she travels to Florida in an effort to save the life of one very special patient, but the source of the epidemic happens to be the nest of a terrifying monster, one that last rose from the depths to annihilate the lost continent of Atlantis.

Leviathan, destroyer, devoted lifemate and parent, the abomination is not going to take the extermination of its brood well.

CHECK OUT OTHER GREAT DEEP SEA THRILLERS

PREHISTORIC BEASTS AND WHERE TO FIGHT THEM by Hugo Navikov

IN THE DEPTHS, SOMETHING WAITS ...

Acclaimed film director Jake Bentneus pilots a custom submersible to the bottom of Challenger Deep in the Pacific, the deepest point of any ocean of Earth. But something lurks at the hot hydrothermal vents, a creature—a dinosaur—too big to exist.

Gigadon.

It not only exists, but it follows him, hungrily, back to the surface. Later, a barely living Bentneus offers a $1 billion prize to anyone who can find and kill the monster. His best bet is renowned ichthyopaleontologist Sean Muir, who had predicted adapted dinosaurs lived at the bottom of the ocean.

MEGALODON: APEX PREDATOR by S.J. Larsson

English adventurer Sir Jeffery Mallory charters a ship for a top secret expedition to Antarctica. What starts out as a search and capture mission soon turns into a terrifying fight for survival as the crew come face to face with the fiercest ocean predator to have ever existed- Carcharodon Megalodon. Alone and with no hope of rescue the crew will need all their resources if they are to survive not only a 60 foot shark but also the harsh Antarctic conditions. Megalodon: Apex Predator is a deep-sea adventure filled with action, twists and savage prehistoric sharks.

CHECK OUT OTHER GREAT DEEP SEA THRILLERS

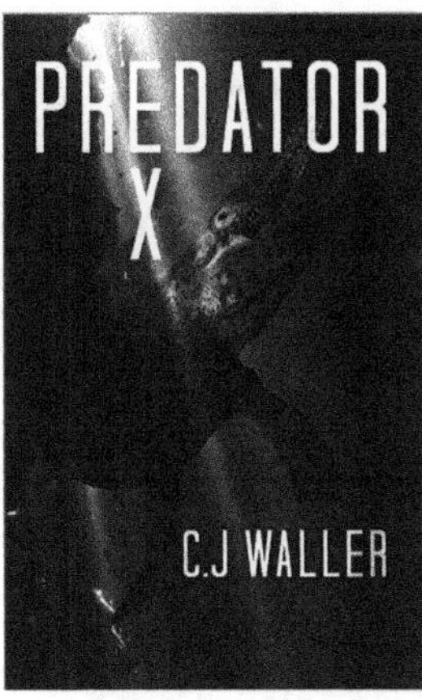

PREDATOR X
by C.J Waller

When deep level oil fracking uncovers a vast subterranean sea, a crack team of cavers and scientists are sent down to investigate. Upon their arrival, they disappear without a trace. A second team, including sedimentologist Dr Megan Stoker, are ordered to seek out Alpha Team and report back their findings. But Alpha team are nowhere to be found – instead, they are faced with something unexpected in the depths. Something ancient. Something huge. Something dangerous. Predator X

DEAD BAIT
by Tim Curran

A husband hell-bent on revenge hunts a Wereshark...A Russian mail order bride with a fishy secret...Crabs with a collective consciousness...A vampire who transforms into a Candiru...Zombie piranha...Bait that will have you crawling out of your skin and more. Drawing on horror, humor with a helping of dark fantasy and a touch of deviance, these 19 contemporary stories pay homage to the monsters that lurk in the murky waters of our imaginations. If you thought it was safe to go back in the water...Think Again!

www.ingramcontent.com/pod-product-compliance
Lightning Source LLC
LaVergne TN
LVHW020045110826
845155LV00029B/637